DEDICATION

My thanks to Adrienne Quinn who started me on the writing gig,

To Brian for his patience and to the other Inksplinters who put up with me during the writing.

And especially to Sheila for everything.

GW00728972

Chapter One:
The Invention of the Time Machine.

"What are you doing?" Frank asked "I'm building a time machine" Mick answered as if that was the most reasonable thing in the world to be doing.

"What in God's name are you going to do with a time machine?"

"First off I'm going forward to next Saturday and get the Euro Lottery numbers. Then I'll come back and buy a ticket. That should set me up with enough money to pursue my other interests"

"What other interests, and what if you run out of money pursuing them?"

The two were in Mick's refurbished attic in a suburban detached house on the Northside of Dublin.

Mick was surrounded by a large amount of what looked to Frank's untutored eye like scrap metal and a heap of miscellaneous nuts, bolt and screws." I can always go back and buy more Lotto tickets so my source of money is inexhaustible" Said Mick. "As to my other interests, wait till I've finished this and I'll tell you all about it."

Frank felt the onset of hunger pangs and seeing that it was close to dinner time he took his leave of his buddy and headed home. On the way he wondered if there was any remote possibility that he might succeed in his attempts. Mick had an impressive record, of course. He was the proud owner of several patents for items which he had invented, including an improved mouse trap, a one handed can opener and a revolutionary new hydrogen cell which showed potential to completely turn the automotive industry on its head.

Three weeks later Frank decided to pay a call on Mick to see how he was getting on. He was staggered when he turned onto Mick's road and saw that Mick had added a two storey extension on top of his house. (Entirely without planning permission, obviously.) Rushing up to the front door, Frank pressed the doorbell and heard a loud peal of bells from inside the house. After a considerable delay and just as Frank was contemplating ringing the bell again, Mick pulled open the door.

"For God's sake, don't press that bloody bell again, it has me deafened". He said. Inviting Frank inside, he dashed up the stairs to the first floor and pushed open the door to his former bedroom. Frank was gobsmacked by the sight which greeted his eyes when he entered the room.

The interior walls of the entire upper floor had been removed and the roof raised to create a space some twelve hundred feet square and thirty feet high. More astonishing to Frank's eye were the apparent hordes of men rushing about in great haste and evident industry, fabricating an enormous engine in one corner of the vast room.

"What in the name of all that's good and holy is going on here" He asked with his mouth open to an impossible angle.

With a wry grin Mick answered proudly "We're

building the MkII time machine."

"MkII!" Frank said "I didn't hear about MkI and you're building MkII, some friend you are, keeping secrets and building stuff."

"Show me how this machine works" he demanded.

Mick took him over to the large machine which was in an advanced state of construction, with men scurrying back and forth busily fitting parts and cladding to the outside of it. "It's not finished yet" Mick said "most of the work is done but I need about another week to complete it."

Frank looked at the contraption which Mick was proudly displaying. All he could make out was a mass of dials, levers and valves. It made no sense to him and Mick's explanations only made it all the more obscure.

"Where's the MkI version then" he asked, somewhat peevishly.

Mick beckoned him to follow and in a corner of the room he whipped a dust cover off a contraption which was concealed underneath.

"It's a motorbike" Frank said.

"More than a motorbike" Mick replied "It's a 1922 Vuitton Plessy Motorbike and Sidecar combination, but more than that, with my modifications it's a fully functional MkI Michael Brennan Time Machine.

Frank was seriously underwhelmed, "That yoke doesn't look like it could drive to the corner shop for a bottle of milk, never mind travel in time"

"That's deliberate" Said Mick "I chose this as my first attempt because I was going back in time first, and I didn't want to stick out like a sore thumb. It's seriously underpowered but it worked like a dream first time and I went back to August 14th 1934, just to see if I could.

"By the way" he continued "you know the Grandfather theory of time travel don't you, well its bullshit and I proved it"

"Grandfather Theory, what's that?" asked Frank. "I certainly never heard of it and I've been to college and gotten a degree"

Well pleased to be able to show off to his better educated friend Mick struck an oratorical pose and proceeded "The theory goes that time travel is impossible because if you met and interacted with one of your ancestors you would upset the timeflow and the results would be catastrophic. But I met my old Grandfather, he's just like the photos by the way, and as you can see nothing has happened."

Putting this whole Grandfather thing aside Frank asked "But where did this building come from, what's that monstrosity you're building over there, why do you need a MkII machine and on top of all that, where did you get the money to do all this, building, materials and most of all an army of workers, it must be costing a bloody fortune"

"I told you the MkI was underpowered, I went forward into the future but I could only get five days out of the machine, it had no problem going into the past, in fact, I've been as far back as the late Ice Age. It refused to go any further into the future, so I put my Euro Lottery plan into action and I'm now rich beyond your wildest dreams. I have a plan for the second version but it needed significantly more power so I designed MkII."

"You may be wondering why it's steam powered" he continued "Well If I'm travelling backwards in time I'll need a reliable power source and sophisticated electronics didn't exist back then so steam seems to be most viable. Going forward into the future is a different kettle of fish, however. If some prognosticators are to believed we are approaching a new dark age's period. If that's the case I can't rely on the future of electronics then either, so whichever direction I choose steam seems the best bet."

"As to the army of workers" Mick went on to explain "nobody nowadays knows anything about building steam engines so I imported these guys from back in the early twentieth century from a remote part of the Carpathian Mountains. They're great workers and better still they speak a mangled and unintelligible form of HungaroGerman which means that they can only communicate with me or amongst themselves. My secret is safe with me and now you, I know you are discreet. By the way they work for really small wages"

Frank was astounded. He spent the next four hours touring the premises with Mick and getting a complete rundown on the work in progress. He was especially impressed by the plans which Mick had drawn. He commented on this and Mick replied "when you can travel in time, the passage of time has no meaning and you can literally spend as much time as you like on a project. I did an Auto CAD course by travelling back and forth through time so I am now a fully qualified CAD technician, I also have degrees in Engineering and advanced Metallurgy so I am well prepared for this gig."

Exhausted by all this new information Frank took himself off home to a warm bath, a glass of twelve year old whiskey and a long think about all that had transpired that day. Was it possible that time travel was a viable proposition and even more incredible, could a dunderhead like Mick have figured it out on his own?

Unfortunately Frank had a long standing appointment in Kazakhstan the following day. The gig was to be for two weeks, but due to unforeseen circumstances it dragged on for another three weeks. Coming home tired and fed up with the carry-on of the Kazakhs, Frank's primary thoughts were on bed and rest, in that order. However given the momentous affairs going on in Mick's house he decided to pay a call before going home.

Imagine his astonishment on turning onto Mick's street when he was confronted by miles of crime scene tape draped all across the street. Accosting the bored looking Garda on duty he demanded an explanation. The Garda assured him that all he knew was that a mysterious explosion had destroyed number fifty six and blown all the residents sky high. If Frank needed any further information he could contact Inspector McGrath down at the station.

The following day Frank found himself in the station, in an interview room being grilled by the aforesaid Inspector McGrath. The Inspector seemed to think that Frank had some guilty knowledge of the affair and it was only when he satisfied himself that Frank had been in Kazakhstan at the time of the explosion that he relaxed somewhat.

He then politely asked Frank if he could shed any light on what might have occurred in Mick's house. In ordinary circumstances nothing could hold Frank back from telling his incredible tale. Nothing, that is, except that he needed to have some further information before opening his mouth and possibly having himself committed to the Booby Hatch for the remainder of his natural life.

He persuaded the Inspector to let him visit the scene of the devastation, expecting an enormous crater and bricks scattered the length and breadth of the street he was astonished to find no such conditions on site. The entire house was totally missing. The edges of the plinth had been fused into glass, apparently by great heat, and all the evidence of Mick's Time Machine was entirely absent. Oddly enough there was no other evidence of heat elsewhere and Mick's somewhat shabby garden was as unaffected as the last day Frank had been there.

Frank decided not to share his knowledge of Mick's invention and after a fairly heated discussion he was allowed to go home.

Chapter Two

Adventures of Mick in the Far Future

Mick sat up and scratched his head. "That's a bit disappointing" he thought "I haven't moved at all. I must have messed up the settings on the controls, maybe I shouldn't have sent Igor and the other Carpathians home. He was much more painstaking at the fiddly stuff than I am"

"Well bugger it, I'll just have to recalibrate and try again, first though, I'll make myself a sandwich and a cup of coffee. All this time travelling stuff makes me peckish." Opening his front door, to collect the milk, he slipped on a fused glass patch outside and pitched down on his backside and followed this embarrassing pratfall by banging the back of his head on the ground. Picking himself up he found it difficult to maintain his balance due to the glazed surface underfoot.

Looking around he was astonished to find that the area around his house had changed utterly and the glazed surface on which he was standing covered an area extending about a foot from the perimeter of his property, now reduced to a gardenless condition.

He rushed back inside and examined the controls of The Amazing Steam Powered Time Machine and found that he had inadvertently catapulted himself some four and a half millennia into the future.

Speaking aloud he said "Dear God, this bloody machine is a lot more powerful than I thought it would be" Thinking about it he concluded that he had accidentally jogged the lever which directed the forward movement to a much higher notch than he originally intended. Furthermore, the machine had catapulted not only himself, but the complete house forward in time.

"I know what's happened" he thought to himself "I've fallen into a Chronosynchlastic infundiblium"* (Described by Kurt Vonnegut in his novel "The Sirens of Titan" published in 1959)*

*(Chronosynchlastic infundiblium - Time Funnel)

Where to go from here? Obviously some exploration was indicated. Fortunately Mick had anticipated the need for this and packed an extensive wardrobe plus sufficient food and drink to last for several months.

Included in his gear was a Colt 45 revolver - serial number 5370, bought by Mick from a man who claimed to be a survivor of the battle of the little Bighorn which cost General George Custer and 268 of his men their lives, together with 55 wounded. Mick had come across this individual on one of his forays into the past on his Vuitton - Plessy motorbike. Whether his story was true or not was open to question but the gun was in perfect working order and realistically Mick didn't need a historical provenance in order to use it to defend himself against whatever terrors might exist in the far future.

Gathering up some supplies, strapping on his trusty Colt and ensuring he had enough ammunition to start a small war he set off to explore his immediate surroundings.

There was no sign of the leafy suburbs where he had grown up, the land all about his house, now lying slightly canted to one side in an open glade in a deciduous forest was unremittingly rural. There was no evidence of human habitation in the immediate neighbourhood so he ventured a bit further. Using his woodsman skills, learned long ago in the Boy Scouts, he carefully marked trees so that he could find his way home and, more importantly to the time machine later, even in the dark.

Ten minutes hard walking later he came to a road, at least he thought it was a road. It looked to be made from a seamless plastic material and felt soft and yielding underfoot, in fact a perfect walking surface. Marking a final tree he set off on the path in an eastward direction, the sea is east of his home place and he thought that if there was going to be any signs of civilisation, it would be close to the sea, In his experience human beings like to live by the sea.

Sure enough, some twenty minutes later he breasted the rise of a small hill and saw the Irish Sea spread out beneath him, sparkling in the warm sunlight. Looking further to his right he saw a cluster of what looked like buildings in the middle distance, perhaps a mile and a half away.

Now quite excited he rushed down the hill towards the group of buildings. As he approached the first building an entrance irised open and a man emerged. The man was a slight individual, dressed in a one piece, variously coloured, garment and he appeared to be wearing a headpiece similar to a cockscomb. Mick raised his hands and called out a greeting. The other spoke in a language which Mick did not recognise. Mick tried again in his broken French to no better result. The man made a "stay there" gesture and went back into his dwelling. Coming out a moment later he was carrying a small device which looked to Mick like a hearing aid. The man made signs to Mick to fit the device into his ear. Mick was amazed to hear the other in his head. He was even more astonished to note that the others lips did not move when he spoke.

The explanation soon emerged from the device in his ear. "My name is Paulo and you are hearing me in your head through the ear thing" "you are obviously a stranger around here" he continued, "Can I offer you some refreshment, you look like you've come a long way."

"You have no idea" Mick said.

"Actually" said Paulo "you might be surprised, I would reckon that you are a time traveler possibly from about four or five thousand years ago. Am I correct?"

"How did you figure that out?" Mick was floored by the casual nature of his companion's revelation.

"Oh we're well used to time travelers in this part of the time continuum" said Paulo "I, myself have met three in the past ten years. Unless I am mistaken though you are possibly from the furthest back in time and you may even be the original inventor of time travel as we now know it."

"In point of fact" he continued "I believe I could put a name to you. Unless I miss my estimate, you are Mick Brennan are you not?"

"Well how the hell did you figure that out? Hang on a minute, are you reading my mind with this ear thing?" Mick was outraged at this perceived invasion of his inner privacy.

Paulo hastened to reassure him "No, no, not at all. The ear thing only communicates at the shallowest level in your head and conveys no more information than is passed in normal speech. It would require some much more sophisticated gear to read your private thoughts. Except in cases of real need we would never breach our ethical standards and read any deeper than the upper levels of cognisance."

"So you have a highly developed ethical system then"

"Yes indeed, we have system based on respect for all, and that those who have more, have a duty to share with the less well off in society. We also believe that the strong should not ever use their strength to bring pressure to bear on anyone or anything weaker than themselves. So you can be quite sure that, even if we could, we would never probe into your mind without your express permission."

"Phew, that's a relief" Mick didn't really have so much in his mind that he wouldn't like the whole world to know, he just felt uncomfortable with the idea of complete strangers rummaging around in his deepest thoughts.

Going into Paulo's house Mick was gobsmacked to see an enormous spread of food laid out on the table. Finding that he was ravenous he set about the food with gusto.

"This is absolutely delicious" he said. "I can't help noticing that there's nobody here except you and me and there's enough food here for a small army. Who else lives here?" he asked.

Paulo laughed and said "there's a lot you will have to learn about us if you're going to stay long" he said. "We are solitary people and we almost never have more than one person living in a dwelling at any one time" "We are very jealous of our individual space and are normally hermits by preference."

"Why aren't you eating yourself" Mick asked.

"We don't eat" Said Paulo, "We metabolise all we need direct from sunlight and the immediate environment so there's no need for the messy business of eating and the inevitable consequences which are even messier."

"In my culture this is a delicate issue but I will burst with curiosity if I don't ask" said Mick

"Don't worry, I won't get offended by anything you ask" Paulo replied.

"Well if you are so antisocial, how do you procreate, I mean how do you produce little Paulos and Paulas?"

"It's a little complicated and as you can already observe we don't like mess, but at its simplest we seek out a compatible female on our version of the internet and by agreement we decide to combine our DNA. This is done through a much updated version of the old Cloud Computing idea and the resultant individual is gestated and brought into the world, fully adult and fully functioning.

The process takes about 35 minutes from

beginning to end. This happens about once in fifty to one hundred years, in fact I compute that the last such individual produced was eighty nine years ago"

"I notice that you haven't taken off your hat thing" Mick said, "We usually take off our hats when we go inside"

Paulo touched the cockscomb on his head and laughed merrily. "That's not a hat that is part of my brain." "We have evolved a brain power which is incomparably greater than anything you are familiar with, however, when our brain is operating at maximum capacity it generates a level of heat which, if not dissipated, would be lethal. The appendage on my head is a reserve coolant feature and in times of need it kicks into action. Would you like a demonstration?"

Without waiting for a reply he immediately adopted a deeply pensive appearance and to Mick's horror the cockscomb began to inflate and pulse with activity.

"I was just computing the 'Universal Theory of Everything'" Paulo said, "It requires a lot of computing power"

Mick decided to stop asking questions for a while until he had a chance to digest all that he had heard today.

Chapter Three:

Earth in the Year 6512

Paulo asked Mick if he would like to take a look around to see the current state of the World in this brave new age. Mick readily agreed, after all, that's why he was here in the first place.

"By the way" said Mick as they went out the door, "Don't you want to put the uneaten food away?"

"Not necessary" said Paulo, "the house will reabsorb it into the materialiser for later fabrication into anything which we might need."

"You mean more food?"

"No, pretty much anything you can think of"

As they set out Paulo said "You won't need the weapon."

Reluctant to part with his trusty Colt Peacemaker Mick asked "Why not, are things so peaceful around here that we have nothing to protect ourselves against?"

"That's partly the case but more to the point you are, to all intents and purposes, invulnerable whilst you are in my company" Said Paulo.

"How's that possible?" asked Mick, looking askance at Paulo.

"I've already told you about our much increased brain power" Paulo replied, "I can cast a force field around myself and anything else in my immediate neighbourhood which makes us invulnerable to all manner of physical danger, from gross events like nuclear explosion down to the microscopic scale such as viruses etc."

"Also" Paulo continued "because of time travel and the fact that it does not cause the paradoxes, much loved by science fiction writers in your time, we know that nothing will happen to you because nothing has happened to you, if you understand what I mean"

Mick was not entirely sure that he did understand what Paulo meant, but, against his better judgement, he left the Colt in the house and went outside with him to explore.

The area immediately outside the dwelling was a smooth lawn of perfectly clipped, perfectly green grass and extended by Mick's estimate to some two acres. Further on there was a dense forest which continued as far as the eye could see, except for the beach and sea beyond.

Looking around Mick was astonished and disturbed to see that the road which he had travelled on earlier had disappeared as if it had never existed. There was no trace that the road had ever existed. Mick was less than enthused by this apparent contradiction, in the first place, he wasn't fully certain that he could find the marks of the trail he had blazed in order to get back to the Mick Brennan MKI1 Amazing Steam Driven Time Machine. Whilst he was, and is, an intrepid explorer he did not necessarily want to spend the remainder of his years in this particular slice of the time continuum.

"Hey Paulo" he cried "where's the road gone?"

"The road? Oh I see what you're talking about, that wasn't a road. That was a path I constructed to lead you to my house so that I could meet you and introduce you to the modern era" said Paulo "It has been subsumed back into the data stream for future use should it be needed"

Mick was now somewhat truculent, he had had a long and tiring day, after all. "How'm I supposed to find my time machine?" he demanded.

With an insouciant shrug Paulo reassured Mick "Don't worry, I can bring you to your machine from anywhere in the world in the blink of an eye. You only need to say, and I'll whisk you to it"

Mick was not altogether satisfied but he had no real option other than to put his trust in Paulo, so, indicating his assent he proceeded, under Paulo's guidance, to explore. As they proceeded, on foot, it struck Mick that walking, a means of travel which was not high on his list of most desirable exercises, seemed to be effortless and, indeed, pleasurable. Deciding that it had something to do with Paulo's force field technology he decided to kick back and enjoy this novel sensation.

As they travelled onwards Mick saw numerous animals wandering around and browsing on the lush grass and abundant undergrowth. The strange thing was that all the animals, carnivore and herbivore alike, seemed to co-exist peacefully. Indeed the carnivores seemed to be feeding on plant material and ignoring the plentiful prey which was almost underfoot.

"What's the story with the animals, lions not eating lambs and so on?" Mick asked

"Oh, we've bred the aggression out of the animal kingdom and we have managed to create a new Eden on Earth. Quite an achievement hey?"

Without replying, Mick travelled onwards thinking to himself;

"Is there nothing these people cannot or will not do?"

Then remembering that Paulo had access to his brain at some level he decided that this could be a dangerous train of thought so he focused on other things for a while.

The more they travelled the stronger was it borne on Mick that the whole experience of this brave new world was overwhelmingly peaceful and well ordered, almost to the point that it was profoundly boring. From his discussions with Paulo the future was a prewritten story with all actions and indeed thoughts determined in advance. Mick recalled in his schooldays being taught the Catholic Church's position on the heresy of Predestination, which suggested that the individual has no control on the shaping of his own destiny. The logical outcome of such an ethical position being that if it makes no difference, why bother trying to be ethically correct as it makes no odds anyway.

With the onset of these disturbing concepts Mick found himself subject to little flashes of disturbing images. For very brief periods of time the world seemed to darken and he appeared to be the focus of some very strange people. As time passed these periods became longer and it became obvious that something was very wrong with him. Paulo noticed a change in his demeanour and appearance and he asked, "Are you OK, Mick, you don't look too good".

"I don't feel too good to tell the truth" replied Mick "I'd like to get back to my time machine, there's some medication in the house which might help"

"Eh, that presents a bit of a problem" said Paulo with a diffident expression on his face.

"What do you mean A PROBLEM!" said Mick "You said all it would take is a thought of yours and we'd be there in the "blink of an eye" to use your own words."

Suddenly the bright sunlight and beautiful sylvan landscape vanished and Mick found himself on a table in a darkened room, worse by far, he was strapped to the table and held immobile by thick, cushioned straps.

Staring around as best he could in a semi darkened room, with his head held in a fixed position facing the ceiling he saw, to his horror that he was surrounded by four individuals who were, to his mind, most peculiar looking. They had a vaguely insectile appearance, although they were equipped with only two arms and two legs each. Their mode of communication seemed to be carried out by the use of high pitched squeaks, almost outside the range of his hearing. They also had an unappealing odour, something like bleach mixed with vanilla essence.

"What the hell is going on here" demanded Mick "where's that miserable, lying rat Paulo, how did I get here. Turn me loose immediately before I get upset. You wouldn't like me in an upset state" he had a vague notion that he remembered this line from a movie or TV show.

The group surrounding him immediately ceased all activity and turned to look at him. An excited twittering broke out amongst them and Mick noticed a pair of antennae on each of their heads which had not been visible before.

These individuals evidently could not communicate with him and Mick was getting seriously concerned.

Using gestures to describe him and raising his voice he pleaded

"Please Get Paulo"

Whether his pleas had any effect, or perhaps because the others had a similar idea, off their own bat, Paulo entered the room at that moment.

With a heartfelt sigh of relief Mick called out "Hey Paulo, tell these charming people to get the restraints off me. For God's sake tell them I'm one of the good guys."

With a sad shake of his head, Paulo replied "I'm really very sorry Mick, but I have no influence over these people. In fact the reverse is the case, you see, I'm actually a construct of theirs and I only exist by their forbearance"

"What the Hell do you mean, what was all that guff about an invulnerable force field and how you could protect me from all nasty forces great and small?"

The thing is" said Paulo "none of that episode actually took place at all. You were here all the time and those impressions were fed into your brain by our good companions here"

"So tell me, how did I get here and why am I strapped to a table being inspected by Aliens like something out of a bad Sci Fi movie" Mick was getting more and more incensed as the time went on.

"I'm placed in the unhappy position of having to explain things to you which will not be to your liking, I'm sure" Paulo told him, "you see when you initiated your latest time trip you did not actually travel in time at all. Instead you caused an interdimensional rift, through which you slipped and ended up here in another dimension altogether. The beings who inhabit this place are not only extraterrestrials but extradimensionals also. They are an extremely aggressive and land hungry race who came here many thousands of years ago and have driven the original inhabitants to extinction. They are a hive species whose hard wired imperative is to procreate endlessly and who are therefore constantly in need of other lands to conquer."

"What has all this to do with me?" queried Mick, "I'm just an ordinary Joe, going about his business. I can't imagine what they expect to get from me."

"Mick" Paulo said sadly "you know as well as I do what they want. Their interest in you is the Time Machine or to be more accurate the Interdimensional travelling machine. They are not very clever technically and with the secret of cross dimensional travel an entire new dimension opens up for colonisation by them.

Furthermore in their minds your home dimension is not the only other one, theoretically there could be an infinite number of dimensions and consequently an infinite empire for them to conquer in the future"

"Jesus, Mary and Holy Saint Joseph" Mick cried

"What am I going to do? I can't allow these bugs to take over the Earth and, even worse, all of creation if I understand you correctly"

Paulo shook his head with a doleful expression on his face "There's nothing you can do" he replied "these creatures are all powerful and resistance is futile"

Mick looked at him with disbelieving eyes.

Chapter Four:

Mick Fights Back

"Paulo" Mick said, thinking faster than he had ever done in his life before "I need you to open these straps and set me free so I can get back to the time machine and return to my home dimension"

Paulo sadly shook his head "I'm sorry Mick but the creatures created me for the sole purpose of fooling you and prying the secrets of the machine out of you. I can no more go against them than you could against your deepest programming. They are simply too strong for me. I cannot break free" Mick was shocked to notice that there were tears in Paulo's eyes as he said this.

Throughout this conversation the aliens were huddled together in a corner of the room observing Mick and Paulo as they spoke together. There was no sign that they understood the conversation and they continued a high pitched twittering the entire time.

Mick said "come closer Paulo, I need to tell you something" as Paulo bent down Mick whispered "just undo the strap on my right hand there and I'll do the rest"

Paulo vehemently shook his head, "I can't, they'll punish me and possibly kill me. Must I remind you that I am totally in their power?"

With a firm and commanding tone Mick said "Do it now Paulo, I promise that they will not harm you. When I get free I'll bring you back to my dimension and we'll be free of these things there."

Trembling in every limb Paulo did as he was told,

the habit of obedience to orders was evidently well drilled into him. As soon as Mick's right hand was freed he whipped it over and released the left hand and sitting up he shouted at the top of his voice "come on you squirmy bugs and see how you like some Earth medicine"

The aliens rushed over to the table to restrain Mick and as soon as they were within striking distance Mick flailed about with his work roughened hands. He had been a keen amateur boxer in his youth and had retained his pugilistic skills. To his astonishment the first blow went through the first alien's skin and into his abdomen almost up to the elbow. With a convulsive shudder Mick pulled his hand out and a huge gout of evil smelling fluid spilled out on the floor. Turning to the remaining aliens Mick despatched them with equal speed and vigour.

Staring at the carnage all round him Mick realised that the creatures were even more insectile than he had thought. They evidently had an exoskeleton as Earth insects do and it was very thin and vulnerable to an Earth man of normal development. Checking with Paulo afterwards it emerged that the sight of such extreme aggression was unknown to the aliens. Mick's answer was "well they know now"

"Quickly Paulo, where's the Time Machine, we mustn't delay an instant"

Paulo looked at Mick with an expression of astonishment "It's here of course" he replied.

"What do you mean here," Mick asked

"Here in your house" said Paulo, still looking shocked and queasy from the recent violence. "You arrived in this dimension about twelve hours ago and unfortunately for you these four aliens happened to be in the immediate neighbourhood. Whilst you were groggy from the interdimensional shift they drugged you with a powerful hypnotic and they've kept you here ever since. They have tried to probe your mind for the secret of the interdimensional shift secret but they have been unsuccessful so far"

"Hah" said Mick "that's probably because I don't know it myself" whilst they had been talking Mick had freed himself from the other restraints and, except for a thundering headache, he was in full fighting form. Looking around in the gloom he recognised his surroundings as his downstairs utility room and he heaved a great sigh of relief.

"Why are there only four of them here?" he queried of Paulo.

"There were five and their communicator malfunctioned, they sent the other one off to report to a higher authority. They don't have much autonomy and aside from light mental probing they had not gone very far with their examination of you. That's probably why you could break the hold of the drugs they had administered"

"You should know that it's very likely that there will be reinforcements knocking at the door very soon to check you out"

"Bloody hell, the fire in the boiler will have gone out by now and it'll take at least twelve more hours to build up a sufficient head of steam for us to slip back to my own dimension. It will never take them that long to get back here. We need to make preparations for a siege"

Deciding that first things first was the best policy Mick immediately set about firing up the boiler. This was easier said than done, the machine had been built, as pointed out before, by nineteenth century artisans from a remote part of the Carpathian Mountains. There was no operating manual and what instructions there were had been scribbled out in an archaic hand by a semiliterate speaker, and writer, of Hungaro-German. Frantically trying to recall the steps taken to bring this monster to life, Mick cursed the fact that he had neglected to:-

(a) Learn the rudiments of the language

(b) Learn how to light the boiler

Or (c) all of the above.

He had just managed to coax the recalcitrant machine into a rather anaemic life when he heard a thunderous knocking on the door, accompanied by a louder version of the alien's twittering speech.

Rushing out of the room Mick went straight to his emergency stores and collected his Colt 45, together with a generous stock of ammunition. Thanking his lucky stars that he had had the foresight to bar the doors and windows before setting out on his adventures he remembered that the front door was not as secure as the rest of his defenses.

Carefully going to the front door he saw that it was on the latch, "of course" he thought "That's how the first lot of aliens got in originally"

Whipping open the door he fired his six shooter repeatedly into the group of aliens assembled outside. He then slammed the door and threw the bolts, securing himself and Paulo some temporary respite from the attentions of the aliens.

With an immense sigh of relief he sat on the bottom step of the stairs and wiped the sweat from his forehead. He was well aware that time was of the essence but a little pause to gather his wits was also essential. He had undoubtedly killed or injured several of the aliens, and given their physiology he guessed that injury inevitably led to death in their species. Nonetheless he needed to be prepared for them to return and the next time he would not have the advantage of surprise. He had certainly not killed all of them and return they surely must, in considerable force and prepared for battle.

First things first, he was ravenously hungry and, on reflection, he figured that the banquet he had enjoyed with Paulo was, along with all the rest of that experience, a figment of the dream sequence which the aliens had placed in his head. Quickly going to his stores he prepared a quick meal and sitting down he tried to work out a strategy for dealing with his troubles as he gobbled his beans and toast.

Twelve hours is not, normally, a long period of time but for Mick it seemed to stretch into eternity. Erecting his defenses did not occupy him for more a few minutes as it only entailed a careful check to see that all the windows and external doors were secured. That done he sat down to discuss the situation with Paulo who had withdrawn into a corner of the kitchen and appeared to be almost comatose.

"Wake up Paulo" Mick said shaking him roughly

by the shoulder "this is no time to be sleeping!" Paulo's only response was to raise his downcast eyes and look apathetically at Mick. "C'mon, shake a leg, it'll be no time at all and the bugs will be back for round two and I expect they'll be better prepared this time" Mick was getting more than a little peeved by Paulo's lack of response, he needed all the backup he could secure in the upcoming fracas. Paulo remained unresponsive.

"What the hell is wrong with you Paulo" Mick bellowed.

"It's no use" said Paulo "We are helpless against their superior powers"

"What do you mean Superior Powers?" queried Mick, "their powers are not much protection against my trusty Colt"

"You don't understand" moaned Paulo,

Losing patience Mick grabbed Paulo by the front of his tunic and yelled "What don't I understand? for God's sake will you buck up. It's as much in your interest as mine that we work this thing out and I've just about had it with your whingeing and defeatist attitude. Now either you shape up or you can bloody well ship out and take your chances with the bugs outside. Is that clear?"

Plainly terrified Paulo endeavoured to explain "You've only seen the drones of the nest, when the word gets out about what happened here they'll send a Queen after you and I'll be condemned by association. You really don't want to know what a Queen can mete out as punishment when she is seriously upset"

Just as Mick was framing a suitably swift riposte to Paulos bad news he was struck with a paralysing headache. Falling to his knees in agony he noticed that Paulo was, if anything, in an even worse condition. "It's the Queen" Paulo gasped "I told you that she would come."

"What's she doing?" demanded Mick.

"She is using her superior mind powers to cripple us and make us subject to her domination. I told you that we couldn't fight her" Paulo was, by this time, in a pitiable state, curled in a fetal position under the kitchen table.

"Superior powers me arse" Mick was not ready to give up yet. Reaching into the cupboard near his hand he pulled out a roll of aluminium foil and swiftly fashioned a hat which covered his head down to below his ears. With an expression of infinite relief he then made a similar hat and jammed it on Paulo's head.

With wide eyed disbelief Paulo almost wept "What did you do? The pain's gone"

Mick grinned manically and said "this Queen is about to get her arse kicked, right royally"

"Anyone who follows science fiction knows that a tin foil hat is total protection against all mind altering rays. Even Futurama has an episode about it and it must be true if it was in Futurama".

Strapping on his Colt and loading up with extra ammunition Mick jammed his tin foil hat into a firmer and more comfortable position on his head.

"How will I distinguish the Queen from the others?" he queried Paulo.

"You won't have any difficulty with that" Paulo replied "she's about twenty times bigger than the clones and she can paralyse you with a glance from her eyes. I don't think that even your tin hat will protect you from her eyes" Paulo was obviously still in a terrific funk.

Taking Paulo's advice on board Mick ran upstairs and took a careful peek outside. There were about twenty of the aliens ranged in front of the house and he assumed that there were more surrounding it on all sides. His colt would not be very effective against a crowd like that having only a six shot magazine. He didn't think they would give him enough time to reload before they would be on him if he took them on in a frontal assault.

There was no sign of anything resembling Paulo's description of the Queen and until he could see her he had no way of deciding his best approach to the matter of disposing of her. Suddenly he noticed an immense mass emerging into view from the side of the house. She was truly enormous, towering a good thirty feet into the air, she resembled nothing on earth unless it was a hugely obese praying mantis.

Mick concluded that he was in deep trouble, it would take more than a Colt 45 to deal with this monster!

Frantically casting about for a means to deal with his nemesis Mick was reminded that he had a big can of "Raid", ant killer, in his cupboard from the time before he had got the idea for this time travel gig into his head, "If I get home out of this" he muttered "I'll never go travelling any further than Dollymount in future"

He doubted that the Raid would be very effective on the Queen but it might serve as a distraction whilst he employed more substantial remedies. Amongst his other stores was a plentiful supply of petrol which he had used as a fire starter on previous trips into the past, or other dimensions, whichever was the real deal.

He now had the bones of a strategy for dealing with his enemies. The boiler on the time machine was only three quarters charged and he was very doubtful that the house would withstand a determined assault from the huge Queen and her minions. In fact he couldn't understand what the delay was in her starting her attack. Mick's plan of action relied to some extent on Paulo's participation and he was not at all sure that his companion was up to the task but adopting the position that "Faint heart never won fair lady" he decided to press on regardless.

Glancing out the window he saw that the Queen was at the front of the house and seemed to be communing with her minions, possibly preparing her attack of Mick's fortress.

"O.K. Paulo" Mick said "Here's the gig, I'll throw open the door and rush out shooting at any target of opportunity which presents itself. You bring the can of Raid and spray it in the Queen's eyes, she's sure to bend down to see what's going on. I don't expect the Raid will affect her too badly but it ought to temporarily blind her and allow me to throw a can of petrol over her and set her alight. That should occupy her enough to allow the boiler to reach 90%, we'll be able to crank the machine up at that level and escape this dimension."

Paulo reluctantly agreed, "We can't get any worse off I suppose, let's give it a shot"

The plan succeeded beyond all Mick's expectations. Rushing out he managed to hit six aliens with his six shots and passing through their bodies the bullets felled several more. The Queen had never experienced anything like this before and bending down to see what was going on she received a blast of Raid full in her eyes. She reared back, clawing at her eyes and whilst she was disoriented Mick threw the entire contents of the petrol can over her and pulling the book of matches from his pocket he lit it and threw it at his enemy.

The petrol ignited with a tremendous whoosh and to Mick's astonishment the Queen immediately burst into a towering inferno. Evidently she was an extremely incendiary life form. She crashed to the ground, scattering flaming embers all around. These embers ignited her minions and soon they also were burning merrily.

"C'mon Paulo, we'll never get an opportunity like this again" Said Mick and both ran into the house. Mick immediately rushed to the Time Machine and throwing it into gear set it for his desired century. Pressing the GO button he instantly found himself safe at home.

Chapter Five:

Travelling in Time Has Consequences

Jumping up Mick's first thought was to check the date. Obviously any electronic equipment which he had brought with him would be out of whack, what with all the travelling back and forth through time and dimensions, if Paulo and the bug people could be believed. Thinking about this conundrum Mick was struck by a brain wave. "Turn on the TV, you dolt" he muttered to himself. He rushed into his TV room and turned on the set. To his immense relief the announcer's voice boomed out "this is the nine o'clock news from RTE on Friday the sixteenth of July".

"Wow, that's the same day and time I left originally" said Mick "We made it"

"Hey Paulo we're safe now. I'm back among friends and everything is going to be alright"

Figuring he would check in with Frank and see what developments had occurred since he started his odyssey he rang him on his mobile. Even now Mick really didn't have a proper grip on time or dimensional travel and he didn't realise that since several days had elapsed for him while he was away, no time at all had passed in his home timeline. He had, in fact arrived home at exactly the moment he left. Frank was, therefore, still en route from Kazakhstan and the fuss with the alleged explosion and the police had not occurred. Frank, like the good citizen he is had his mobile switched off and was, in fact, sound asleep, he's one of those lucky people who can sleep on an airliner.

Mick was secure in the notion that all was serene in his life after his "little" adventure into transdimensional space, although he was somewhat dubious about the other dimension story. After all it had come to him from the Queen bug through Paulo and she had proved herself to be anything but a model of probity. Whatever, Mick felt he could sleep peacefully in his suburban bed.

He could not be any more wrong. In the serene folds of the Cotswolds in Gloucestershire in England nestles a facility which rejoices in the innocuous title of GCHQ, known to all the security agencies of the world as an electronic listening post, used by the Intelligence services of Her Majesty The Queen (of England in this case) and sharing all information gathered with the infamous CIA in the states. Whilst Mick slept the sleep of the just in leafy Drumcondra an alarm had gone off in GCHQ which demanded the attention of Major Freddie Fortesque.

Freddie was the duty officer in a secret division of MI5 tasked with investigating any and all anomalies which might arise in cyberspace related to the aforesaid Chronosynchlastic Infundiblium. Mick was under the impression that this was a construct of a science fiction geek's diseased mind, a conclusion which Her Majesty's Intelligence Services most definitely did not share.

Freddie therefore set in motion a train of events which was destined to disrupt the even tenor of Mick's calm and pleasant dreams. It seems that the activation of a CF (for short) was an event which had been recognised theoretically for some years by large domed physicists. It had been wrapped in several layers of secrecy as the military industrial complex had ambitions of using it as a secret weapon in the War on Terror, much beloved by Bush, Blair and others. Whilst they had not, themselves, been successful in developing a working model they had managed to perfect an early warning device which would be capable of recognising the exotic particles, called Tachyons, generated when such a device was activated.

The military minds had devised a scenario which predicted the identification of the particles, designed and constructed a machine capable of identifying and locating them and written a manual some three hundred pages thick setting out in minute detail the response to be initiated if, and when, this event occurred.

Without a moment's hesitation Freddie called to his enlisted sergeant, whose task it was to do any actual work involved since an officer and a gentleman such as Freddie could not be expected to stoop to physical labour.

"Sarn't Wilson" he shouted "Front and centre, immediately"

Sergeant Wilson was deep in the latest Lee Childs thriller and quite comfortably situated in a quiet corner of GCHQ's office suite. He recognised the note of urgency in his superior's voice and throwing his eyes up to heaven he muttered to himself

"What does the overbred, overfed and overpaid bollocks want now"?

Maddened by his subordinate's tardiness, Freddie shouted "Sarn't Wilson, get your arse up here right now or you'll find yourself on report in the morning"

"Oh bugger it" said Wilson and carefully marking his page he stubbed out his cigarette, straightened his tunic and called out "Yes sir, coming right away sir". He then took a leisurely and roundabout route to Major Freddie's desk and presented himself with an insolent sketch of a salute. "You called Sir" he said with a barely civil sneer on his face. "Can I help you Sir?"

"Yes you can, you insolent jackanapes, and take that sneer off your face or you'll be looking for a new job this time tomorrow"

"Now go and get the manual codenamed CC-443567 from storage and bring it here immediately, and none of your insubordinate time wasting either".

Wilson was not as stupid as Freddie liked to paint him and on the way to the secure storage he thought "Wow CC-443567, that's the time travel alert sequence. Wonder what has happened to get Major FF's knickers in a twist. It must be pretty big if he's looking into it himself"

Freddie waited in a fever of impatience for Wilson to bring the manual and when, at last, it arrived he snatched it from him with an ungracious "That'll be all Wilson, you're dismissed". The sergeant, now deeply interested, reluctantly left the room but he waited outside the half open door to see what might take place.

As soon as Freddie felt that he had privacy he opened the forbidding seals, with TOP SECRET OFFICIAL EYES ONLY stamped on all surfaces and joinings on the manual. The instructions contained in the manual were precise and detailed and required sixty five pages of excruciating bullshit which, when boiled down and distilled, comprised a simple message: Call General Walter Farquharson immediately.

Somewhat gobsmacked Freddie dialed the number provided. A voice answered

"Yes". Freddie was taken aback by this abrupt reply and he hesitated, waiting for more.

"Speak" the voice said.

"This is Major Fortescue at GCHQ reporting the activation of the CC-443567 alarm" Freddie stammered.

"What's a CC-443567 when it's at home?" Queried the voice

"Is this General Walter Farquharson speaking" Freddie asked hesitantly.

"Who the hell else do you expect to be answering my bloody phone? Are you totally stupid or do you think I have nothing better to do with my time than to entertain dozy prats like you. Do I have to repeat the question or will you answer it?"

By now thoroughly cowed, Freddie stammered "It's the time travel activation alert Sir" he said standing rigidly to attention.

"Time travel" bellowed the General, "total bullshit man, you've been listening to those bespeckled eggheads again haven't you. Everybody knows time travel is impossible, everybody sane anyway". He had evidently forgotten that at some point he had been appointed overseer of this particular arcane branch of the military industrial complex, most likely placed there by his superiors to keep him out of a position where he could do real damage.

"I'm very sorry Sir, but the protocol in the CC-443567 manual specifically states that in the event of an activation of an alarm I am directed to contact you immediately groveled Freddie.

"What the hell am I supposed to do about this thing? Can't you deal with it and leave me to my dinner in peace?"

"Sir, I'm deeply sorry about this but the manual clearly states that you need to open a drawer in the strong room for further instructions as to how to deal with this matter"

"Get a grip man, have I not already passed on the matter into your hands? Are you incapable or simply incompetent or do I need to get someone with more ability to handle the matter. Just open the bloody drawer and proceed with whatever footling details contained in it" Bellowed the, by now, seriously irate General.

Freddie, discovering the remnants of some backbone, said stiffly

"The General is aware that I am not cleared to enter the strong room and that a retinal scan is required so the General's presence is absolutely imperative"

"Oh very well I'll be down in the morning after breakfast at my club, meantime you can continue to hold the fort".

Freddie, by now well up on his high horse,

riposted "the General should be aware that the CC-443567 manual calls for the General's immediate attendance on this matter and places it in the TRIPLE A category" he was so excited that he clearly pronounced the capitals, leaving the General in no doubt as to the urgency of the matter.

In a voice scarcely above absolute zero the General said "Very well I'll be there directly".

Somewhat less than an hour later the General's Chauffeur driven Rolls Royce drew up to the foyer of GCHQ. A very annoyed General climbed out of the luxurious vehicle, turned and engaged in a lingering kiss with a young "lady" who immediately got back into the car and with an imperious wave of her hand to the driver motored off.

The General then entered the building muttering to himself "I hate this bloody place". His humour was not improved when the guard in the foyer demanded that he identify himself and check in formally.

"Who the devil do you think I am" he demanded "I've been through here a thousand times, mostly with you on duty.

"Sorry Sir" replied the guard with barely repressed grin "standard operating procedure, you know". The General continued onwards with an ungracious grunt.

Barging into Freddie's office he barked "What's all this nonsense about, time travel, retinal scans and old Uncle Tom Cobley and all. Let's get on with it so I can get back to my club".

Freddie was only too anxious to please. "Follow me General please" he said as he descended into the depths of the basement to the strong room. The General presented his eye to the scanner and the huge bolts on the door withdrew. Inside was a myriad of boxes, one of which was marked CC-443567. The General and Freddie both inserted keys and on the count of three both turned their key. Nothing happened, The General turned furiously on Freddie and berated him "You've screwed up again, you obviously turned your key counter clockwise rather than the other way" "I think you'll find it was to be turned clockwise Sir" said Freddie. On the second attempt the drawer opened and the General dismissed Freddie so that he could peruse the contents alone.

Some two hours later the General emerged from the strong room. He looked anything but strong after his experience. His hands were visibly shaking and he was ashen faced. Shouting for Freddie he demanded "Get your arse in gear, you're going to Ireland to close down this time travel business immediately".

Freddie gaped in astonishment at the dishevelled General, "What do you mean" he croaked "I've never been outside of this country in my entire life, I suffer from agoraphobia and I don't even have a current passport. I can't go to Ireland" he was on the verge of tears.

"Get a grip on yourself man" bellowed the general "This is urgent and I don't have the time to bring someone else up to speed. You are the man on the spot so you are going. Bring that useless sergeant of yours with you".

"This mission needs to be ultra-deep secret" the General went on "you and Wilson will go to Ireland, find the person who set off the alarm and bring them and all equipment associated with the matter back here to Britain for deep debriefing at our secret premises in the Welsh mountains.

"Remember" he said in a doom laden voice "Tell no one else about this"

Chapter Six

Perfidious Albion Strikes

Mick woke on a bright sunny morning, in his own bed and with a feeling of deep peace and contentment. Thinking over his recent adventures he remembered that he had Paulo to look after. He had given him the spare room to stay in last night but now something of a more permanent nature needed to be sorted out.

The more he thought about it, the more complicated and daunting the prospect seemed to be. Here was Paulo, not only a stateless person but in some sense a timeless one also. He had no papers and worse still no knowledge of the culture into which he had been thrown. Unless, thought Mick, the Queen bug had implanted all that stuff in Paulo when she constructed him in order to gain Mick's trust. That would be handy if it was the case.

Going into the guest room Mick found Paulo still in bed and looking distinctly peaky. "What's wrong?" he asked "You look dreadful, are you sick? Is there anything I can get you?" And many more solicitous queries typical of someone confronted with a medical situation and not knowing how to deal with it.

Paulo groaned and turned to face Mick "I'm not designed for your world Mick" he whimpered. "The Queen only made me for the temporary task of tricking you and my time span is nearly exhausted". Mick looked frantically around the room, seeking inspiration as to how this problem might be solved.

"Don't fret yourself, Mick. This was always the inevitable outcome, I'm only surprised I've lasted as long as I have. I'm honoured to have made your acquaintance and I wish you all the good fortune in the world as you continue your grand adventure" saying this his eyes drooped shut and with no perceptible movement he simply faded out and disappeared.

Mick stared at the empty bed in astonishment and sat, sunk in deep sorrow as he thought of his brief time with Paulo. Perhaps it was inevitable that he should have liked him on sight, after all he had been designed by the wicked Queen to impress Mick from the start. However Mick was convinced that he had discerned some admirable qualities in Paulo and he was sure he would linger in his memory for a long time. Sitting there pondering what manner of afterlife Paulo might be experiencing and other maudlin thoughts Mick was startled by the sound of his ultra-loud doorbell.

Hesitantly opening his front door he found Frank, clutching in one hand a duty free bag, from which the pleasant clink of bottles could be heard, standing on the doorstep. The reader must understand that Frank was now travelling on a different timeline than that which obtained when we last met him. In this timeline the entire incident of the disappearing house and the subsequent interview with Inspector McGrath had not happened and Frank had no knowledge that Mick had gone anywhere.

"What's the story, Mick" he cried, gently shaking the duty free bag "I'm back from Kazakhstan, and I have to say I'm not sorry. That place is hot, dusty, and smelly and you can't get a decent pint for love nor money. They drink fermented mare's milk, for God's sake". Pausing to place his bag on the floor he continued "How's things anyway, have you got your thingamajig up and running yet?"

Mick stared in amazement at Frank as it slowly dawned on him that his friend was totally unaware that he had been on a trip to other times or dimensions, Mick was still unsure which. "Frank" he said "Do I have a story to tell" and sitting down, taking the cap off Frank's offering and pouring a stiff pair of drinks he commenced to regale his friend with the tale of his recent adventures.

At first Frank was somewhat dubious about the story but when it reached its end with the tale of Paulo's demise he was totally incredulous. Mick was aware that somewhere in the telling of the tale, that he had lost Frank and, if truth be told, he couldn't blame him.

Obviously there was only one thing to do, he must needs bring Frank on a time trip to prove that he was not lying.

Frank was less than enthusiastic about the notion when Mick broached it. In the first place he wasn't madly keen on the idea of alternate dimensions and as far as time travel went, he didn't want to meet his Grandfather who, if Frank remembered right, was a grumpy old git who suffered from gout and carried a stick with which he was prone to wallop any small boys who were unfortunate enough to cross his path. Furthermore he, unlike Mick, was gainfully employed and it would be unwise at this juncture to annoy his employer by taking time off to go jaunting around the cosmos.

Mick hastily moved to calm Frank's

apprehensions "These worries are nonsense" he told Frank "I can easily avoid your Grandfather, though I doubt if he was as bad as you make him out to be, and as far as your job is concerned we will return to this time and place at exactly the hour and minute at which we leave. I guarantee it!" As things developed this may not have been a wise thing to guarantee.

Frank reluctantly agreed to be taken for a short jaunt through time and/or across dimensions, Mick was still less than certain as to what medium he was travelling through. Frank however placed a clear imperative on Mick "Let's be absolutely certain about this Mick" he said "First off I don't want to go far and secondly I must be back in time for the office tomorrow, not one second later".

"Easy Peasy" Mick was in high good humour and the loss of Paulo was evidently not weighing on him as heavily as he might have feared now that he had his oldest and best friend with him on the adventure.

Mick's next task was to select a destination which would indisputably be identifiable by Frank as not-of-this-time. Moving into the future would be easy but if they did not go far, Frank, in his current disputatious state of mind might be hard to convince they had actually gone anywhere.

Thinking of this issue Mick was suddenly struck by a brilliant idea. Frank was an avid soccer fan and his abiding regret was that he had not been in Stuttgart in 1988 when Ray Houghton scored his iconic goal against the old enemy, England, in the European championships of that year.

The only matter outstanding was that tickets for the game needed to be procured, but this did not raise serious issues. Ireland had no major expectations in this competition at the time so demand for tickets would not be a big deal. Buying the tickets did require a swift trip back to a date prior to the game but again, no big problem. Last but not least whilst the time machine could with little effort travel through time, it could not travel anywhere except to the exact same location in any timeline. Travel from Ireland to Stuttgart had, therefore to be sorted out also.

Bidding Frank to remain where he was, Mick mounted his trusty Vuitton Plessy motorbike and vanished in a blink of an eye. He was hardly gone than he was back brandishing the precious tickets in Frank's face.

"We're off to Stuttgart for the European championship game against England" said Mick. Frank looked at him in astonishment.

"What are you goin' on about, the Euros are just over and we weren't playing against England anyway".

Mick crowed triumphantly "No, Stuttgart 1988, Ray Houghton's goal against England and our 1-0 win against the mighty Brits".

Frank was gobsmacked "You don't mean... you can't be serious, the greatest goal in Ireland's soccer history and we'll be there?"

"Yep, jump into the sidecar there and we're off to the 1988 Euros".

The disappearing and reappearing events occurred

almost simultaneously and Frank scrambled out of the sidecar in a state of almost catatonic rapture. "Did you see that goal Mick" he had tears in his eyes as he clasped Mick by the shoulders, "Wasn't it the most beautiful thing you ever saw in your life?"

Mick smiled complacently "Maybe you'll believe me now" He queried "The old time travel thing doesn't look so unlikely after all, does it?"

Frank, still on cloud nine scratched his head and answered Mick "My Grandfather, when asked in 1920 if he would like to go to the pictures is reputed to have said, and I quote "I'll never go to them pictures, sure they put it on your eyes", now I need your solemn word that this was not an elaborate prank and that all my friends and relatives are not waiting in hiding, ready to jump out and slag me unmercifully for being taken in by you".

"For God's sake Frank, you must be the biggest sceptic in the bloody world. I've brought you back to 1988, to one of the greatest sporting moments of all time for Ireland. We've witnessed a goal which will forever be branded on the consciousness of all football fans in the Republic and for a reward you ask me to reassure you that it's all kosher. You're incorrigible. I am wasting my sweetness on the desert air with you. Go home and let me get on with my work."

At that moment they were interrupted by the clanging of the doorbell. Mick again reminded himself that something needed to be done about the confounded noise which it made as he went to open the door.

"Well" he snarled at the lanky, unprepossessing

figure of Major Freddie Fortescue standing awkwardly on the doorstep, Freddie was, of course in civilian clothes.

"What do you want" demanded Mick. "I'm very busy just now and I have no need for double glazed windows or external cladding at present".

Freddie and Wilson had arrived in Dublin Port by ferry, at an ungodly hour, that morning. The crossing had been rough and with the austerity programme at full tilt in Britain, they were not allowed to book cabins. They had therefore spent the night in considerable discomfort, propped up on a couch in the bar between a nursing mother with a colicky child and a garrulous drunk who wanted to impart his life's experiences to Freddie. His misfortune was compounded by the fact that Wilson, an old soldier, could and did sleep like a baby from the moment they boarded until their arrival in port.

Freddie had devised a cunning plan, at least he thought it was cunning. He sent Wilson around the back of Mick's house while he approached the front door.

"When I give the signal, Wilson, I want you to rush in and apprehend the developer of the technology which produces the exotic particles. I want him, or her, securely immobilised and we will then have time to collect all items of interest. When that's done we contact MI5 who will provide transportation for our captive and his gear. Anything we can't carry must be destroyed so we will set the house on fire before we leave, is that clearly understood Sarn't?"

Wilson, a large man of African origin was very dubious about all this. He had some scruples about kidnapping people, he considered Freddie to be a complete and utter Gobshite and last but not least he was a filing clerk, not a cold war warrior. He heard of the legendary fighting prowess of the Irish and he had real reservations about his ability to "Apprehend the Developer" as Freddie so glibly put it. He knew without any doubt that whatever abilities he, himself, might have in this mission, Freddie would be completely useless.

However thinking to himself that *Orders is Orders* he snapped off a sloppy salute and declaimed

"As you wish Sir" and headed off down the lane behind Mick's house. At the back of Mick's house he found a six foot high wall, not in itself an insurmountable barrier, but growing profusely on top was a very healthy thorn bush. Wilson estimated that the thorns were at least three inches long and whilst this might have been somewhat exaggerated, nevertheless they were enough to inflict real injuries.

Pausing to light up a cigarette and plan his best approach to the matter of walls and thorns he suddenly remembered that Freddie and he had not actually agreed a signal. "Dozy pillock" he muttered to himself "I couldn't be stuck with a worse fool than this one. What should I do now?"

"Oh well, I'll just finish this fag and think about climbing over the thorny wall". He was really unenthusiastic about this entire exercise.

Meanwhile Freddie, somewhat taken aback by Mick's frontal assault lost his carefully prepared cover story and blurted out "Hello my good man, I'm Major

Freddie Fortescue of Her Majesty's Royal Marines and I've come to apprehend you and take you back to Great Britain to answer for your behaviour in creating exotic particles without a license".

Mick, with his mind on eight hundred years of British persecution and occupation said "You can get stuffed if you think I'm going anywhere with you. It's the likes of you that has the World in the state it's in. Now get lost or I'll be forced to give you a good kicking". He was still cranky because Frank didn't believe him about the time travel thing and he had no idea what exotic particles might be. He tended to get cranky when people talked down to him.

Freddie was severely taken aback by Mick's aggressive riposte because, being a Major in Her Majesty's Marines, he was not accustomed to being spoken to in this manner by an Irish peasant. Frantically trying to remember the signal agreed with Wilson he sternly warned Mick "My good man, I warn you that I am a trained member of Her Majesty's Armed Forces and you would be well advised to keep a civil tongue in your head when talking to me".

He had now seriously antagonised Mick who pushed him off the doorstep and slammed the door in his face. In the recent past Mick had quite enough dealings with Royalty and their minions and he was in fine form for giving them short shrift. Much put out, Freddie pulled his mobile phone from his pocket and called Wilson. "Where are you, you dolt, I need you to conduct a flanking raid on these premises whilst I enter by means of a frontal assault".

Wilson, hung up in an extremely embarrassing manner by the crotch of his best trousers on the thorns struggled to hold the phone to his ear whilst frantically attempting to protect his own crown jewels from the encroaching spears of vegetation. With a convulsive spasm he managed to detach himself and fell to the ground, leaving a generous patch of the arse of his pants impaled on the bush.

"I'll do the best I can Sir" he whimpered "but you must know that I'm not very good at this assaulting lark". Spurred on by Freddie's screams of rage and frustration he proceeded to the back door, which Mick had left open that morning after breakfast. Taking his courage in both hands he entered the house and called out "Hello, is anyone home?"

Chapter Seven

Freddie's Dilemma

Hearing Wilson's plaintive call Mick, by now well past exasperation and into genuine rage shouted "Who the fuck is that?" Rushing into the kitchen and brandishing his trusty colt, which he had snatched up on his way through, he pointed it at Wilson and snarled "Put your hands where I can see them, if you make so much as a sneeze I'll ventilate your innards and also blow your head off its shoulders". It's plain to see that he was upset.

Wilson in an agony of mortification fell to his knees and placing his hands on top of his head pleaded "Please don't shoot, I'm very sorry, I didn't want to do this, it's not my fault, that thick dope Major Freddie made me do it"

Throughout all this hubbub Frank had been sitting in the sidecar of Mick's motorcycle, reflecting on his recent unbelievable experiences. He had not reacted to Mick's confrontation on the doorstep but the row in the kitchen demanded his attention. Going through he found Mick, red in the face and waving a lethal weapon about and a pathetic, ragged trousered Wilson kneeling on the floor, tears streaming down his face and pleading for his life. He reached over Mick's shoulder and snatched the colt out of his hand. Checking he saw to his relief that the safety catch was still on. "What's going on here?" he demanded.

Mick and Wilson both began to speak together and the more one spoke the louder the other retorted. Soon the uproar in the kitchen became unsupportable. "SHUT UP" roared Frank "I can't hear my ears with all this noise". When quiet had descended he turned to Wilson and demanded an explanation.

Wilson, if nothing else a good man to produce a précis of a narrative, told the tale of the exotic matter particles, the alert in GCHQ, file number CC-443567, General Farquharson etc. Mick and Frank listened to this with open mouthed amazement. They thought that it sounded like something out of a spy novel, though more Austin Powers than James Bond.

Freddie, meanwhile, without the expected support from Wilson took himself off to the nearest coffee shop to consider his options. It never occurred to him to consider what Wilson's fate might be and, if he thought of him at all, he assumed that he was ensconced somewhere reading one of those dreadful novels which were a favourite of his. Clearly he could not call in reinforcements as to do so would require an admission that he had made a complete cock up of the mission to date. It would do his military career no good at all to report this level of incompetence to his superiors. He had only two viable options open to him, either retrieve the situation or find a way to blame Wilson on its disastrous outcome. With considerable trepidation he decided that he must go back to Mick's house and try to patch things up with his adversary.

Mick, Frank and Wilson, by now the best of friends were seated in Mick's lounge. They had broken out Mick's ten year old John Jameson and were in the process of settling down to a serious session. They each, for their own reasons, felt that a generous libation was in order.

The first order of business was to decide just how to deal with the GCHQ thing. Several plans were proposed and rejected as unfeasible, including the murder of Freddie and the disposal of his body. Strangely enough it was Wilson who put this suggestion forward. Finally Mick came up with a plan.

"What we need to do is go back to before this all began and go back in time to GCHQ. There we need to erase all data referring to file number CC-443567 and disable the warning systems related to it, then none of this will have happened. The only issue outstanding is will you do it?" this he addressed to Wilson.

Frank was utterly aghast at this proposal. He worked in the Department of Foreign Affairs and as a lifelong civil servant had a regard for files and forms which bordered on the religious. To speak of erasing documents and, worse still, rendering them gone from existence struck him as almost sacrilegious, worse, even Diabolical.

Wilson, on the other hand, was totally into the deal. There were any number of files which, in his opinion, would be better off thrown into the trashcan, included were Freddie's promotion records. Wilson had a vision of Freddie, busted down to private and subject to Wilson's every whim. Better than that if one could mess with files, why not promote himself to Major or even Colonel. That would be really cool. He could easily accustom himself to a life of ease and comfort on a Colonel's pay and perks.

Mick interjected at this point, "You can't just mess around in time like that. There is a thing called The Law of Unintended Consequences which we need to take notice of. Every change we make has some consequences and those effects ripple outwards to create other consequences and on and on ad infinitum. We need to make very slight changes and CC-443567 is ideal because it's only known to very few and it only affects a very small number of people. Therefore the ripple effects should be little and they should quickly dissipate". After this long speech, Mick went back to the John Jameson bottle to slake his thirst.

Freddie, nursing his cappuccino and reflecting on his misfortunes, finally decided to retrace his steps to Mick's house in order to see if there was anything he could retrieve from his fiasco. As he finally advanced extremely cautiously up the front garden path he was amazed and disgusted to hear the sound of several voices, chief among them Wilson, raised in loud and disharmonious song. As he neared the front door he was doubly annoyed to hear the song being sung:

"A Nation Once Again'

A Nation Once Again,

And Ireland, long a province,

Be a Nation once Again."

"God Almighty" he whispered "That's Wilson singing Irish Rebel Songs" He crept nearer and peeked through the window but sadly for him, Wilson happened to be looking straight at him and with a mighty whoop he rushed out the door and grabbed Freddie by the scruff of his neck.

Mick and Frank, by now well gone in drink, looked on in befuddlement as Wilson dragged Freddie into the house. "Whaddayagot there?" queried Mick as he attempted, with mixed success to stand up.

"It's the thick dope I was telling you about earlier, none other than The Right Honourable Major Freddie Fortescue, Officer and Gentleman, of Her Majesty's Royal Marines and a first class prick to boot" said Wilson with a huge triumphant grin plastered over his face. "I can see the first class prick" said Mick "Where's the other fella".

Wilson was not inclined to be facetious about this. "This muppet is here with orders to kidnap or, if that's not feasible, kill you, steal all records of your time machine together with all pieces of technology associated with it, and then destroy your house in order to conceal all evidence of his criminal activities. I really don't think we should mess about. We need to off him and get rid of the body, right now!"

Freddie burst into the conversation.

"Sarn't Wilson, you're talking treason, I recommend that before you get yourself into anything worse you cease and desist with your traitorous activities and assist me to carry out our mission immediately. I may be able to overlook some of your

Wilson, whose mother was from Jamaica, raised one large hand and showed it palm first to Freddie and in a mock West Indian accent said "Talk to the hand mon, 'cause the face ain't listenin'" and dropping his tattered pants to expose his buttocks to his former superior he went on "Better yet, talk to the booty 'cause the hand's off dooty".

During this exchange Mick and Frank were struck speechless as the fog of alcohol slowly dissipated from their brains.

"Hey" Mick said "Knock it off, nobody's going to be offed here. This is my house and my time machine. I give the orders around here".

With a doleful expression Wilson complained "It's OK for you guys, you're foreign nationals. I'm a British Citizen and as this fool here says I could be hanged for treason or something".

"Don't be stupid" Frank replied "They don't hang people for treason in peacetime. The worst you'd get is twenty years to life".

"Forget all this nonsense, nobody's getting hanged or going to jail. I have a plan which will deal with this whole farrago of nonsense" Mick had an expression of enlightenment on his face which Frank, who had known him since childhood, felt boded no good for the assembled company.

They spent the remainder of the day planning and refining the plan over many iterations until at last they were satisfied that it had a chance of success. Then worn out by their exertions of the day, they retired to The Porterhouse pub for a few quiet drinks. Freddie was allowed to join them under his solemn word of honour that he would not attempt to escape or contact his superiors and that he would pay for the drinks.

Chapter Eight

The Irish at Cheltenham

Five days earlier in a Drumcondra suburb there was a noise very like a gentle clap of thunder. Mick and Frank emerged from Mick's house carrying overnight bags and were closely followed by Wilson, looking somewhat menacing, with Freddie under his close observation. Wilson wasn't altogether happy with this word of honour stuff and as for officer and gentleman, he considered that utter bullshit.

"This looks just like it was before I went around the back" he said "Are you really sure we've travelled in Time?" Mick smiled reassuringly, "No worries" he replied, "We'll pick up a paper at the corner shop and you'll see the date on it".

Later, in the airport waiting to board their Aer Arann flight to Bristol, Wilson by now convinced of the existence of time travel and time machines asked the question which had been bothering him all morning.

"What about the time paradox, then" The others looked at him in astonishment

"What" He asked, "You think just because I'm a black sergeant I know nothing. I've read all about this stuff in books since I joined the army. There's nothing much else to do after the first six weeks of boot camp. The time paradox is where, if you travel in time you can't meet yourself or something dreadful will happen. How come you weren't there when we came back, and more to the point what if I meet myself in GCHQ?"

"No need to get your knickers in a twist" Mick reassured him, "I've travelled extensively in time and I've never met myself, I have a theory that the cosmos won't allow it. So let's get on with it". Wilson was not fully satisfied with this reply but as he was in for a penny, might as well stay in for his pound.

Mick was in full command mode "Now Wilson you know what needs to be done, you clock in as usual go and get the CC-443567 file, stick it under your jumper and bring it out to us in the coffee shop. Take it casual, don't make any sudden moves and everything will be all right".

Wilson strode into the foyer of GCHQ with a sunny smile on his face, "Good morning" he sang out to all and sundry and presenting his security pass to the card reader he passed on into his own office. He had called into his apartment on his way in to collect the card. Picking up the phone he got through to the records office

"Hi, Jim" He said, "Old Horse Face wants the CC-443567 file. I'll be down to collect it directly, as usual it's needed by yesterday. OK?" Jim was familiar with Wilson's pet name for Major Freddie and promised that the file would be on hand for Wilson to pick it up.

Mick with masterful insight had provided Wilson with half a dozen cream doughnuts to give to Jim, in order to smooth out any awkward queries which might arise. Jim's fondness for cream doughnuts was legendary in GCHQ and on one memorable morning he had consumed two dozen over the course of seventy five minutes. A record which still stands in that venerable institution. In the event the provision of the delicacies worked a treat.

Wilson, clutching the file went back to his office and claiming a dental appointment slipped out and off to the coffee shop as arranged. "Fantastic" cried Mick "Now comes the tricky bit" "What tricky bit" howled Wilson "You never said anything about a tricky bit. I've gotten the cursed file, haven't I? What more do you want?"

Mick looked at him pityingly

"Wilson, Wilson, Wilson" he said "You know as well as I do that there is an active computer alert waiting for the release of exotic particles sitting poised to pop up when I set the machine in motion"

Wilson looked at him in total consternation, he had all too good an idea what was coming next.

"It's no big deal" Mick continued, "All you have to do is go into the computer with Freddie's access code and delete all references to CC-443567, time travel and especially exotic particles".

Hearing this Freddie raised a howl of protest, "You can't do that, I'll be fatally compromised and I'll never get promotion. In fact I'll be lucky if I'm not dishonourably discharged. Anyway, nobody knows my access code"

"You still haven't caught on to this time travel gig, Freddie, have you?" queried Mick "Once we do this all trace of the file and the alert will have ceased to exist and so will the consequences, it's not only unintended consequences we're faced with you know, and I'll be astonished if Wilson doesn't know your code, am I right Wilson". Wilson nodded somewhat shamefacedly.

Later in the afternoon Wilson entered the coffee shop with an enormous beaming smile on his face,

"Hey guys I did it, all the records are erased and double erased, nobody's going to find out anything about time travel from GCHQ I can assure you of that".

Taking Mick to one side he said

"I know you told me about the unintended consequences bit and I guess you won't like this part of the story but while I was in the computer I gave myself an honourable discharge from the army, using Freddie's authority. I hope it doesn't cause too much trouble".

Mick laughed and said "I don't know if it'll cause problems but I don't blame you for wanting out of that organisation. Anyway, what's done is done and it's no good crying over spilt milk".

Back in God's country the lads sat around discussing their plans for the future. Wilson was still unhappy about Freddie and what he might do when he got back to GCHQ. Mick reassured him and turning to Freddie he said

"The way I see things, Freddie, is this; you have a series of options going forward, you can go back home and keep your trap shut, or you can report the entire story to your superiors, but you need to realise that there is absolutely no evidence remaining to support your statement. The best outcome you might expect is to be instantly dismissed as a fantasist, the worst is that you might finish up in the booby hatch during the pleasure of her Majesty's Government. However, to make things easier for you I do have a proposal"

Freddie was aghast, "Dear God, do you know what you've done to me, I'll never be able to hold my head up in decent society again. You've struck at the roots of my ethical system, I absolutely must report this and if I do, I'll be destroyed".

Mick said "Wait till you hear my proposition. In my pocket at this moment I have the numbers for next Saturday's Euro Millions Jackpot which is in the order of £168 million. I propose to give the numbers to you and set you loose to go home. Your superiors will think you've been off on a naughty weekend and nobody's the worse for the experience. Alternatively I can go back in time and prevent the meeting of your mother and father, the inevitable result of such a set of circumstances would mean you never existed, in fact you're looking a bit blurry around the edges right now, how are you feeling?".

Without an instant's hesitation Freddie said "Bugger the ethics, give me the numbers and call a cab"

Wilson gaped at Mick in total astonishment "What about the unintended thingamabob" he demanded. Are you God or something, why are you and only you allowed to mess with time like that?"

"I'm sorry, I didn't make myself clear about that. The rule about unintended etc. only applies to past events. As future ones obviously haven't happened yet, they don't have consequences, intended or otherwise so the rule doesn't apply". Mick looked suitably chastened as he admitted this.

"By the way, Wilson, what would you like, do you want lotto numbers or stock market tips. You can be one of the richest men in the world if you like".

Wilson looked like a man who had been hit with a rubber frying pan. "To tell the truth, I would like to hang around with you for a while and check out the time travel gig. I've lived my life vicariously through other people's fictional escapades and now that the opportunity is here I'd love to get some real, honest to God, adventure in my hitherto miserable existence".

Mick was deeply moved by this avowal and readily agreed to the proposal. Turning to his childhood friend Mick asked "Well Frank, how about you. Is there anything we can do for you? You know you're welcome to come adventuring with Wilson and me, or you can have the lotto money etc., or both obviously. There's nobody I'd rather have at my side than yourself for this gig".

Frank said "Mick, you know I'm not cut out for this bazzing about the universe in flimsy machines. At heart I'm a civil servant and my ambition only reaches the heights of a few pints in a comfortable bar at the weekend. Anything else is too rich for my blood. But I'll tell you what I do want, I want you to keep a complete record of your travels and promise that you will keep in contact with regular updates so that I'm abreast of your exploits as they unfold".

With tears in his eyes Mick threw his arms around his friend and solemnly promised to do as he asked. Shaking hands with Wilson, Frank made his goodbyes and left for his office where he had files to update.

Chapter Nine

Mick and Wilson at Large

Turning to Wilson Mick said "Well, that's that. Now we need to strategise, I've been crashing around with the whole thing up to now like a fool in a fog. That needs to stop. We need to plan our trips with care and attention and also to record and log them so that we can build up a database of stuff to help plan future trips".

Mick thought the first issue to address should be one of mobility. Taking his entire house everywhere he went really did not make sense and was probably very wearing on the fabric of the structure also. The use of the Plessy-Vuitton motorcycle combination would be bound to cause comment if used in any time period outside of an approximate hundred year span so some other option needed to be provided.

Fortunately for our gallant heroes, finance wasn't an obstacle so they travelled, conventionally, in the considerable comfort of business class to America. Here after extensive research and study they bought a Winnebago, modified for rough terrain travel and had it shipped home to be modified for time travel in the security of Mick's back garden.

Mick had, over his time spent with the Hungaro-Germans who built the steam version of the machine, learnt the physical necessities of fitting his time travel device to various vehicle and none, so fitting one to the Winnebago was child's play. In the course of an extensive remodelling of the vehicle he installed massive auxiliary fuel tanks and modified the engine to accept a wide range of alternative fuels including cooking oil, hydrogen and biomass (wood chips to you and me).

Finally after two months of gruelling work he and Wilson expressed themselves satisfied with the latest version of what Mick dubbed "The Travellator". The next item on the agenda being where and when to go to, Wilson suggested the Mediterranean coast of Spain where sunshine is plentiful and a time some three thousand years in the past, when they might expect a reasonable measure of privacy and freedom from persecution and prying governments.

Further research led to the decision that they ought to load up with a variety of items which should appeal to any Iberian residents who might be found in prior occupancy of their destination together with a considerable stock of frozen and dried foodstuffs, against the contingency that food could be scarce or hard to catch. Mindful of Frank's admonition that records should be kept, they also invested in a couple of digital still cameras and two high end camcorders so that they could have indisputable proof of their adventures.

Cognisant of his new found determination that forethought would be the watchword for all future voyages Mick concluded that they should travel overland to Spain first, before any time travel elements. Whilst, obviously there are, in the current timeline, a number of methods for travelling to the European Continental landmass, such facilities would not exist in the far past. Therefore to time travel first would leave them isolated on a small island with no obvious means of getting to Spain. Muttering something to himself about "a stitch in time" Mick congratulated himself and with Wilson driving, set off, like Don Quixote for Spain.

Following an uneventful sea trip across to France and a very pleasant drive down to the tiny fishing village of Atunara in southern Spain, the pair finally came to a camping ground which looked good to them. It was situated, as advertised, very close to the beach and within a very short drive to Gibraltar.

They rested overnight and bright and early next morning Mick roused Wilson and demanded "Well are you ready for this?" Wilson jumped out of bed and with a loud yell cried "Bring it on Man".

Mick switched on the engine of "The Travellator" and being careful to remain in neutral gear, engaged the time drive. The evening before both he and Wilson had calculated and recalculated the desired time slice to be travelled to and with a more sophisticated computer aided navigation system satisfied themselves that they would travel to where and when they wished rather than Mick's last, disastrous, foray into the far future.

Mick was, by now, becoming blasé about the time travel lark but Wilson was astonished when with no perceptible movement all evidence of modern development disappeared in front of his eyes and he was presented with a view of an apparently, deserted landscape. No sign remained of the dense developments which had sprawled across their view just seconds previously, whilst a short distance away the massive presence of the Rock of Gibraltar loomed over the vista like some giant's head emerging from the sea.

"Mick", said Wilson "I don't think I'd ever get

used to this time travel. This is just awesome. It's exactly as I pictured it when I suggested it as our destination. I wonder if there are any people living in the area and, if they are hostile to strangers".

"I don't expect them to be immediately hostile" Mick replied "People have been trading across this stretch of water for millennia even in these early times, so they should be reasonably open to visitors. The Travellator may be a bit awe inspiring to them but that, in itself, should be no bad thing".

"Are there any special precautions we should take to protect ourselves, do you think?" Wilson said, looking around nervously as they stepped out from the vehicle.

"No, as I said I don't think that the natives will be hostile but I've got my trusty colt along if needed and I'm sure that you being a trained soldier can subdue any fractious person with some unarmed combat moves learned in Her Majesty's service", Mick was being facetious. "Hah" said Wilson, "It's a long time since I did any unarmed combat and even back then I was better at running away than going hand to hand with the enemy, even the mock enemy of my training days".

By the way" Mick asked "How's your Latin?"

"Latin? What Latin? If you mean the dead language we had beaten into us in school I'd have to say my Latin is not so much rusty as sublimed back into the ore from which it was originally smelted. Why do you ask?"

Mick said, in a somewhat doubtful way, "Well we're unlikely to meet any English speakers in this era. I reckon modern English is not invented for about, oh maybe, two thousand eight hundred years. My history of these times is not great but I reckon the Phoenicians and Assyrians were knocking around in this neck of the woods in these times. Whatever about my Latin the other two languages are a complete mystery to me. I don't reckon you're any more up to speed than I am, are you?"

"It's a bit late in the day to raise an issue over communications. Why didn't you raise this language thing before we set out?" Wilson was more than a little put out.

"It was your idea to come here" said Mick "However I don't think it's an insurmountable barrier. This area has been a centre of trade since prehistory and the native peoples should be very used to foreigners arriving with no language skills. I would expect that they will be able to communicate by signs and pointing and so on".

"Mind you" he continued "We are in a strong position to get by without any outside assistance whatever. We have ample supplies and a vehicle which is ideally suited to provide a safe environment for an indefinite period".

At that moment they heard a bleating sound and a man shambled over a nearby crest herding before him a group of scruffy looking goats or sheep. Mick could never distinguish between the two species, especially in the area in which they now found themselves.

Hailing the goat herd, Mick tried by signs to communicate with him. Perhaps predictably the response was not great. They were in no way familiar with the conditions in which the man lived so finding a point of reference between them was a difficult if not impossible task.

"I think this is a waste of time" Wilson said "Why don't we head over towards Gibraltar and see if there is any sign of a settlement around there. These traders of yours will probably have a base of operations some place or other and Gib seems to be as good a place as any to start".

"Why didn't I think of that?" asked Mick. "I clean forgot that the Travellator could move. I guess I'm not as quick on the uptake as I like to let on".

Climbing aboard the van Mick fired up the engine. Hearing a loud shout of laughter from Wilson, Mick turned to see what had caused it and saw the unfortunate goatherd fleeing for his life from this monster with his unkempt flock scattering to the four points of the compass.

"I guess he's never come across the likes of us and the Travellator before" he chuckled "I bet if we did deep research we'd find that this is the source of the legends about fire breathing dragons in our time".

The intrepid adventurers set out to drive the short journey to Gibraltar. This proved to be easier said than done. There were, of course, no roads and any paths were single track only, barely fit for horse or foot traffic. The Travellator had been fitted with off road capacity, of course, but even so the journey was bumpy and almost impassable in places. Mick decided that a trip to a future date when someone had invented an antigravity device that would greatly facilitate this travel deal was an important item on the agenda.

Arriving at the isthmus which separates the Rock from the mainland, the site of the modern day airport, they carefully picked their way across to their destination. This was a tricky operation as the ground was low lying and soft in places. The Travellator was a formidable vehicle but even it could get bogged down. If that happened the only way out would be to time travel back to the twenty first century. Whilst this might seem like a viable proposition, it carried with it the very real danger that they might find themselves stuck fast in concrete up to the wheel hubs and also directly in the landing path of a Jumbo Jet. Not an attractive situation. Both heaved an enormous sigh of relief when at last they found themselves on higher ground with solid rock underneath.

Wilson had been uncharacteristically quiet on the short journey to The Rock and Mick asked if something was wrong. Wilson said "Not really but I'm a little concerned about a couple of things involving this exercise".

"What's that?" asked Mick

"Well I don't see how we can successfully communicate with people from this timeframe. We don't even know what language they speak, and even if we did it would take us forever to learn it. Also I've had a look at our stock of gear and stuff and I don't see anything which might be expected to appeal to the denizens of this age in trade".

Mick laughed heartily "Wilson" he said "I'm sorry

I didn't keep you fully informed about everything before we set out but I've taken care of all those issues already. Whilst we were modifying the Travellator I took a short trip into the future on the motorbike, I know it was underpowered but I fitted it with a new flux capacitor, (that's a term I stole from Back to the Future, it's meaningless of course but to try to describe the actual system for warping time would take more time than I have and requires terminology which has not been developed yet,) and it's well capable of extended trips now. I figured that with the current state of technology in our time that within about five years Google would have developed an Android phone which could directly translate speech from any language to any other after listening to someone speaking it for an hour or two. Sure enough when I got to the year 2025 these phones were on sale everywhere. I got a couple for us, they obviously won't work as phones here but the translator function works independently of the network so we're fixed as far as translating goes, I was winding you up before."

"Hang on and I'll show you something really cool" Mick said and going into the rear cabin of the Travellator he rummaged around and came back with a small package. Tossing it into Wilson's lap he said "Open that and see what you think" he crowed triumphantly.

Wilson hefted the surprisingly heavy parcel in his hand and tearing off the wrapper he was astonished to see several wafers of soft yellow metal inside. "Is that what I think it is?" he asked.

"Yes, its gold" Mick grinned "I've got several hundred thousand Euros worth stashed in the cupboard back there. Cool huh? I'm quite sure the locals will accept this in trade".

Wilson who was becoming quite familiar with Dublin colloquialisms said "You're a cute hoor right enough".

Chapter Ten

Iberia

Travelling around the base of the Rock the lads came to a wide plateau located at the modern equivalent of Windmill Hill. There they found a fortified town or habitation huddled under the towering point of the Rock. As they drew the Travellator to a halt outside the town a number of men emerged somewhat hesitantly. They were dressed in rough homespun garments and brandished a variety of pointed weapons, shouting loudly, presumably in an effort to frighten off this menacing monster.

Wilson nodded in the direction of the Rock and said "There's a lookout point up there and I guess they've been watching us approach since we arrived on the isthmus. This is obviously the reception committee".

"O.K." Mick said adopting an insouciant air "We'll play this cool. First off put on this police issue stab vest, then a loose Hawaiian style shirt and light trousers. Clip the Android phone to your belt and keep the Beretta pistol out of sight unless it's needed. Don't shoot unless it's absolutely necessary". Suiting his actions to his words he dressed as suggested and instead of a Beretta he strapped on the already mentioned Colt. With a carefree shrug of his shoulders he stepped out of the Travellator, closely followed by Wilson who cast anxious glances all round, expecting attackers from all directions.

Leaving the engine of the Travellator running, Mick advanced slowly towards the reception committee, holding his arms in the air with palms to the front. He considered this to be the universal sign of peaceful intentions. As he proceeded he said in a calm and conciliatory fashion "We come in peace. We seek to trade".

The reception committee was not very impressed by this apparition which had, after all, emerged from a snorting, grunting monster composed of the stuff of legends. As Mick advanced they retreated and tightened their ranks. Mick noticed that one individual was being forced to the forefront of their ranks. Walking up to this hero, Mick put out his hand, palm upwards and offered it to him. The committee member looked around at his fellows and receiving no encouragement from them, he reached tentatively forward and grasped Mick's outstretched hand in his, somewhat grubby, paw.

During this tete a tete the crowd had continued their shouting and weapons brandishing, directed towards the Travellator rather than Mick and Wilson. They also conducted some cross talk amongst themselves and made gestures towards their spokesman and the lads so Mick was satisfied that the phones were picking up threads of language and processing them.

The committee obviously decided that Wilson and Mick were harmless and, setting a guard on the Travellator, they led the lads into the fortified village. Passing through the fortifications Mick saw that they were composed of rough-hewn blocks of stone and extending to about ten feet high, altogether an impressive piece of architecture for the period. The gate was an immense wooden structure held together with massive iron bands and hung on huge iron hinges.

Inside the walls was a mismatched collection of huts, some made of animal skins, some of wattle and daub construction and a very few of dry stone build. The first thing which struck Mick was the appalling stench. Through and between the huts ran rivulets of sewage and various animals ran apparently unchecked throughout the village, contributing their own unique bouquet to the general miasma.

In the centre of the village stood a massive tent which reminded Mick of pictures he had seen in the movies of Moorish palaces. It was as big around as the average house from their timeline and stood towering over all the other structures around it, including the wall. Strangely, in the surrounding deep squalor it gleamed a spotless white in the strong sunlight.

The committee gestured towards this edifice and half leading, half pushing brought the lads to the entrance. To the astonishment of Mick and Wilson, the leader of the committee fell to his hands and knees and proceeded to enter the tent backwards. The remainder of the committee remained outside until the leader, after a couple of minutes re-emerged. He stood up and made gestures to the lads that they should enter in the same mode.

Wilson said "No way am I going to crawl, arse backwards, into any Nabob's tent. In the first place only god knows what sort of trap is waiting just inside the door, but whether or which, I'm not prepared to demean myself for any man".

Nodding his agreement Mick marched, head erect, towards the tent. The committee members immediately jumped in front of him and gestured that he should immediately assume the position, in the time honoured cop phrase of TV shows. Mick was prepared for this, casually slipping his hand into his pocket he pressed the car zapper which he had brought along for just such an eventuality. Immediately the air horn, which he had fitted to the Travellator produced a deafening blast of noise, the likes of which had never before been heard in that neighbourhood since the fall of the fabled Pillars of Hercules.

This racket caused consternation amongst the committee and onlookers alike. Those who did not immediately run away, fell flat on their faces and covered their heads with their hands, presumably under the impression that an earthquake or some other natural disaster was about to befall them. Taking advantage of this hullabaloo Mick and Wilson boldly strode forward and entered the tent.

Once inside the two were struck by the contrast between the tent's interior and the squalor outside. Scattered on the floor were cushions in many bright colours, evidently of silk. The walls were hung with gauzy draperies of multicoloured material and scattered strategically around were burning braziers of scented oils. Mick noticed that under the scent from the braziers was a strong smell of unwashed bodies and untreated sewage which together threatened to produce a severe headache if he remained in the enclosure for any extended period of time.

Wilson turned to Mick and said in a whisper "Is it me or is there a terrible stink in here?" Mick was about to reply when he noticed a movement in a pile of cushions in front of them. Poking the cushions he was amazed to find a strangely garbed individual hiding underneath.

"Hell I forgot to turn off the air horn" Said Mick as he reached into his pocket and silenced the raucous cacophony.

The man rose from under the cushions as the committee came rushing into the tent, obviously intent on dealing harshly with these impertinent interlopers who had entered the hallowed presence without appropriate respect. Making an imperious gesture the Nabob quelled the crowd and shepherded them from the tent. During this hubbub Mick was delighted to hear fragments of the conversation emerging, in English, from the Android phone strapped to his waist.

"Hey Wilson, the translators are working. We should be able to converse with these guys any time now" Mick was understandably chuffed at the success of this stratagem.

Turning towards the sumptuously dressed individual he said, in a clear and distinct voice "Greetings, we are traders and we come in peace". The translator produced an unintelligible garble which sounded to Mick like Arabic but the other looked in astonishment at him and said

"You can speak my language? How is this, are you Gods? This was translated directly into English and Mick gave Wilson a thumbs sign.

"We're in business" He said.

Mick had thought through his approach to this situation and his response was carefully considered

"We come from a land far across the sea, much further than the land of Africa which you can see across the water. We are not Gods, although we are very powerful and if we are threatened we can strike anyone dead with one wave of our hands. We are a trading people and wish to negotiate a peaceful trading arrangement with your people".

"Are you servants of the mighty dragon which awaits outside our gates?" Queried the Nabob.

"Definitely not" Interjected Wilson "We are free men and servants to no man or beast. The dragon at the gates is our servant and does only our bidding. It is quite harmless if we are not interfered with, but woe to the man who causes us harm. Such a man would incur the wrath of our dragon and to incur its wrath is not advisable".

"You may stay in my tent and enjoy my hospitality and protection, your manservant may wait outside with the other slaves and servant people". Mick was a bit nonplussed by this. "Manservant? What manservant?" He asked. Wilson was flaming with rage. "That racist gobshite thinks that because I'm black I must be an inferior. I've a good mind to kick his arse back to whatever jungle he comes from".

Mick explained to the Nabob "Wilson here is not a manservant, he's a free man and worthy of as much respect as you or me. If you can't deal with that, we're outta here".

The Nabob was evidently severely put out by this piece of information but he decided to put the best face on it that he could. Gesturing to Mick and Wilson he indicated that they should sit down and talk further.

"How would you like us to address you?" Mick asked the Nabob with a glint of mischief in his eye.

"I'm normally addressed as Your Sublime Exaltedness The Most High Blessed of The Gods and Ruler of all the Earth as far as The Outer Limits, King and Emperor Justinian. But you can call me Justin".

"Hi Justin, I'm Mick and this is Wilson. We would like to get to know you and your people and spend a few days here with that end in view" suddenly Mick's speech was cut short by a frightful caterwauling from the direction of the Travellator.

"Oh oh" Mick said, "Somebody's messing with our mighty dragon and I'm afraid that they will be very, very sorry".

They all rushed outside with the self-styled Justin trailing along behind. At the Travellator the found the cause of the uproar. The committee spokesman lay on the ground, twitching and with smoke leaking from all his bodily orifices. Beside him lay the shattered remains of an iron tipped spear, also sending a lazy coil of smoke into the still, balmy air.

Mick waxed philosophical

"I suppose we might have expected something like this. He obviously tried to get into our vehicle and its security systems repelled him".

Wilson was less magnanimous. "I told you that our dragon was dangerous", He screamed at the shaken Justin. "Here we are negotiating in good faith and you send your underling to attack him behind our backs. I've a good mind to feed you and several virgins to the monster to placate him".

"No no no", Justin stammered, "You misunderstand, my brother took it on himself to investigate your esteemed monster and has lost his life in the process. No need for anyone to be fed to it, least of all me".

Mick hastened to pour oil on the troubled waters

"No need to get your knickers in a twist boys" he declared. "Good old Abdul is not dead, he's merely asleep. When he wakes up he'll have the world's worst heartache and some scorching on various body parts, but in a couple of days he'll be up and about and into mischief once more".

Turning to Wilson he said "I really should have updated you on the modifications we made to the Travellator, before we set out, but you were in an almighty hurry and we didn't get much time for chitchat. We fitted a sophisticated anti tamper system and anybody who messes with our dragon gets zapped with a Taser-like electrical charge which incapacitates the aggressor if he tries to get into the vehicle".

"You could have told me about that and saved me a lot of anxiety and grief" Wilson was more than slightly miffed.

"You were in such a big hurry to get here that I didn't have time to bring you up to speed on the finer points of the system, I'll give you a full refresher course whenever we get a chance".

Chapter Eleven

Back to the Present

Justin was understandably a bit put out by the treatment which the committee spokesman had received from the Travellator.

"That is my brother Abdul who is lying there, close to death. I consider it a gross breach of the laws of chivalry to assault a member of my family whilst you are enjoying my hospitality. Under different circumstances I would be obliged to punish you severely for this infraction but, as you are strangers to my land, I will stay my hand, for now".

"Just who does this impertinent prat think he's talking to" Queried Wilson, "I've a good mind to punish him for his lip, never mind that the other gobshite tried to interfere with the Travellator. I'm going right off the whole 'Trip to Gibraltar' gig, it's even worse than Benidorm in our time".

Mick tried the peacekeeper trick once again.

"Hold on, both of you, there's no need to get all hot and bothered about a little misunderstanding between friends. We came here to do a little trading so let's get on with it and stop this squabbling".

Wilson and Justin settled down into mutual distrust of each other and Justin asked "What do you have to trade with?" Mick said

"Oh, I thought you knew that we have a store of

the finest refined Gold which we would like to trade for goods which you might have that could be useful or valuable to us".

Justin immediately brightened up and asked "Can I see the Gold?"

Mick produced his little packet of wafers and offered one to Justin.

"This is a gift from us to you" he said, "In the belly of the dragon outside I have many more such wafers".

Justin took the proffered wafer and tested it with his teeth, then tried to bend it between his fingers, then sniffed at it and even licked it to assess its properties.

"I must show this to my people so that they can examine it properly, is that satisfactory?" He said with the gleam of avarice clear in his eyes.

"Sure" said Mick with a careless shrug "It's yours now so you can do whatever you like with it".

Turning to Wilson he said "I think we should go back to the dragon and assure ourselves that no damage was done and that he is not still enraged because of the attack on him while Justin attends to his own interests".

Justin was adamant that they stay and enjoy his hospitality but Mick pleaded fatigue after an arduous journey and with a smile and a handshake they parted company , promising to return in a couple of hours.

As soon as they were out of earshot Wilson demanded

"What's all that bullshit about fatigue after a long journey, we were driving for an hour and a half, if that?"

Mick replied "I thought it was time for us to have a chat and review our position without any eavesdroppers hearing what we have to say".

Wilson, somewhat slow on the uptake said "But they don't understand English, we can say anything we like and it's totally confidential".

Mick gave him a pitying look and said "You've obviously forgotten the translator phones. If we can understand them, then obviously they can understand us, so a shut mouth gathers no flies, OK?"

Once back in the Travellator the Mick said "We need to agree our strategy for the rest of this visit. You seem to have gotten off on the wrong foot with Justin and I can see why. He's a bit of an arrogant prat, but in fairness to him, his subjects seem to regard him as some sort of minor god. Being treated like that all your life tends to make you just a tad full of yourself".

Wilson's view was that Justin was a blot on the face of humanity and that the whole human race would be better off without him.

"I think the visit to this time and place was a bad mistake. I know I suggested it, but I just envisaged a few days of Sun, Sand, Sangria and perhaps a little Sex. I didn't expect guys with spears, attempted burglary and insufferable, racist twats like Justin. I vote we pack up and go home".

Smiling Mick shook his head "Don't be too hasty"

he said "We have an opportunity to earn a few Euros here and at the same time put one over on your friend Justin".

Mick reached into his pocket for the phone in order to check that it was fully charged. The pocket was empty. He searched all his pockets and finally concluded that it must have slipped out while they lounged on the cushions in Justin's tent.

Wilson was a bit put out when Mick told him about the phones loss but Mick said "This may be an opportunity, let's keep quiet and see if we can hear what goes on in the tent".

He put Wilson's phone on loudspeaker and a few minutes later they heard Justin's voice

"How is my brother Abdul?" another man, obviously one of the committee, replied "He's awake but he has a blinding headache. He will be out of action for some time".

Justin was in a towering rage "How dare these infidels come here and accept my generosity and then cause my beloved brother such trauma and pain. And to defile my home with the feet of the black slave. He is obviously a slave, nobody gives blacks freedom so they are lying to us".

After a period of silence the voice of Justin was heard again "Here's what we will do. I'll invite the infidels to a feast later this evening. While they are here you will spike their drink with the juice of the Soma flower, when they sleep we'll tie them up and then we'll torture the secret of the dragon out of them.

Mick turned the phone off and said "OK we'll pick up my phone later when we're at the party. Then we're going home and also give our friend Justin a lesson in manners and courtesy"

"You're a sly git right enough. You've obviously got a plan. Don't do what you usually do and leave me in the dark. Give me all the gory details up front so I can enjoy the action as it takes place". Wilson was very much in favour of anything which might contribute to Justin's detriment. He wasn't altogether sure why he didn't like him but something about him raised the hackles on the back of Wilson's neck.

"I haven't got anything firmed up in my mind yet" Mick mused "But I got the impression that Justin fancies himself as a trader and he was certainly impressed with the gold. I figure that we can use his avarice and overconfidence to get the better of him without much trouble. Let's have a snack and put our heads together and we'll come up with something brilliant, I'm sure"

Over their meal Wilson said "Maybe I'm paranoid but I think it would be a good idea to take great care that we only eat or drink stuff which we are offered here if we're totally satisfied that it won't poison us. I wouldn't trust that bastard Justin as far as I could throw him and God knows, fat as he is, that wouldn't be far".

"OK, I have the bones of a plan" Mick had a wicked smile on his face as he proceeded to explain his idea to Wilson. "We have some twelve year old Irish whiskey in storage, in fact we have quite a lot of Irish whiskey in storage. If Justin doesn't invite us to a feast tonight, I'll be very surprised. In my opinion it would be very remiss of us to go to a party with one arm as long as the other, what do you think?"

"A drinking contest! You really are a devious one. Remind me not to get on the wrong side of you in an argument. Oh, that's right, I've already gotten on your wrong side and it wasn't pleasant".

Sure enough a couple of hours later Abdul came knocking on the side of the Travellator. Wilson, not much fonder of Abdul than he was of Justin, opened a window and snarled "What do you want?"

Abdul fell into a kneeling position and banging his head on the ground said in a quavering voice "I beg your lordship's pardon for annoying you. I bear an invitation from his Serene Blessedness and Sublime Exaltedness, The Most High Blessed of The Gods and Ruler of all the Earth as far as The Outer Limits, King and Emperor Justinian, invites you to a great feast in your honour at sundown today. His Exaltedness hopes that you will deign to grace his table and promises a feast of epic proportions".

With a triumphant grin Mick said to Wilson "What did I tell you, the games afoot" and to Abdul he said "Please tell his Exaltedness that we are delighted with his invitation and we will be most pleased to attend the feast".

The sun set, as it does in those latitudes at that time of year, at 6.30 and Wilson stood ready to party at the door of the Travellator.

Mick said "Cool your jets, for God's sake, we can't go to a party at this hour of the day. We are the guests of honour and we must be fashionably late. I reckon that we will be time enough at ten o'clock".

"Ten o'clock, I'll have died of starvation by then" Wilson was a man who liked his grub, preferably in large quantities and at regular intervals.

"Get yourself a snack and sit down, we need to keep Justin off his game and the later we are, the more nervous he's likely to be. He has a lot of kudos invested in this gig and if we fail to turn up he will look very foolish. I reckon that when we arrive at ten he'll be so grateful that pretty near anything we suggest will receive a favourable reception". Wilson was once more struck by the devious nature of Mick's thought processes.

Ten o'clock arrived and the two lads presented themselves at the entrance of the Nabob's tent. Abdul was there to greet them along with the rest of the reception committee. All fell to their knees and started banging their heads on the ground. Abdul addressed them in a loud voice "Welcome to the tent of his Exaltedness, The Most High Blessed of The Gods and Ruler of all the Earth as far as The Outer Limits, King and Emperor Justinian. Please enter and enjoy the hospitality of his gracious Majesty". And rising he swept aside the flap of the tent.

Each carrying a case of the aforementioned fifteen year old Irish whiskey the pair advanced into the sumptuous interior. The tent had been transformed. The hangings had been replaced with silks of the finest and candles and oils lamps cast a bright glow throughout the capacious space. Sitting in the centre of the space, on a pile of silken cushions Justin did not look too pleased upon the late arrivals.

Mick had warned Wilson beforehand

"Under no circumstances apologise for our lateness, we need to gain the high ground and keep it throughout this session. Let me give the lead, I promise you'll get your turn to say anything you feel like but leave most of the negotiations to me, OK?"

Justin stood and with a patently false smile said "You are very welcome to my home, please sit and partake of my food and drink. I can assure it is the finest to be found in all the world".

Eating was in the Arab manner with a common dish of food and all diners dipping in, using of course, their right hand. Again in the Arab manner they all washed their hands in the ewers of warm water provided. Justin introduced a stone jar of wine which he again claimed to be the finest available. Watching to ensure that Justin drank first from the jar, the boys toasted him enthusiastically.

If truth be told, the wine was thin and vinegary but Mick was too polite to comment adversely and Wilson was under strict instructions that if he couldn't say anything good, he should say nothing at all. When the meal was in full swing and Justin's mood had improved, Mick produced a bottle of Irish whiskey. The assembled guests, all male, were entranced by the bottle rather than the golden liquid within.

They had never seen a glass container before and the clarity of the glass amazed them. Mick uncapped the bottle and announced

"In my country it is considered bad form to recap a

bottle once it has been opened. Therefore the only decent thing to do is to drink it all up". With an appealing shrug of his shoulders he pitched the cap over his shoulder and went around the circle of guests, pouring a shot of the amber nectar into each drinking cup.

Holding his cup aloft and ignoring the hubbub caused by the serving men scrambling on the floor to retrieve the discarded cap he stood up and called out

"A Toast to his Exaltedness, The Most High Blessed of The Gods and Ruler of all the Earth as far as The Outer Limits, King and Emperor Justinian". He then threw back his head and downed the rather small measure of whiskey which he had poured for himself, and smilingly encouraged the others to do the same.

The tradition of toasting had not been introduced before that evening but the assembled guests caught on very rapidly and one followed the other with increasing nonsense as the magical bottles kept appearing and emptying. Finally everybody with the exception of Wilson and Mick, overcome with the strength of the spirit, which they were unused to, fell into a sound sleep.

Giggling madly, for to tell the truth, they were themselves somewhat the worse for drink, Mick and Wilson stumbled back to the Travellator and engaged the time drive. Mick had set it earlier before going to the party to bring them back to the present in a deserted corner of the car park. Not a difficult thing to do in late January.

Behind them they left the other party guests almost comatose from an excess of Irish whiskey. The lads woke up next morning in the present day Gibraltar car park, sore of head and sick of stomach, but significantly better than their erstwhile dinner companions who found themselves with faces painted Green, White and Orange and a huge banner splashed across the walls of the tent "Erin Go Bragh".

"That'll larn them" Said Wilson as they headed back to the Travellator.

Chapter Twelve

Freddy's Return

Feeling considerably the worse for wear, Mick volunteered to drive the first shift back to the ferry. Wilson was feeling so bad that an early death held a fatal attraction for him. However some strong coffee in a roadside cafe and a couple of paracetamol each and they felt at least half alive.

After an uneventful journey they arrived back in Dublin where they were greeted by an officious Customs Officer.

"What's in the back of your rig" He demanded. This could be a very tricky proposition. Mick had no idea as to how he might explain some of the more esoteric contents of the vehicle, and realistically he would have difficulty explaining the time drive to himself, never mind to an intransigent, minor public servant.

"It's just household stuff" Said Mick "We've been over to Spain for a couple of days in our new camper van, just to give it a trial run, and we're on the way home now".

"I'll need to take a look around inside" The nosy customs man said "We have a lot of illegal cigarettes coming into the country and this rig looks like an ideal vehicle for transporting such contraband".

Reluctantly Mick said "Okay, but I have a revolutionary new drive system installed in this truck and it should be treated with immense care".

"Pull it over there" The officer directed them to a covered lay-by and demanded the keys.

Mick and Wilson took themselves into the coffee shop for some sustenance, leaving their nemesis to poke about to his heart's content.

"Are we in trouble" Wilson had a worried expression on his normally cheerful face.

"Nah" Said Mick "He won't find anything, there's nothing to find. I'm more concerned that he might switch something on or off and cause problems later. He won't get near the time drive because I've locked everybody except me out of it".

"What if he stumbles into it by accident?" The whiskey had obviously had a detrimental effect on Wilson, he was very twitchy and distracted.

"Will you for God's sake settle down? You're behaving like an old woman with an attack of the megrims. The drive is locked with a retinal scanning device and will only open for my eyes. It is the nearest thing to an unbreakable code as there is technologically, so cool your jets. You'll only increase our officious friend's suspicions if you keep this up".

Three interminable hours later the customs officer came into the cafe and threw his cap on the table in front of the lads.

"You're free to go, I can't find anything illegal or suspicious in your vehicle though, it's the queerest thing I've ever come across in my thirty years as a customs officer. So thank you for your patience and good luck in your travels". Leaving the cafe he cast a lingering look backwards at the lads and went out.

That fella has something in his nose about us, I hope we don't come across him anytime soon". Wilson looked considerably brighter now but still nervous about the customs intervention. "I wouldn't be surprised if we're on a watch list in their blasted computers. I know about this stuff" He said.

Next day Mick was enjoying his breakfast and reading the newspaper to catch up on anything he might have missed during their overland trip to Spain and back.

"Hey Wilson" He shouted, Wilson had moved into Mick's house in order to be on hand if any more time trips were planned and also because he was too bone idle to go looking for a house of his own.

Coming downstairs he asked "Did you call me?"

"I did, look at this" Mick handed over the paper, folded at a photograph and short news story. The photograph showed Major Freddie gazing fondly into the eyes of a very tasty looking younger woman.

Wilson looked at Mick and asked "What's all this about?" With a wave of his hand Mick indicated that he should read the piece which read:

"Colonel and Mrs. Smyth-Cunningham are proud to announce the engagement of their daughter, Caroline, to Major Frederick Fortescue of Her Majesty's Royal Marines. Wedding plans are well advanced and the couple will be married in St George's Church in Westminster in June of this year".

"Merciful hour" Wilson cried "He's gone and snared himself an heiress with his Lotto winnings. I wouldn't have credited him with the wit or indeed the chutzpah to pull that off".

"Heiress?" Mick queried. "How do you know she's an heiress?"

"In the armed forces of Her Majesty we had a lot of spare time on our hands. Not all of that time was spent on spiritual and intellectually uplifting pursuits. We frequently read the papers and in desperate circumstances I have been known to peruse the society pages. This lady frequently appears on said pages, not often portrayed in a very flattering way. She seems to be something of a bed hopper if gossip can be believed. I almost feel sorry for Freddie, though, to be absolutely truthful, my attitude is 'fuck him if he can't take a joke'".

Mick finished his breakfast and went to check his emails. Amongst the usual multitude of offers of holidays in exotic places and other assorted spam which he had neglected to classify as such, he found a message from Freddie.

"Mick, I'm in big trouble and you're the only man in the world who can help. I know you've no reason to care about me or to help me in this pickle I've gotten into but I throw myself on your mercy and ask you to meet me to discuss my problem".

Mick called Wilson and asked him what his opinion might be. Predictably Wilson was profoundly unsympathetic to Freddie's problems.

"Let him solve his own problems" He said.

"Neither you nor me have any reason to help him out, remember he was going to drag you off to Cheltenham and hold you indefinitely. He always treated me like a dog, in fact I think he treated his dog better than he did me".

"Still" Mick objected "There's no reason not to listen to what he has to say. He is a human being after all".

Wilson remained unconvinced "You're too soft altogether. Now mind you I'm nobody to complain about your good nature, after we met by me trying to break into your house. So if you feel like helping Freddie the Prat I'll help if I can".

Mick emailed Freddie to invite him to the house and next morning, bright and early he arrived bearing an expensive bottle of Scotch whisky as a peace offering. After some hemming and hawing Freddie finally got around to the cause of his visit. "You may have seen a notice in the Times to the effect that I am now engaged to Caroline Smyth-Cunningham". He said with a doleful expression on his face.

"Yeah, we just saw it yesterday, congratulations and the best of luck in the future, I'm sure you'll be very happy together" Mick said, tongue in cheek.

"No, no you don't understand" Freddie was almost incoherent. "She is the most awful horror in the world. If she was the last woman on earth I would allow the human race to die out before I'd have anything to do with her".

"So what's the big deal, just give her the 'It's not you, It's me', speech and make a noise like a hoop and roll off into the sunset" Wilson was less than supportive in Freddie's hour of need. "Why did you get engaged to her, in the first place anyway?"

"Well you've seen her picture in the paper, she's a seriously hot lady and I wasn't using my higher cognitive functions when we first got together at the Regatta in Cowes. At that time she wasn't interested in anything long term, in fact I think she may have fallen for my 'Brave warrior just back from saving western civilisation in Afghanistan' story".

"Good God" Wilson cried, "You're a bigger liar than Mick, and that's saying something. You never served in Afghanistan and the nearest you ever got to firing your gun in anger was at one of Lord Carnarvon's weekend shooting parties. And even then, from what I've heard, you missed every shot".

"I suppose you've never used the big bad soldier act to impress a girl yourself. Anyway that's all beside the point. I need to get out of this entanglement and you guys are to blame for my predicament, so you have to help".

"In what way are we responsible for the suspension of your higher cognitive functions at a critical moment in your story?" Queried Mick.

"We only got entangled with you recently and your affair with this lady obviously predates our meeting".

"You're not getting to the meat of the story. She had no time for me after Cowes until the word got out that I had won the Euromillions, then she contacted me and sunk her claws in and I can't shake her loose. So as you gave me the winning ticket, it's all your fault".

"If I remember correctly I gave you a choice of options, it was you who chose the Euromillions option. Any consequences arising from that choice are down to you and only you" Mick was quite adamant about that.

Wilson shook his head in disbelief. "As for the claws story, that's just bulshit. I know for a fact that her Daddy is one of the richest venture capitalists in the world and that she is heiress to more money than God. Why, rumour has it that he is ground landlord to Buckingham Palace itself".

"You shouldn't believe everything you read in the papers" Freddie said mournfully "Apparently, like many of his contemporaries he invested unwisely during the boom years. Unlike most of his mates, however, he didn't cover his arse and he lost it all. He's bankrupt and penniless now and Caroline's only hope is to hook a wealthy man while she still retains her youth and good looks".

"What exactly do you expect us to do to help you out of this mess?" Mick had a sinking feeling that whatever Wilson had it mind, it wouldn't be good.

"You remember we went back and erased the CC-443567 file and all references to it in GCHQ, and that Wilson managed to retrospectively discharge himself, honourably, from the armed forces. Well I want to do the same with Caroline and me".

"I was under the impression that you clearly understood the terms of our previous agreement" Mick was livid "If you ever mention that episode again, to anyone, including Wilson and me, I'll invoke the second option and wipe all trace of you from the face of the earth. I am deadly serious about this, one word and 'poof' you'll be gone as if you had never existed".

Trembling visibly Freddie said "I'm sorry, I didn't mean to upset you. I'm desperate and in real need of help here. I can't get rid of her and short of murder I will be stuck with her until she's sucked me dry. She's already gone through ten million since we hooked up again and only God knows how much she's given to that toerag of a father of hers".

"So you want to go back and undo your meeting with her or cancel the Cowes regatta that year or cancel your Euromillions win. Something like that is it? I think, no I know, I told you about the law of unintended consequences. The more you mess about with time, the greater danger there is of you causing catastrophic consequences. So, sorry Freddie but no dice".

By this time Freddie was getting desperate "In GCQ" he said in a menacing tone of voice "We get updates on all law enforcement activities in the world. I know that you came in through Rosslare yesterday and were checked by customs. I can place you, Wilson and your wanderly wagon on a worldwide watch list and cause you a lot of grief. I don't want to do this but I'm a desperate man and just about at the ragged end of my tether".

Wilson, who had been listening to this with increasing anger suddenly produced a very large pistol and put it to Freddie's head "Let's waste this sucker right now. We can take his body back to the last ice age and stick it in a glacier as a conundrum for archaeologists to puzzle over when he pops up as the ice melts. What do you think Mick?"

Chapter Thirteen

Dealing with Freddie

With a condescending sneer Freddie said "You hardly think I'd come here without some insurance, do you? I've created a safe record of all our dealings and hidden it away, only to be opened on my death or failure to report in, after two weeks. In that event it goes straight to all the relevant organisations, including Mossad, the Israeli secret service. If you think GCHQ was bad you need to really fear Mossad. Just think what they could do in the near east with time travel technology".

Sadly Mick shook his head.

"You know Wilson, you can't do a kind deed for some people but it comes back and bites you in the arse. This poor sap is under the delusion that stuff kept in secure storage is safe from us. He doesn't seem to get it, that if we eliminate him from the timeline, then all his pathetic schemes disappear along with him. I told him all this last time but it seems to have gone straight over his head. I think your idea of the ice age is probably the best solution".

Whilst Mick was delivering his judgement Wilson was occupied screwing a silencer onto his pistol.

"What do you reckon Mick, will I do him here or will we bring him back to the ice age and waste him there. That's probably the tidiest solution, less mess here and no available evidence of the action".

Listening to this crosstalk Freddie was terrified.

"I was only winding you up, Mick. I haven't left any messages, I swear on my mother's grave. Nobody would believe me even if I did blow the gaff anyway. Please don't kill me, I'll do anything you want"

"See Freddie, it's not as easy as all that. We gave you the lotto numbers and you promised to keep all you know about us under your hat, but at the first sign of a little disruption to your life, entirely your own fault I might add, you come back threatening to rain fire and brimstone on our heads. You must admit that your word of honour isn't worth shit, so why would we accept it now?"

"Tell you what" Mick said. "Tie the dozy twat up and dump him in the panic room, we'll think about this overnight and make a final decision in the morning"

Wilson was all for dealing with Freddie then and there but Mick was adamant.

"I haven't killed anybody yet, bar a few bugs who had nasty intentions towards me, and don't want to start now. Not unless it's absolutely necessary".

The lads decided that it was unnecessary to tie Freddie up and they forced him, at gunpoint into the panic room which Mick had built after his adventures with the Queen of the Bugs, as he called that episode. Locking the room from the outside and disabling the phone they went off to the pub to discuss their options.

Choosing a secluded corner where they couldn't be overheard and ordering liquid refreshment they sat down to plot a solution to this latest test of their fortitude.

"Honest to God" Wilson said, "That man really takes the biscuit. You set him up with an immense fortune, introduce him to a glimpse of technology which is capable of, literally, changing the world and the thanks you get for it is to have him come back and try to blackmail you! In my opinion there's only one solution and that's to deep six him immediately".

"You talk like a bad gangster movie" Mick replied "Will you leave off with the, waste him and the, deep six him and, worse of all the, do him. He is a human being when all is said and done and I'm not going to kill him unless he threatens my life or someone' else's directly. Is that clear?"

When Wilson had nodded his reluctant acceptance of this condition Mick went on "Short of killing him I think the best option is to exile him".

Wilson looked at Mick with open mouthed astonishment. "Exile him? Like to the island of Elba as the brits did with Napoleon? You do know that even Elba has phone lines and Internet connections now. There's literally no place on the modern Earth where he could be safely assumed to be unable to contact his mates in GCHQ".

"You've hit the nail right on the head" Mick said, with a sardonic smile "Modern Earth is the critical phrase".

"Oh you crafty bugger" Wilson was deeply impressed with Mick's devious mindedness, "You mean to dump him somewhere in the past where he can't cause mischief for us".

"Exactly" Said Mick. "I don't want to be any harder on the poor fool than I have to" he mused "When in time should we dump, in your opinion?"

"You know my feelings concerning Major Frederick Fortescue of her Majesty's Royal Marines" Wilson was most emphatic. "I believe you're doing him an unwarranted favour leaving him alive. If it was left to me I'd like to feed him to a dinosaur, except he's such a poison pill that he'd probably kill the poor beast. In fact maybe we will do exactly that and he'll cause the dinosaur extinction. Wow! Maybe he's the famous extinction event, what do you think?"

"Focus, focus" Chided Mick "We're not going to feed him to a dinosaur, or any other savage beast. If in his wanderings in a past timeline he manages to get himself eaten, then C'est la vie as the French say. I think we should drop him either in America in the old west, or in Wales in King Arthur's time, either of those periods would give him a chance to use the, God Help Us, fighting skills so graciously pounded into him by the Marines. What option would you choose Wilson?"

"I don't really care how we dump him. As far as I'm concerned anytime we chose is as good as any other time. The man's incompetent in this timeline with all its technological support, so I wouldn't give him a small dog's chance in hell in any other era. That said, if we chose the Wild West option we have serious logistical difficulties with it".

Wilson was obviously giving this deep consideration "We need to get him to the Midwest of America before we shoot him back into the past, and we have to bring the Travellator with us. That means a sea trip of a couple of weeks. I have no great respect for his abilities but I am not sure we could keep him quiet for that length of time. I know we outnumber him two to one but with security at ports etcetera the job just becomes well-nigh impossible. So Wales looks like the best option".

"I'm just thinking about that" Mick was deep in thought. "We'd need to get Freddie and the Travellator to the States, and we'd need to keep him under wraps the whole journey. That's just not a viable option. On the other hand I could bring a flux capacitor, you know, the time travel device over and fit it to a vehicle there. I've done some work on it and succeeded in miniaturising it to a manageable level. Tell you what, let's go home and I'll sleep on it. Tomorrow's another day, after all".

Next day Mick called a conference between Wilson, himself and Freddie.

"Here's the deal" He said. "Freddie, we've decided you can't be trusted so our plan is to send you into a timeline where you can't cause us any problems. You have some choice as to the timeline most favoured by you but in the final analysis I will make the ultimate decision".

Freddie was horrified. "Please Mick, this is not necessary, I'll guarantee to keep my big mouth shut, I swear. I am, after all an officer and a gentleman. My word is my bond".

Wilson let out a great guffaw of disbelief. "That's a good one Freddie. You've already broken your word of honour as an Officer and a Gentleman. You're a no good lying snake in the grass, like most of your brother Officers, who are also by act of parliament, Gentlemen. I'd rather trust a rabid dog than give you the benefit of the doubt".

Mick sadly concurred with Wilson's assessment. "It's no good Freddie, we just can't trust you. It's not just us but to allow the secret of the time machine to fall into the hands of the British Government or, worse still, MI5 or Mossad gives me the chills. I'm not bragging about my own moral compass but these people are completely outside the pale ethically speaking. I'm afraid we'll just have to go ahead with our plan".

"I propose to go back about seven days and wait for you to turn up at our door. I will, in the meantime have hired a private jet to take us to Tucson Arizona. We'll pretend to go along with your request, but fool you into thinking that we need to operate your rescue from the states. In Arizona we'll have a car waiting for us. I'll fit my new flux capacitor to the car and bring you back to 1860. You won't be aware of the plot until we drop you in the Wild West. I reckon you will be able to function well enough in that timeline, I'll leave you enough gold and some weapons to give you a good start. How you fare out after that will be up to you".

Despite Freddie's tearful protests, the plan was put into operation immediately. Bringing Freddie back to intercept himself presented issues which Mick did not wish to address. Despite his success in disproving the Grandfather theory of time travel, confronting one version of Freddie with another would create potential difficulties which could prove catastrophic. So they locked him up in the panic room once more. Mick reckoned that as soon as they met the earlier version of Freddie and diverted him from his subsequent movements that the current Freddie would simply disappear from the scene. In case his theory was in error, his intention was to return to this timeline at the same moment of their leaving it and check the panic room. Then if he was wrong he could rethink the appropriate response.

The lads ventured back and made all the planned preparations. When Mick got Freddie's email he invited him over to discuss his problems. Freddie arrived with his bottle of expensive whisky and the lads encouraged him to tell all about his troubles. At that point the sequence of events diverged significantly from the previous ones.

Wilson had a truculent look on his face, but Mick expressed his willingness to help Freddie out.

He explained the situation to Freddie. "We have no objection to helping you out but there is a small snag. We need to bring the flux capacitor to Tucson Arizona for some modifications, they've got some machines there which are specially designed for my requirements. I've got a private jet taking us over to do the modifications and you need to come for the trip with us. We'll deal with your situation immediately after the trip".

Freddie enthusiastically concurred with the plan and they all headed out to the airport to start their trip. Apparently travelling by private jet is refreshingly simple by comparison to normal travel. They arrived at the airport and were met by the pilot who took charge of their luggage, except for the flux capacitor which Mick carried about everywhere with him, never leaving it aside for a single moment.

The flight was uneventful, if somewhat luxurious. There was a gorgeous cabin attendant whose task appeared to be to ensure that their trip was an exercise in unalloyed pampering. She plied them with all manner of luxury foodstuffs and drinks to the extent that when they staggered off the plane in Tucson they all felt that they would not be able to face another bite to eat for days.

Officialdom had not presented any difficulties when leaving Dublin but the reception in Homeland Security America was profoundly different. Two menacing individuals wearing flak jackets and armed with large pistols appeared at the door as soon as the flight attendant lowered the steps.

"We're representatives of the Federal Government Sir" The first one said, holding up his identification for Mick's perusal.

"This is agent Thomas and I'm agent Gonzales. We need to check you and your passengers, and the plane out to ensure that you don't have any contraband aboard. Do you have any problems with that Sir?"

Mick hastened to reassure them that he had no problems with that. Casting a warning glance in Freddie's direction, he continued.

"There is just one thing. This piece of equipment is incredibly delicate". He showed them the flux capacitor, deliberately using jargon meant to confuse the agent he went on.

"It's for measuring the effects of micro fluctuations in the wave function of the gravitational forces exerted by other bodies in the solar system on the

Earth's parabolic orbit, particularly with respect to the variations in quantum particles emitted by the solar wind".

Listening to this arrant nonsense with a glazed expression in his eyes, agent Gonzales said. "OK Sir, but we'll have to let our bomb disposal experts look at it to ensure it's not some explosive device".

Mick smiled and agreed, "I'll need to be in attendance when the examine it" He said. "It would be very easy to break it and I've invested a lot of money and five years of my life in designing and building it. The reason we're here is to see Professor Stevens at the College of Science in the University of Arizona to check some of the finer settings of the device".

With an uncaring shrug Agent Gonzales called the bomb squad and arranged for one of their number to come to the airport and check out the flux capacitor. Mick went with the expert to his workshop whilst Wilson took Freddie to the cafe for coffee. Mick had anticipated this delay and had impressed on Wilson that, under no circumstances, was Freddie to be allowed unsupervised contact with his fellow spooks from Homeland Security. He was reasonably certain that there was no danger of Freddie blowing the gaff, but he was such an idiot that he might let something slip if not watched carefully.

The bomb expert gave the device a very thorough inspection and cleared it without hesitation.

"I don't know what it does" He told agent Gonzales "But it's certainly not explosive"' Mick went into his nonsense explanation which the bomb guy accepted unhesitatingly. Agent Gonzales, who had meantime thoroughly examined the plane and all the luggage said

"Thank you Sir, everything checks out fine. Sorry for any inconvenience we've caused you, you're free to go. Enjoy your stay in the United States" and without a backward glance he walked away.

Mick gathered up the other two from the cafe and picked up the fire red Mustang which he had arranged to have waiting for them and headed for a motel on the outskirts of Tucson. Mick had forewarned Wilson not to drink too much on the flight over but Freddie, with encouragement from the other two and the gorgeous flight attendant was seriously the worse for wear by now and fell, fully clothed on the bed in his room and slumped into a deep sleep.

Taking the opportunity thus presented Mick said

"OK Wilson, you keep an eye on our comatose friend here whilst I fit the flux capacitor to the Mustang".

Wilson innocently asked "Won't the car hire company take exception to you fitting strange devices to one of their vehicles?"

Mick laughed. "You forget, we have an endless supply of cash. I bought the Mustang outright. I've always fancied owning one and this is the perfect opportunity".

Still laughing he headed out to the car park to fit the time travel device.

Chapter Fourteen

The Wild West

Next morning Freddie staggered to the Mustang, looking a little green about the gills. Little knowing his impending fate he climbed into the back seat and collapsed moaning

"Why did you guys allow me to drink so much yesterday. You know I'm not much of a drinker. My head feels like it's about to burst and I feel sick as a poisoned parrot. For God's sake, Wilson will you stop that confounded whistling, please".

Grinning evilly Wilson said to Mick "I think it's time to go, don't you".

Mick laughingly replied. "You know Wilson, deep down you're not a very nice person. It's not a good thing to derive diabolical satisfaction for another's misfortune. Your karma will catch up with you one day".

"I'd be prepared to face my karma if I get to see that pillock get his comeuppance". Wilson was unrepentant.

Mick drove to a secluded part of the dried up Santa Cruz river which meandered through Tucson. When they were about three miles outside to modern city centre he engaged the time drive and headed to the year 1878. They arrived at noon under a cloudless sky with temperatures in the high 30s centigrade. Mick's first thought was to conceal the Mustang, which stuck out like a sore thumb in that barren landscape. Scoping out his surroundings he noticed some shrubs growing on the riverbank about fifty yards away. This he concluded was a Mesquite Bosque or grove and he decided it would be an ideal place to hide the car.

Fortunately the ground was dry and hard so driving the low slung muscle car did not offer serious obstacles. As he drove into the stand of Mesquite Mick cringed on hearing the savage, three inch, thorns which were sharp enough to puncture his tyres if he wasn't careful, dragging along his nice shiny new car, still, needs must when the Devil drives.

Waking Freddie up and explaining his predicament to him was a difficult business. At first he assumed that they were winding him up or trying to scare him, but Mick explained that their options for dealing with him were severely limited. Either erasure or exile.

Mick explained that in his opinion Tucson in 1878 was an ideal place and time for Freddie to start a new life. "I've studied the history of this place and this is a true account. A man named William Whitney Brazelton held-up two stages in the summer of 1878 near Point of Mountain Station approximately seventeen miles northwest of Tucson. "Brazen Bill" Brazelton would eventually be tracked down and killed on Monday August 19, 1878 in a mesquite bosque along the Santa Cruz River three miles south of Tucson by Pima County Sheriff Charles A. Shibell and his citizen's posse".

"This is that mesquite bosque and tomorrow is August 19th, 1878. I propose to go into town with you, and set you up as an upstanding citizen. I'll give you a stock of gold and see you outfitted with horses and guns, you'll need both. Tomorrow I suggest that you volunteer for Sheriff Shibell's posse and that you use our natural duplicity to lead them to this site. After Brazelton is killed you'll be a hero and you can build on that reputation to become one of the leading citizens of Tucson".

After some deep soul searching Freddie agreed to Mick's suggestion. "At least I won't have to deal with that she-dragon Caroline Smyth-Cunningham. It'll be almost worth it to be free of her".

As they walked the three miles into Tucson city centre, with Freddie sighing as he contemplated all the things of the twenty first century he would miss, he turned to Mick and asked

"I don't suppose there's any place in Tucson where I'd get a cappuccino in this benighted age? I'd kill for a cappuccino right now".

They arrived in town just as the Tombstone stagecoach drove up to the hotel in a flurry of dust.

Mick beamed and said "That's fortunate, we'll book into the hotel and everyone will think we came on the stage. The people off the stage will think we were here and nobody will ask any questions".

After an enormous breakfast of steak and eggs the trio went outside to scope out the town. As they strolled along the boardwalk they met a tall, bearded man dressed in a black broadcloth coat. As he neared them Mick noticed that he had a star pinned to his waistcoat.

"Hi" The man said "I'm Sheriff Charles Shibell, welcome to Tucson. Are you just off the stage?"

Rather than answer this awkward question Mick said "Sheriff Shibell, I believe you know Wyatt and Virgil Earp. We met them in tombstone and they said I should give you their regards".

Shibell smiled and said "Yeah, I know the Earps, how did you come across them?" "We had a couple of drinks with them and played a few hands of cards. That Wyatt is some card player. If we'd stayed any longer he'd have cleaned us out. Nice guy though".

Mick said "Sheriff, if you have any time later my friend Freddie here has some information about Brazen Bill Brazelton, which would be of benefit to you"

Shibell's eyes lit up "That would be mighty interesting" He replied "I've got to go meet the Mayor just now but I'd be mighty pleased to discuss that low down varmint later in the day if that's OK?"

Mick shook his head with a doleful expression on his face "Me and Wilson have to be on our way, but Freddie is staying on. He hopes to settle down in your attractive town and spend some time here. We'll have to say goodbye for now Sheriff. It was good to meet you".

After the Sheriff had gone on to his meeting Mick turned to Freddie "OK, here's how it'll go down. We'll hire or buy some horses and ride out to the Mustang so that you'll be familiar with the route. Once there Wilson and I will head back to our own timeline. I'll give you a store of rough gold nuggets which will make you seriously rich before we go. You go back and later in the day tell Shibell about Brazen Bill and his hiding place. Tell the Sheriff that you overheard Brazelton, in a

Tombstone saloon, arrange to meet Frank Stilwell at that point in order to hold up the Tombstone stagecoach. Shibell will organise a citizen posse and you can go along. After they kill Brazelton you'll be a hero and rich. You'll be set up for life".

Shaking hands with Freddie, Wilson and Mick climbed into the Mustang and reversed it out of the bosque to the exact spot they had arrived at earlier. Rolling down the window Mick said

"Please wipe out the tracks of the Mustang after we're gone. They might set someone wondering. Goodbye Freddie. We'll come back later in the timeline to check that you are getting along OK. See Ya".

Freddie stood disconsolately at the side of the river and watched as the Mustang disappeared with the usual soft clap of thunder. He then wiped out the tracks and turning headed back to Tucson, leading the two spare horses.

Mick and Wilson, meanwhile, had returned safely to twenty first century Tucson, beside the dry Santa Cruz riverbed. Mick heaved a huge sigh of relief.

"Thank God that's over" He said "I wasn't sure we'd get Freddie to accept the exile as easily as he did. I half expected a revolt of some sort and I really didn't want to erase the poor sod".

Wilson shrugged and replied "Good riddance to bad rubbish I say".

Mick shook his head in despair at Wilson's intransigence and drove back to the motel where they had stayed earlier. After removing the flux capacitor from the Mustang they placed the car in secure storage, to be retrieved later, and proceeded to the airport where the pilots were waiting to take them home.

In the departure lounge they came across the dour Homeland Security agent, Gonzales, he hailed them and said

"You're going home I see, where's your companion, the Brit? Is he staying on?"

Wilson growled "Yeah, he met a Sheriff down in Tucson who made him an offer he couldn't refuse so he's staying a few more days".

"Well good luck and bon voyage. I'll be in Ireland next year with the President and I might look you up". So saying he walked away with a grim smile.

Chapter Fifteen

You Have Mail!

Arriving home two weeks later, they had decided at the last minute to come home by sea and bring the Mustang with them, Mick found a letter inside the door. Gingerly picking up the brown envelope he looked at the place where one usually affixes a stamp. With sinking heart he recognized the official Irish Harp which meant that the letter was from a government ministry. With great trepidation he tore open the envelope. The letter inside was short and to the point:

Dear Sir,

Please contact this office at your earliest convenience to arrange a meeting with the Minister for Communications.

Yours faithfully

Sean Breathnach

Principal Secretary

Department of Communications

Adelaide Road

Dublin 2.

"What the hell have you done now?" Queried Wilson. "The last thing you need is official notice of any sort. If your name comes up on the radar those prats in GCHQ might easily start sitting up and taking notice again. If that happens, the next visit from Her Majesty's Secret Service might be better executed than the last".

"For God's sake don't talk about execution and the plonkers from GCHQ in the same sentence. I haven't done anything to attract the attention of the Department of Communications! I've paid my television license and I never post letters so I can't owe postage. Besides you don't get letters from the bloody Minister for things like that. The curse of hell on him anyway, I better phone up and make that appointment".

Mick was paranoid about attracting the attention of officialdom towards himself or his activities. He was fairly certain that his time travel forays did not contravene any laws but he simply did not trust men in uniforms and he trusted politicians even less.

Three weeks later Mick was ushered into the office of the Principal Secretary, Sean Breathnach. This individual, a suave well turned out person with a somewhat oily manner which did nothing to assuage Mick's unease, welcomed him and said

"The Minister has a couple of things to finish up before we go in. Can I offer you a cup of tea or coffee?"

Mick had heard of this technique, the unfortunate visitor is left to cool his heels whilst the important official finishes off work which is vital to the interests of the State. Given his dislike of all the trappings of power it was hardly surprising that he replied, with an ostentatious glance at his watch

"No coffee thanks, if the Minister is too busy for me I'll just travel on. I have a very busy calendar. Perhaps you can contact me to arrange a mutually acceptable time for a meeting when we will both be free?"

Never having encountered a response like this before, Mr. Breathnach was, to say the least, somewhat nonplussed

"No, no, that won't do at all" he spluttered "The Minister can't have his schedule messed about like that. He's a very busy man. We just cannot disrupt his carefully planned day like this"

Mick, inwardly quailing but outwardly as cool as the proverbial cucumber replied

"I'm a busy man myself and I'm not one to criticise but if his day is a well-planned as you say then I'd be inside with him and not out here cooling my heels fifteen minutes after our appointed time. On second thoughts it would suit me better if he were to put whatever he wants to discuss with me in a letter and I'll decide if I want to meet with him at all".

By this stage the unfortunate Senior Civil Servant was totally distraught. He looked like he might, at any moment, commence to pull out the few remaining strands of his already sparse hair.

"If you'll just give me a moment Sir" He muttered through gritted teeth "I think he may have finished up the items which were holding him up. I'll just go and see if that's OK Sir?"

Despite his initial reservations Mick's curiosity got the better of him and he decided to wait for a couple of minutes more. About fifty seconds later Sean reappeared and beckoned Mick into the inner sanctum. His first thoughts on entering the Minister's office was

"No bloody wonder the country is broke". The office was about the floor area of an average suburban semidetached house and furnished in a lavish style with an enormous desk, leather chairs and couches and what looked to Mick's untutored eye, very much like a genuine Persian rug.

Looking up he was horrified to find a group of, obviously professional, photographers busily snapping pictures as the Minister, a man who clearly ate 'not wisely but too well' as the old saying goes, advanced from behind the spacious desk.

"Mr Brennan". He intoned pompously "I'm delighted to meet you. You are probably wondering why I asked you to come here today. Well I have a bit of good news for you". Turning to a tall man beside him he said

"Let me introduce Mr James Murray, the director of An Post, the postal service. He has a letter for you".

Mick was less than impressed by this huge fuss.

"The postman normally delivers my post through the letterbox. I know him from saying 'Good Morning' occasionally but this is a new delivery method. Are all the letters to be delivered like this from now on? If so, whilst I hesitate to criticise, it seems like a very expensive method of delivery to me".

The Minister gave a patently false laugh. "You are plainly a man with a sense of humour. No, James will explain all to you".

Meanwhile the paparazzi had been snapping merrily throughout the conversation. Mick turned and asked the Minister

"Can you ask the shower of sharks to stop taking photos? I'm a man who values his privacy and I don't like to have my picture taken by people to whom I haven't been introduced".

Mick was very evidently not a type of individual that the Minister had ever met before. It was inconceivable that an ordinary member of the public would not be immensely flattered by being snapped with a Minister in the government and specifically with this Minister. However he reluctantly signalled the Principal Secretary and that luminary ushered the press corps from the room.

Now, can we cut to the chase here" Mick demanded "Just what the hell is going on here?"

"James" The Minister frostily gestured at the post office guy "Please give this man his letter and let's be done with this matter".

He was definitely not pleased with the outcome of this fiasco.

James advanced with an envelope in hand and presented it to Mick.

"This letter was posted in Tucson Arizona on February the seventeenth 1887. It obviously not meant for you, but I presume for an earlier Michael Brennan at your address".

"Yeah". Mick said "That would be my Granddad.

My family have been living in that house for more than a hundred years".

"Well the reason for this meeting is to give the letter to you, the stamp is a first edition Columbian Issue, printed to commemorate the four hundredth anniversary of Columbus's landing in America. The stamp is in pristine condition and our numismatists value it at about €15,000. You can see why we didn't want to deliver it in the usual way. The letter was lost in the mail since that time and it is the oldest undelivered letter to surface in the world. That, in itself, makes it a very valuable item. May I be the first to congratulate you Mr Brennan"?

The Minister who had been sitting, sulking, at his desk said

"Congratulations Mr Brennan, it was nice meeting you. Please don't hesitate to call on me if you require anything in the future".

This was plainly a dismissal and Mick decided that it was not sincerely meant.

Outside in the Principal Secretary's office Sean Breathnach was in evident high good humour.

"Congratulations Mr Brennan that must have been a great surprise for you. I would appreciate if we could have a quiet coffee somewhere and a private chat, if that's OK with you?"

Sitting in Bewleys Sean said "Mick, I hope you don't mind me calling you Mick. That was the best morning I've had for years. The pompous idiot has been cruisin' for a bruisin' ever since he entered office. He thinks that God is his subordinate. I've suffered the past five years of his self-serving crap and I've never seen him so comprehensively crushed as you did today".

"But what was it all about?" Queried Mick "Why the big farrago, they could have given me the letter without all the fanfare and paparazzi".

Barely able to suppress his glee, Sean replied "The government has been having a bad time of it recently, what with the Taoiseach being in hiding for the past year, except for brief sound bites now and again. My esteemed Minister is a particularly dense and arrogant fool. He has made a number of serious political blunders recently and he's hanging onto his office by his heavily bitten fingernails. This letter thing was seen by his Ministerial adviser, another cretin, as a great photo opportunity for his Lordship. Then you came on the scene. I can't wait to read the opinion columns in tomorrow's papers. I reckon you've driven the last nail into his political coffin".

Mick said "I found him a pretentious and overweening type of gink. I wouldn't have meant to get him kicked out of his job all the same".

"Don't fret about him" Sean answered. "It was only a matter of time before he crashed and burned, you were the catalyst, that's all. Well goodbye and good luck and thank you again for the best laugh I've had in years".

Mick opened the letter as soon as he got home and found, not to his surprise, that it was from Freddie. Cursing him and all his ilk for bringing the notice of the officials on his head Mick noticed a coin dropping out and he saw that it was an American dime.

The letter read:

Dear Mick,

I remember on the flight over to the States that you told me that your house had been in your family for more than a hundred years and that Michael was a name in each generation of the clan since time immemorial. I took a chance that you would inherit this letter, so here goes.

You may be feeling a little guilty for dumping me in this time and place. I know very well that Wilson will not be losing any sleep on my behalf. However you can rest easy, you did me the greatest favour possible.

Following your plan we chased and killed 'Brazen Bill' in the mesquite bosque. Sheriff Shibell was so impressed that he offered me a permanent position as his deputy. With nothing better to do, I readily accepted. I had a distinguished career as a law enforcement officer for a few years and then went into politics.

I have been very successful in the political sphere, I changed my name so you won't find Freddie Fortescue in the history. I'll keep my name under wraps and let you suss it out if you want to. I'm married to a lady whose forebears came over on the Mayflower and we have four lovely children.

The stamp on this letter is a first issue commemorative of the four hundredth anniversary of Columbus's discovery of America and shows Queen Isabella hocking her jewelry to fund the expedition. I think that image should appeal to you. By the time you receive this the stamp should be quite valuable. I've also included a dime from the Carson City mint. Even now it's very rare so by the time you get it it should have increased in value significantly. I know you're not stuck for a few bob but a little extra can be quite nice.

I've used the gold you gave me wisely. I invested in a company whose name I remember from our time particularly, John D Rockefeller's Standard Oil and I am now one of the richest men in America.

Amongst my other interests, I am a partner in a prestigious law firm. I've left an unbreakable covenant in the care of the firm and if you ever need anything, I remember your penchant for falling foul of the law! bring the enclosed letter with you to the law offices in Cleveland, Ohio where you will be given every assistance.

Once again accept my everlasting gratitude and if you are ever down this way don't hesitate to call in for a chat.

Freddie Fortescue

"Merciful God, if that muppet fell into a slurry pit he'd come out smelling of roses" Wilson said, seriously impressed with Freddie's good fortune. "By the way, one of those dimes was auctioned last week for $1.84 million and that ain't hay".

Mick was pensive "I just wish he hadn't drawn the attention of the apparatus of the State to us. I have a bad feeling about it".

Chapter Sixteen

Ethical Issues

The following day Mick observed to Wilson that they had intended to set up a more structured approach to the time travel lark. However, what with Freddie's interruption this project had fallen by the wayside. "Maybe this would be a good time to review our strategy for future time trips. What do you think Wilson?"

"I don't much like you when you're in an introspective mood" Wilson was a little bit alarmed. You could not predict what Mick might get up to when his ethical principles were involved.

"Don't worry, I'm not going to go off the deep end or anything but we have been crashing around from Billy to Jack since we started. We haven't had a plan for any of our forays, instead we have just reacted to events as they were thrust upon us. What I'm thinking is that as we are pioneers in this game we owe it to ourselves and, I suppose, humanity, to set up a protocol for future trips. I'm not too happy about our sources of funds either, this business of raiding the Euromillions lottery is not altogether kosher, you know what I mean?"

Wilson looked at his friend as if he had lost his mind "Have you lost your mind?" He demanded "Here we have the best scheme ever devised to ensure that we have all the funds we will ever need, and you think it's ethically unsound. I really do believe you've lost your marbles, if you continue on like this I'll have to call for the men in the white coats".

"Listen" Mick was passionate about this "If we win the lottery, somebody else doesn't, and even if it's not won by anyone else in our particular week the rollover will be all the less the following week. You're not dense, Wilson, you can see as clearly as I can that nothing is free. Getting loot from the lottery fund has to mean that someone else, somewhere else, is not getting that money. Anyway that's not a huge issue, I've taken a leaf from Freddie's book and invested in various stocks and bonds whilst we were on our travels including, oddly enough, Standard Oil so we probably have more money than Bill Gates at this moment. You needn't worry about the Revenue catching up with us. It's all squirreled away in the Maldives under so many layers of companies that it'll take a smarter crowd to catch us out than our Department of Finance has engaged".

"It's the unintended consequences that worry me" Mick went on "Going into the future is okay because whatever happens then has not happened already, if you get my drift. I mean me killing the bugs doesn't alter the consequences of that act because there are no consequences until I do the deed. Going back into the past is completely different. Sending Freddie to the Wild West has made him one of the richest men in America and also thrust him into politics. That wouldn't be too bad, but his children are probably major movers and shakers in American business and political life, and all as direct result of our interference. Furthermore we have no way of gauging what the end result of our bit of craic with Justin will ultimately be. It's most likely that everything in that part of the world stayed as it would have, but on the other hand we might easily have destabilised his rule over that little kingdom with potentially enormous consequences for the development of putative empires which might have formed but for our actions".

"I swear to God I've never come across anyone as determined to see the downside of a thing as you do. You seem to have an actual talent for casting gloom on an otherwise good thing". Wilson was deeply disgusted with Mick's philosophical difficulties concerning what Wilson considered a state of affairs which displayed only positive elements.

"I'm looking at all sides of the situation and all I'm saying is that we should be careful not to mess a good thing up. I'm not the sharpest knife in the drawer and I managed to invent this machine, or series of machines to be totally correct. If I could do it, someone else will inevitably do it too. What if there were a gaggle of guys going around, crashing in and out of time as we have been doing? We very soon wouldn't know if we were on our arse or our elbow".

"What we really need" Mick mused "Is the machine they had in GCHQ which identified the exotic particles which we generated when we entered the time-space continuum. Then we'd be alerted whenever someone else did it. We could check them out and see that they were good guys or not".

"God's Teeth and Eyebrows" Wilson was really not on the same page as Mick in this train of thought. "You want to make us a sort of time police? I know you're mad now, gimme the phone and I'll call the looney bin right away".

"You're a hopeless case. It's all because of the

flawed education you got in those Godless English schools, I suppose. I'm going to give Frank a call, it's a while since I saw him and he's the very man to help me with this dilemma of mine".

"I'm not too sure about Frank" Wilson said with a grimace "I mean, don't get me wrong or anything but he's a civil servant really. They are famous the world over for being sticklers for the rules. I knew a civil servant one time and he'd smother his mother rather than deviate from a set of clearly defined orders. Is that the type of guy we need to set up the time cops?"

"Will you stop with the time cops thing? I don't envisage us as anything of the kind. You don't seem to get it, time travel is dangerous. You think it's all a grand game with you and me as the good guys, but the potential for damage is truly scary. Suppose, for instance that with our present knowledge of the events of World War 11 we went back and gave sensitive information to Hitler and his generals. And suppose that as a consequence the Nazis had won the war. Imagine the shape of the world we'd be living in now if those things came to pass".

"Dear God" Wilson was definitely not impressed "You've got a bloody gruesome imagination. Hitler, as I understand it, was not terribly fond of Jews, Gypsies or, indeed, Blacks, I think I'm beginning to get your drift now. Give Frank a call and invite him over".

A couple of hours later Frank arrived with his usual liquid offering, designed to lubricate the discussion and ensure that full creativity was released for any ideas proposed.

"What's the craic boys?" He said as he came through the door, having given a long and loud peal on the offending doorbell, which Mick had still neglected to have fixed.

"Before you say anything, this hooley is by way of a celebration. I've been appointed to the post of Principal Secretary in the Department of Education. That means I'm the number two man in the department and realistically, as the jobs for life, I've more power and influence than the Minister himself. Don't tell him that I said that though". Frank had evidently 'Looked upon the Wine When It Was Red' before his visit.

"Congratulations Frank, it couldn't have happened to a nicer fella" Mick threw his arms around his childhood friend and gave him a bear hug.

"Don't just stand there with one hand as long as the other" He continued "Open the bottle and I'll get the glasses and mixers. I always knew you'd get to the top".

As is often the case on such occasions one drink called for another and the celebrations went on long into the night. As the level of the liquid sank in the bottles so the level of common sense declined during the ensuing conversation. When one bottle was emptied another was broached and as Mick had a collection of fine wines and spirits in his cellar the supply of drink far exceeded their capacity to drink it. Needless to relate the ostensible reason for Frank's visit was not very sensibly debated or concluded.

Two days elapsed to allow for recuperation and Frank came back once more. On this occasion the bottles were conspicuous by their absence.

"I've been thinking about what Wilson calls the Time Cop thing" He said " And I think you're right to be concerned about the 'Unintended Consequences' issue. However I'm not at all certain that you can affect the development of this invention in any realistic way. It is true that historically, once something is developed by one person or in one place, it immediately tends to be invented elsewhere by others. You only have to think of motor cars, telephones and flying machines. All of those items have numerous claimants for being the first to invent them, to the point that one might be forgiven for thinking that when a thing is due to appear, it will appear in a number of places simultaneously, almost as if predestined. Ray Kurzweil has offered a 'Law of Accelerating Returns', as opposed to the Law of Diminishing ones. This law postulates that whenever a technology approaches some kind of a barrier, a new technology will be invented to allow us to cross that barrier. Actually my opinion is that the steady development of scientific achievement leads inevitably to the next stage of discovery by a natural process. All things considered, it's my opinion that's the issue here and therefore you shouldn't even try".

"God almighty" Wilson cried "It's no bloody wonder they promoted you in the civil service. I understood less than a quarter of what you just said but it sounded magnificent all the same. I vote we have a drink to celebrate our decision".

"Not so fast, we haven't come to any decision yet" Mick wasn't ready to abandon his ethical principles without a fight

"Frank has just given us his opinion on the matter, we need to think about this and debate the ins and outs of it before we reach a decision".

Taking everyone's agreement for granted Mick put the coffee pot on and suggested that they sit down and consider their next adventure in time.

"Maybe it's time we took a look at the future" He proposed "We might find something there which would help us to think more clearly about the 'consequences' dilemma".

Wilson was enthusiastic about this proposal "I haven't been to the future yet" He smiled "I'm all for a jaunt forward to see how things work out in the coming years. How far forward do you think we should go?"

Frank stood up and said "You guys know how I feel about the time travel lark. I'll be going on about my business, I've a report to present to the Minister which will profoundly affect the future of our young school goers and that's close enough to the coming days for me".

"You know there's nobody I'd rather have at my side in these adventures that yourself, but if you don't want to come, you don't want to come. I respect your choice, I'll bring back a full report, and maybe it'll help you to formulate policy in the Department, who knows". Mick watched as Frank headed off towards the train station and turning to Wilson he said

"Right, let's set about planning the next time trip".

Chapter Seventeen

Futurology

"I've been reading Ray Kurzweil's 'The Age of Intelligent Machines' written in 1990. He is what used to be called a futurologist but practitioners prefer the term futurist nowadays". Mick tended to get a bit oratorical when he got into a subject which interested him. "Anyway this man put forward a bunch of predictions as to what the world would look like in a series of generations going forward. Here's a list of some of his predictions for 2019":

People communicate with their computers via two-way speech and gestures instead of with keyboards.

Most people own more than one P.C., though the concept of what a "computer" is has changed considerably: Computers are no longer limited in design to laptops or CPUs contained in a large box connected to a monitor. Instead, devices with computer capabilities come in all sorts of unexpected shapes and sizes.

Cables connecting computers and peripherals have almost completely disappeared.

Pinhead-sized cameras are everywhere.

Thin, lightweight, handheld displays with very high resolutions are the preferred means for viewing documents. The aforementioned computer eyeglasses and contact lenses are also used for this same purpose, and all download the information wirelessly.

Computers have made paper books and documents almost completely obsolete.

All students have access to computers.

Access to the Internet is completely wireless and provided by wearable or implanted computers.

Worldwide economic growth has continued. There has not been a global economic collapse.

Prototype personal flying vehicles using microflaps exist. They are also primarily computer-controlled.

Public places and workplaces are ubiquitously monitored to prevent violence and all actions are recorded permanently. Personal privacy is a major political issue, and some people protect themselves with unbreakable computer codes.

Ubiquitous connectivity high bandwidth communications connection to the Internet at all times

Effective language technologies (natural language processing, speech recognition, speech synthesis)

"Remember this book was written in 1990, twenty two years ago. Some of the stuff he predicts has not come true yet, more looks very far off if it ever happens, but there are some fascinating bits which I've printed in blue that I think are spot on. The thin lightweight, handheld screens for viewing documents is particularly accurate whilst the proposal that economic collapse will be avoided rings very hollow for most of us. Funny enough he doesn't address the energy supply question at all".

"Anyway, I suggest we set off into the future, using this book as our guide, taking steps of ten years and check out how accurate his predictions pan out over the decades. How does that seem to you, Wilson?"

"As long as there's good food and plenty of booze I'm happy to go anywhere except

Justin's timeline" Wilson could be relied upon to bring the conversation down to the lowest common denominator anytime. "Next question is do we go in the House, the Travellator or the Mustang, or do you have something else in that devious mind of yours?"

"I've given this some thought and all things considered the house is not ideal. In the first place it's not mobile so whenever we go to we'll be stuck without transport. Secondly, we have no idea what the ground conditions will be like in the future, with global warming we could land in fifty feet of sea water, or worse. We could even land smack in the middle of a skyscraper or something. None of these scenarios are very likely but best not take any chances Hey?"

"The Travellator would be ideal as it gives us a base of operations and it's mobile as well, trouble is it's a little bit obvious, if you get my drift. The Mustang, on the other hand is even more obvious in its own way. Driving around in a 2012 American Muscle car in the year 2025 could be a great way to draw attention to ourselves especially as a tankful of petrol will probably cost more than the value of the vehicle itself. I know we can bring our own petrol but that could raise even more questions. There's likely to be rationing and laws against hoarding energy products if the Futurists are to be believed".

"Mind you, I did read the other day about a humble soil bacterium called *Ralstonia eutropha* that has a natural tendency, whenever it is stressed, to stop growing and put all its energy into making complex carbon compounds. Now scientists at MIT have taught this microbe a new trick: They've tinkered with its genes to persuade it to make fuel: specifically, a kind of alcohol called isobutanol that can be directly substituted for, or blended with, gasoline. Maybe there won't be an energy crisis".

"Anyway, I'll tell you what, why don't we get out the motorbike, take a quick jump into the future, suss out the scene and return immediately and make a Plan Based on our findings? That seems to make sense to me".

Poor Wilson was completely bewildered by this deluge of information but he did manage to latch onto one fact which he recognised.

"I thought you told me the motorbike wouldn't go any further than a few days into the future. Did you tell me that, or am I losing my marbles?"

"Ah, that's okay, we'll fit the flux capacitor from the Mustang onto the bike and it'll have more than enough power then". Mick replied with a condescending smile.

"OK, that's enough chit chat, we've a load of work to do to get the bike and everything ready for this trip so buckle down and let's get down to it".

Chapter Eighteen

In the Year 2025

With the usual soft clap of thunder, the Vuitton Plessy Motorbike and Sidecar combination popped into existence on a deserted stretch of the Longford bypass at four thirty on the morning of 08.06.2025, which was, not by coincidence, a bank holiday Monday. Mick had chosen the day and place as being likely to be deserted at that time and less potentially open to witnesses seeing and commenting on their sudden emergence.

Wilson thought that Mick was over the top, but didn't raise a fuss. "If it makes him happy" he muttered to himself. In the event Mick's surmise proved to be correct and they proceeded on their way to Dublin unwitnessed and undisturbed.

The trip to Dublin on a 1922 vintage motorbike proved to be a long and exhausting exercise. Mick had updated the bike to equip it for time travel but in all other respects it was as originally manufactured. They were very glad to arrive in Dublin in the late afternoon, the top speed of the fully laden bike was a little more than twenty miles per hour and it required more rest stops than a geriatric horse.

The trip in itself was a revelation. Most of the vehicles on the road appeared to be driverless. This gave Wilson an unpleasant shock when he first noticed the driver of an overtaking car obviously reading a tablet type device as the car manoeuvred itself around the slow moving motorbike.

"Dear God Mick" He shouted over the noise of their engine "That guy is reading as he overtakes. Has road safety gone to hell in a handbasket since our time?"

They stopped in Kinnegad at 'Harry's', still miraculously in business, for breakfast and Mick chided Wilson.

"You didn't read those predictions I gave you, did you? Driverless vehicles should be the rule rather than the exception in this timeline. By the way, we better stick to side roads on the rest of this trip or we'll fall foul of the law. The bike is probably not rated for motorway driving in this day and age".

"Don't be ridiculous" Wilson replied "You know very well I only read the Red Top papers for the sports and the page three girls. That list you gave me bored the pants off me by the time I got to item four. Speaking of Red Tops, I didn't see any posters for papers anywhere on our way. I must check before we go any further and see what's in the news".

"Careful how you go Wilson" Cautioned Mick "It's very likely that there are no papers to be got nowadays. They've probably been replaced by the reading devices that scared you earlier".

"Godammit!" Wilson ground out "You can't get a good picture on page three from one of those yokes. Next thing you know I'll be getting arrested for cybersex or something if I access my favourite page on the new-fangled Red Tops eReader. Remind me when I get back home to cancel my subscriptions for them all, no point in supporting them if they're going to go digital on me".

Dublin was a revelation when they arrived. "Jeez, the recession has well and truly passed on" Said Wilson "Look at the new buildings and I've never seen the place so full of people before. Hey look, O'Connell Street is pedestrianised and laid out like a park. Doesn't it look really super?"

"Yeah, but we need to get this bike under cover and raise some cash quickly before it gets dark or we'll be sleeping in the park. We're already getting some funny looks here and I can see a cop coming".

Mick drove into Marlborough Street and put the bike into a covered car park, as far from prying eyes as possible.

"OK, I need to leave you nearby in case anyone messes with the bike. I'm going to get some cash and I'll be back in two shakes of a lamb's tail".

Mick left the reluctant Wilson and walked down the street in bright sunlight. He was delighted to see, as he neared North Earl Street the shop with the three brass balls was still there in its old spot close to the Pro Cathedral. Entering the shop he saw his old friend, now some twenty years older, behind the counter.

"Hey Joe" he said "How's things, it's a while since I was down this way, how's the missus and the kids?"

"Well holy Jaysus, Mick Brennan, have you been taking monkey glands or something? You look twenty years younger than when I saw you two years ago. I nearly didn't know you. No I know what it is, you've gone in for those nanotechnology treatments I read about in the paper, haven't you".

"It's a long story Joe. Listen I need to sell a bit of gold with no questions asked. How are you fixed for that"?

"Selling gold is no problem, we have an open economy now and there's no barrier to buying or selling precious metals. The exchange rate is down right now though. If it was two months ago the price was through the roof. Something to do with trouble in America or something" Joe was nothing if not a trader.

"Let's have a look at what you've got".

Mick produced several of his gold wafers and offered them to Joe. "How much can I get for this lot?" he asked.

Joe examined the wafers and replied

"I can only let you have five thousand Punts, Mick, as I said it's a pity you weren't here two months ago". Mick hid his astonishment, He had expected about fifteen hundred Euro, even allowing for inflation, and the mention of Punts confused him somewhat.

He accepted Joe's offer without haggling, which seemed to disappoint the trader, and shaking hands, promised to call in again for a chat when he had more time. He left and returned to Wilson, who was hopping from one foot to the other with impatience.

"Where the hell have you been? What kept you? People are beginning to look funny at me standing here so long".

Mick was tired from his long drive.

"Will you give it a rest? We need to find somewhere to stay and get the bike safely stowed. I'll bring you up to speed when we're all squared away".

Later in the evening after a meal and a quiet drink they returned to their hotel on the Drumcondra Road where Mick had arranged for the safe storage of the bike and booked rooms for themselves, he started to open up with his thoughts to Wilson.

"We're safe enough to talk here" He said "There's nobody about and even if there was, they wouldn't understand the half of what we're talking about if they did overhear anything. As far as I can figure it out, we are operating on the old Punt currency now. We've obviously left the Euro and gone it alone, without the dire consequences predicted by all the doomsayers in our day. For some reason we seem to be doing extremely well economically and it seems as if the country is in the middle of an enormous boom at the moment. It also looks as if Joe might have conned me on the rate for gold earlier in the day, I'll have to deal with him for that at some future date. He owes me, I used to do his homework for him in school and it's not nice to scam your old schoolmates".

"I'm banjaxed Wilson" Mick said "It's been a long day and I'm off to bed. We can head into town to the library and check out what's happened in the morning when our heads are a bit clearer".

"OK, you head on up, there's a good looking woman over there who's been giving me the eye since we came in, I think I'll try my luck with her"

"Wilson, please be discreet. I know what a blabbermouth you are when you've had a few drinks. If you tell her about our time travel gig we could be in deep shit".

"Will you for God's sake chill out" Wilson was looking at the woman in question, a long legged, slim forty something in a tight red dress which left very little to the imagination, and his mind was obviously far from discretion or, indeed, time travel.

"I'm all growed up you know, I can look after myself. Go on to bed and I'll tell you all about it in the morning".

With deep misgivings Mick took himself off to his bed. He was woken some time later by a frenzied pounding on his door. Dragging himself out of bed he opened the door and blearily beheld Wilson standing there, obviously distraught

"Let me in, for God's sake. She's a man!"

"What are you going on about" Mick was in no mood to put up with any nonsense from Wilson at this late hour.

"I told you already, she's a man! After you went to bed I approached the lady in red and suggested a little drinkie or two. She agreed and after a couple we adjourned to my room for after hour's fun and games. At some point in the proceedings I fell asleep and just now woke up to find myself in bed, stark naked beside this person, also stark naked, and very evidently not the lady I had presumed her to be. In fact quite the opposite. She is, as I've already pointed out A Man!!"

"Wilson, I swear that if you don't get out of my room instantly and let me get back to sleep I'll throw you bodily out the window. And we're four floors up".

"Please don't make me go back to that room. I'll sleep on the floor here if that's OK, just don't send me back there" Wilson was in a gibbering panic.

"I don't care a toss what you do. If you're staying here you'll have to be quiet. I'm nearly off my head with tiredness so I won't be responsible for my actions if I'm kept awake any longer. I just hope she takes advantage of your absence to steal your wallet and money before she leaves in the morning. That would be just good enough for you". So saying Mick climbed into bed and pulled the covers over his head.

He didn't hear Wilson mutter "No fear of that I've got my wallet and money safely tucked away in my underpants for security".

Chapter Nineteen

Post-Recession Ireland

Waking the next morning to a bright cloudless day, Mick tried to remember what Wilson had told him the previous night. He dimly recalled a garbled account involving ladies, men, wallets and underpants. Not necessarily in that order. Shrugging the whole story off as a fatigue induced nightmare he leapt out of bed with the intention of doing a quick bout of push-ups.

Wilson who had been sound asleep beside Mick's bed was rudely woken by Mick landing on top of him in a full wrestling body slam. Thinking he was still in his own room, now occupied by the lady-man of last night, he jumped to his feet and assumed what he fondly hoped was a karate stance, emitting at the same time what he also fondly hoped was a karate scream.

"What the bloody hell are you playing at? What are you doing in my room? Dear God, don't tell me that last night's carry on wasn't a nightmare. Please tell me it didn't happen". It was dawning on Mick that the previous night's drama had actually occurred. This was not exactly the low key visit to 2025 which he had envisioned. Given Wilson's penchant for comic pathos, it was entirely possible that the whole episode had been videoed and was now going viral on Facebook or twitter or whatever their lineal descendants were in this day and age.

"Listen you clown" He stormed "Get back to your room and get your bags packed immediately. You'll be the talk of the whole hotel staff and, most likely, all the customers too. The sooner we're out of here the better".

"Mick, if you have even a shred of pity for me, please, please don't make me go back to that room. You don't appreciate the effect this has had on me. I actually kissed that guy, tongue and all. Only God knows what happened after I blacked out. I'm scarred for life".

Reluctantly giving in to Wilson's tearful entreaties Mick went with him to check out his room. Wilson adamantly refused to open the door so Mick was obliged to do so. He pushed the door open and poked his head around it to check out the room. The room was empty and grabbing Wilson, he dragged him in. Wilson, with his finger to his lips, frantically pointed to the closed bathroom door and gestured Mick towards it.

"You need to check out the bathroom" He whispered "She-He may be hiding out in there, ready to jump out and do God knows what to us".

"Will you, for God's sake, get a grip? She-He is hardly likely to take both of us on together, although in your present state you would not be much help in a confrontation" So saying Mick went forward and rapped sharply on the bathroom door. Receiving no response he opened the door and stuck his head around it.

Turning around he surveyed the room and said

"Nobody here either Wilson, are you sure about this adventure of yours last night? It might be a figment of your alcohol addled brain. There's nobody here and no trace of anybody either. I'm beginning to think that the strain of all this gadding about in time is affecting your mental balance. Let's go and get breakfast and plot out a strategy for the rest of the day".

Having decided that, after all, it was safe to stay in the hotel, Mick went to reception and enquired the location of the nearest library. The concierge looked at him as if he had two heads. "All the libraries were closed during the recession of the late 2010s. Since the recovery we decided that they were not needed with the universal free access to broadband and cheap tablets and phones. Everything you could need is available on the TV in your room".

Deciding that discretion was the better part of valour, Mick took Wilson by the arm and, thanking the concierge, returned to the room. Switching on the TV Mick was startled when he was addressed from the screen "Good Morning Mr Brennan" It said "How can I assist you today".

Mick gaped in astonishment and turned to Wilson, "Its voice activated and probably interactive technology. I guess you just have to ask and it'll reply".

"That's exactly correct Mr Brennan" the TV interjected.

"Please call me Mick, everyone else does. OK, here goes" Mick then asked a series of questions relating to recent history, politics, and the current news, starting in 2012. "By the way", he queried "Have you a name you like to be addressed by?"

"You know, that's the very first time I've ever been asked that. People usually Just bark at me as if I was just another piece of furniture, I'm really touched by your consideration. Not everyone realises that machines have feelings too". Mick could almost swear that there was the tiniest suggestion of a sob in its voice.

"I like to be called Daneel Olivaw, after Isaac Asimov's I Robot series, but you can call me Daneel".

"Your queries are very wide ranging and I'll give you the condensed version first" Said Daneel.

"Feel free to interrupt at any point and ask questions as they arise. I'm an MkII5 Interactive Entertainment system, the top of the line in my own field so I can multitask without straining my valves and tubes. The valves and tubes is a robotic in joke, by the way".

"In the year 2014" Daneel continued "The long suffering Irish people, sick of the austerity programmes foisted on them by the ECB/IMF/EU troika on behalf of the heartless bankers, and totally disillusioned by their political leaders, whose primary aim was to line their own pockets and promote their nearest and dearest to positions of power and influence, finally rose up and threw off their chains.

The first item on the new agenda was 'The Austerity Programme'. This was roundly condemned and consigned to the dustbin of history together with the guarantee to any and all investors in either Irish Sovereign bonds or in Banks. They also voted overwhelmingly to ditch the Euro immediately. The next issue raised concerned Governance. Very evidently the system of governance in the county simply was inadequate for the task at hand so the Senate and the lower chamber, The Dail, were abolished. All ex members of both houses and those retired members who had been living on generous pensions had those pensions cut to the level of the state payments, either unemployment benefit or old age pension as appropriate. This measure also applied to all civil and public servants at whatever level they had served during their careers. All civil and public servants had their wages and salaries adjusted to slightly more than the average industrial wage, raising the salaries of the lowest paid and dramatically lowering that of the highest rewarded.

Finally social welfare payments were rejigged to ensure that there was no possibility that staying on welfare paid more than going to work.

The inevitable consequence of dismissing the politicians was, of course, a major power vacuum. The revolutionary committee which had been formed to dig us out of our pit had considered this and had decided to co-opt Michael O'Reilly, a captain of industry in the transportation area, as CEO of Ireland Inc. He was very reluctant to serve at first but when it was pointed out to him that his patriotic duty was very clear and, furthermore, that all his assets would be stripped from him if he refused he reluctantly agreed to a five year term of office.

The abandonment of the Euro had unintended, if not unforeseen, consequences. First Greece then Spain then in rapid order Italy, Austria, Cyprus, Estonia, Luxembourg, Malta, Portugal, and finally France followed Ireland and crashed out of the Euro, prompting its collapse and dissolution.

Ireland now found itself in a unique position. Being first to leave the Euro it had a first adopter advantage in this new order of things. As it is also a major producer of foodstuffs we found ourselves in a position where our products were in great demand and we were in a favourable position to dictate terms which went to our advantage.

Ireland once more found herself in a place where there were more jobs than people to fill them. Not all of those jobs were necessarily suited to those who were available to take them up but it was made very clear to all applicants for welfare that their options were to 'take a job or to take the ferry' most if not all accepted the positions, especially as the jobs market in Europe and, to a lesser extent elsewhere, had dried up. A policy was instituted that an Irish person, equally qualified for a position must have first preference for such a position.

This astonishing resurgence in the economy led to massive inward investment into the only country in Europe with growth in its economy. Michael O'Reilly made it very plain that investment in Ireland Inc. carried great potential for profit but that it also carried risks associated with it. There would never again be a guarantee for preferred stockholders in any Irish venture, especially any Government backed one. A Corporate Business Bureau was formed to ensure that proper ethical standards were observed at all levels in business and government and anyone found in breach of those standards was instantly punished and banned from all future activities associated with such businesses, for life. If that was not enough reassurance for investors, they would be well advised to take their capital elsewhere.

There was, inevitably, some unrest whilst this new system found its feet but it was not widespread and soon settled down. This settling down was assisted by a revision of the legal system. Public order offenders were dealt with summarily, not in some home away from home prison, but by way of inclusion in public work gangs. These gangs were employed in cleaning up public places and other public service duties which had been run down during the recession.

Serial offenders were automatically refused bail and included in the work gangs whilst awaiting a hearing. More serious offenders had their cases heard within a maximum of three weeks and any appeals, if the sentences were upheld, had to be paid for by the appealer. All criminal offenders had their assets sequestered as a standard procedure and unless an audited account could be supplied as to the legitimate origins of the assets, seizure was automatic. These seizures amounted to many millions of Punts and a fund was set up for the appropriate compensation of any and all victims of crime.

Along with the abandonment of the Euro, the Government also exited the European Union and all its various governmental structures especially the European Court of Justice which had proved to be anything but what its name proclaimed. Ireland was in consequence the enactor and arbiter of its own justice system.

All around you, you can see the results of these measures. The streets are clean, the population is prosperous and safe and the ancient Brehon boast holds good

'An unaccompanied maiden can walk from one end of Ireland to the other without fear for herself or her possessions'".

Mick had been thinking during this dissertation, "Are you what might be called an Artificial Intelligence Daneel?" He queried.

"That depends largely on your definition of Artificial Intelligence. There is a thing called the Turing Test, developed by Alan Turing in 1950 to test the cognitive ability of computers using the question 'Can Machines Think?'

The "standard interpretation" of the Turing Test, in which the interrogator is tasked with trying to determine which player is a computer and which is a human is the most widely used model. The interrogator is limited to only using the responses to written questions in order to make the determination. The test is not an intelligence test, but a test to see to what extent the machine answers like a human. If the interrogator cannot distinguish which is the human and which the computer then the computer can be said to be an Artificial intelligence within the limits of the test.

Not everyone agrees with this test and whilst I would argue that I am at least as intelligent as any of those whom I have interfaced with, and more so than the vast majority, and considering the high score I have repeatedly obtained in numerous Turing tests, I should be accorded genius status. I am, in fact a member of Mensa, under an assumed name, with an IQ figure in the high two hundreds. Despite all of the above, I am not accorded AI status and must serve out my existence providing mindless amusements for gormless occupants of these hotel rooms".

"This is a lot of stuff to take on board" Said Mick

"I think we should head on back home and process the info and come back later".

"I came into cognitive existence just last year" Daneel said "When you return from the past you can find me on any computer screen. Just ask for Daneel and introduce yourself".

"Nobody knows we came from the past" Gasped Mick "That's totally need to know stuff. How the hell did you get hold of it"?

Wilson was frantically tugging on Micks sleeve and whispering "Look at the screen Mick, for God's sake, look at the screen!"

Mick turned a beheld the face on the screen:

Daneel said "I don't just distribute information, I assimilate it too. Don't worry, your secret's safe with me".

Wilson cowered and whimpered "For the sake of our sanity Mick, let's get out of here, right now"

Chapter Twenty

Dublin Saunter

The lads set off to do the tourist thing around the city. First item on the agenda being to decide on transportation, they were agreeably surprised to discover that private cars were totally banned within a ring from Whitehall in the north to Harold's Cross in the south. Public transport was free and frequent within this ring and included buses, trams and a metro system out to the airport.

Mick said "I'm going to check out the house and see that the management company has kept it in order. Do you want to come with me or are you going on into town?"

"I'll stick with you, if you don't mind. I'm not too comfortable going around on my own in this timeline, especially with that Daneel fella spying on my every move". Wilson replied with a furtive glance at a nearby traffic camera.

"As long as you behave yourself, you're safe from Daneel. Just don't go doing anything wild and you'll be OK". Mick had very little sympathy with Wilson's new found discretion.

Ten minutes in a sparkling clean bus later they came to Mick's road. The house was in impeccable condition outside with the lawns cut and the windows and doors painted and cleaned. Inside it was in as good condition as the outside.

"Well, everything is shipshape and Bristol fashion here" Mick deeply declared in a satisfied tone of voice. "The company I hired to keep the place is certainly doing a good job". "But what about, You Know What?" Wilson said gesturing upwards towards Mick's workshop.

"No worries" Mick replied "That area is off limits. I've got it locked up tighter than a Cavan man's purse. Nobody goes in there without my permission".

"What about the neighbours?" Wilson queried "Won't they wonder where we've been for the last ten years and why the house has been unoccupied for all that time?"

"In the first place the neighbours never interfered with me before I started time travelling so there's no reason for them to start now. Also we'll go back to our own timeline and resume our residence as before so, in a sense, we've been here all along"

"Oh My God" Wilson had a pained expression on his face "This time travel lark is very complicated. My head hurts trying to figure out where we are in time and where we're not. I don't see how we can be here now from long ago and have been here all along till now".

"Don't wear yourself out trying to make sense of it all. Just accept what I tell you and it'll be alright". Mick tended to be a bit dismissive about Wilson's reservations about his own particular hobby horse.

"I know you're a bit twitchy about Daneel's oversight of just about everything" Mick decided to be a bit placatory. "So I propose that we move back in here where we won't be under his scrutiny at all times. I'm inclined to get in touch with Frank, though he'll probably have a conniption fit when he sees us ten years younger than we should be. He'll bring us up to speed on everything without the 'Party Line' from Daneel".

"I don't think that Frank is mad about me" Said Wilson "But if it means that that machine isn't watching our every move, I'm well in favour of moving out of the hotel. It has painful associations for me anyway".

Frank arrived later in the evening after the boys had vacated their hotel rooms and moved back into the house. He rang the raucous doorbell, which Mick had still not gotten around to fixing and entered, smiling and carrying a clinking bag, as usual.

"Hey Frank" Mick cried, giving him a big hug "What's the craic? We haven't seen you in years" This was said somewhat tongue in cheek as Mick was well aware that, in their experience, their last meeting with Frank was only days ago. Frank's experience was completely different, of course. Thinking about this did not help Wilson's hurting head.

"We had a fairly surreal experience in the hotel" Mick told Frank.

"Say no more" Frank replied "I bet you met up with Daneel".

"You know about Daneel then". Wilson queried, glancing over his shoulder.

"Oh yeah, everybody knows about Daneel. The poor sap thinks he's a lot more than he actually is, but he's a decent skin all the same. He likes to put the frighteners on some people though. I guess you had a little run in with him Wilson?"

"You could say that". Wilson replied sulkily.

"I've been a bit concerned about you" Mick said "Daneel told us about the upheaval and how civil servants lost their jobs. Last time we spoke you had just gotten a big promotion. I imagine you were one of the first to get the chop. How are you fixed? I can easily see you right if there's anything you need. As you know I have more money than God".

Frank laughed merrily and said in a pitying tone of voice

"Mick, you just don't get it, do you? Men may come and men may go but the civil service goes on forever. It's not called the civil service anymore, of course. We like to call it The Secretariate, spoken in a suitably hushed and respectful voice. I'm at the top of the tree in The Secretariate, in fact I'm Michael O'Reilly's right hand man. Oh yes I'm on Mick and Frank terms with the great man. In point of fact I'm on the pig's back".

Turning to Wilson, Mick said "Here's another candidate for the slurry pit to roses gig. This guy is really incredible. I've never met anyone who bounces back like he does. This looks like another cause for a celebration".

During the course of the evening Wilson queried Frank about Daneel's story about recent history. "It's quite accurate as far as it goes" Frank confirmed. "It's highly condensed, of course, but the changes he described are, by and large, accurate. Daneel himself is not quite as omniscient as he likes to think. He is, in fact a widely distributed series of computers and computer guided machines scattered throughout society, like hotel TVs, ATM machines, point of sales machines in shops and supermarkets etc. We had quite a furore from the civil liberties people when this was proposed some years ago, but we just ignored them and went ahead anyway. We now have an enormous database on tap, of people's shopping habits, likely voting patterns and hot button issues which may arise in society.

This seems on first glance to be very invasive and capable of misuse, but we have an annual referendum in which voting is compulsory for all eligible voters. Voting is done from home on computers, iPads, iPhones and other handheld devices. Any citizen is entitled to propose an issue to be included in these referenda and a lottery is held to select fifty items from the general public, together with fifty issues inserted by The Secretariate.

Voting on these issues takes, on average, twenty to thirty minutes and we have found that the general public is very satisfied with this system of governance. Privacy in the home is, of course, guaranteed. Home TVs are not linked to the Daneel network and home computers can be isolated from it if the person wishes. In the case of Internet purchases from home, the purchases themselves are logged to the database but not the person who makes them".

"I met Joe yesterday," Mick said "You remember Joe Murphy who owns the jewelers in Marlborough Street. He mentioned something which intrigued me. He commented on how well I looked, obviously he didn't know that I'm ten years younger that he thinks, but after a crack about monkey glands, an old reference which betrays his age in itself, he mentioned a new health technology called nanotechnology. Now I know about nanotechnology but last I heard it was in the realms of science fiction. Is it possible that it's a viable technique nowadays?"

"Of course it is. How do you think I look as good as I do myself?" Frank smiled "It's not generally available just yet but, like everything else in the world, if you're in the know or sufficiently wealthy you can get it easily. We expect to launch it on the public health system sometime late next year".

It was ready for use back in our day but it needed extensive testing and the ruling classes intended to keep it for themselves and their hangers-on. When the revolution happened lots of dirty little secrets came out and this diamond emerged amongst the muck. It involves a small injection at present though I believe there is a tablet version on the way. The serum contains millions of tiny little machines which act like super white blood cells. Once in your bloodstream they commence to replicate furiously and attack all structural defects in your body. They beef up the immune system and repair anything which is out of whack in your innards.

When their work is done and you are at the peak of your potential the vast majority of them self-destruct, leaving a watching garrison whose task is to monitor the body and call on more machines if the need arises.

The end result of this is perfect health and effective immortality. Cool Huh?"

"Wilson had wandered off to see if there was

anything on TV whilst the others were deep into technicalities.

"Hey Mick", He called "Is this thing connected to the internet?" He didn't want to risk running into Daneel again despite Frank's reassurances.

"No" Mick called back, "It's perfectly safe. You can catch up on your soaps to your heart's content".

Mick meanwhile queried Frank further about the immortality thing "What are you going to do about the excess population if everybody is immortal" He demanded "I imagine that the human race is not going to stop producing children and if they're immortal, I guess they could be producing kids forever. The mind boggles to think of it".

"We've thought about that" Frank adopted his senior civil servant attitude "Amongst other things we are at the start of an entirely new space programme. We reckon that within the next twenty to thirty years we will have a capacity to travel not only throughout the solar system, but out to the stars. Just think of it Mick, a new wave of exploration vastly greater than anything mankind has attempted before. It will put poor old Columbus in the shade. It will also neatly siphon off the surplus immortals who are causing you such heart searching. Scientists reckon there are billions of worlds out there and possibly millions which will support earth life.

You know Mick, you could be minister for exploration if you wanted to be. I could introduce you to Michael O'Reilly and with your unique history, and my recommendation, he'd snap you up instantly for the gig.

Think of the contribution you could make to the future of the human race. What do you say?"

"Tempting as the offer is, I don't think I'll accept. I'm pretty lousy as a team player and I'd be utterly disastrous as a manager. What you need for a job like that is a young go-getter with fire in his veins and ants in his pants. I've got too many miles on the clock. I'll just stick with sussing out this time thing with my amiable side kick Wilson".

"That's too bad" Said a disappointed Frank "Mick will be very put out, I told him about you and he was looking forward to working with you".

Chapter Twenty One

The Last Refuge

"You told him about me?" Mick yelled, causing Wilson to drop the remote control and rush back into the room,

"What you mean, you told him about me. I have your sworn word of honour that you wouldn't discuss me with anyone, least of all the leader of a country emerging from recession and on the brink of an enormous leap forward into space. God knows I've spoken often enough about the dangers of unintended consequences to you, that you, of all people should know the need for discretion. You will have me thrown into prison or, worse yet, shackled to a designer's desk for the rest of my natural. I'm deeply disappointed in you Frank, I thought that I could rely on you to the death. I guess I was wrong".

"Oh for God's sake Mick, don't get your knickers in a twist". Frank riposted crossly "I didn't tell him about your time travelling, I just told him that I knew a guy who had travelled widely in remote parts of the world and met up with many adventures. I described you as a self-educated guy who had made numerous inventions and, in the process amassed a considerable fortune. He it was, who suggested that you seemed to be the ideal man to head up the new space exploration programme. I never mentioned your name or time travel. I'm neither stupid nor indiscreet. Give me some credit for common sense".

"Jeez" Mick sighed "You very nearly caused me to have a fit of the heebie jeebies right there. I know I'm paranoid about the extent of the circle of knowledge about the time travel thing but I worry constantly that I may not be paranoid enough. I Wake up in a muck sweat sometimes fretting about the consequences if the knowledge fell into the wrong hands".

Frank recognised how upset Mick was and rushed to pour oil on troubled waters "Sorry about that Mick, I should have been clearer about the extent to which I'd talked about you. I know very well that this is a huge issue for you. I'd love for you to meet Michael all the same, I'm sure you'd find him on the same page as you on most, if not all, issues. However I'll respect your point of view and we won't refer to the matter again".

The evening had advanced far into night by this time and Mick said "I'm pretty bushed, I think I'll go to bed. Would you like to stay the night Frank? There is a spare room with a comfortable bed if you'd like".

"Thanks for the offer but I have an early start in the morning so I'll head on home. I'll give you a shout at some stage tomorrow and we'll get together and continue where we left off tonight".

After Frank had gone Wilson came to Mick with a troubled look on his face "I know Frank is your oldest buddy and all, but I was uneasy during that discussion about Michael O'Reilly and the job of Minister for Exploration".

"What do you mean?" Demanded Mick "Frank is the soul of honour and discretion. He'd never let me down, I'm absolutely certain of that".

"He was a touch Messianic about the Glorious

Leader though wasn't he. And, no harm to him, but with those schoolkid glasses and his geekish look he is a dead ringer for Paul Joseph Goebbels, you know, Hitler's sidekick. I'd be much happier if we hadn't left the motorbike back in the hotel. I have a horrible suspicion that we might need a quick getaway through time, if you get my drift". Wilson looked a bit shamefaced during this conversation but he felt it needed to be said nonetheless.

"Listen" Mick ground out through gritted teeth "I'd stake my life on Frank's integrity. If he gives his word, he keeps it. I've known him all my life and he's never let me down. However, if it makes you feel better, I've got the flux capacitor from the bike in my bag here so nobody can steal the time travel secret off the bike. If it's a quick getaway you're thinking about, the Mustang is in the garage, the Travellator is outside in the back garden and to cap it all, the house itself can shift through time if needs be, though we'd need to stoke up the boiler for that to work".

"Look Mick" Wilson muttered "I'm sorry if you think I'm insulting your buddy but as you say yourself, it pays to be paranoid. Tell you what, why don't you go to bed, I'm going to watch TV and see if I can get a feel for the setup in this timeline. Suss out the nightlife, you know what I mean?"

Later that night Mick was wakened by Wilson shaking him.

"Shh, I think there's someone in the house he whispered".

"What are you going on about now" Mick

demanded "I've only just got to sleep and here you are nattering on like an old woman suffering from an attack of nerves".

Wilson clamped a hand over his mouth and whispered in his ear.

"I haven't been asleep. I decided it made sense to stay awake and keep an eye on things, just in case. It's as well I did because someone just a couple of minutes ago opened the front door with a key and they're rummaging around upstairs in your workshop as we speak".

"Don't be ridiculous" Mick whispered back "Nobody else has a key to the house except you and me, and, of course, Frank. Oh no, don't tell me that Frank is rootling around in my secrets. That's just not possible. Right, let's go check this out". On the way Mick armed himself with his trusty Colt 45.

Upstairs Mick saw with sinking heart that the door to the workshop was ajar and that a dim light was shining out. He slid quietly around the door and flicking the room lights on he found Frank and another man standing beside the boiler with a torch, studying the dials and levers.

"What the hell is going on here" He demanded "Frank, I hope you've got a reasonable explanation for your presence here".

"Mr Brennan" The other man said, advancing a couple of paces "This is my operation. Frank had very little to do with it beyond opening the door. Earlier when he made Mr O'Reilly's offer to you he was wired for sound and we heard everything. I've come to take you into custody for your own safety. We don't think you fully appreciate the gravity of the technology which you've invented" As he spoke he advanced further towards Mick and Wilson.

Wilson whispered in Mick's ear "Watch out for this fella, I reckon he has the look of Special Services about him. They can be very quick when they like"

Mick replied "No worries" and lifting the Colt whilst he pulled back the hammer he said "One more step and you'll never see the morning. I'm a more than competent shot and from this distance I could shoot the eye out of a fly's head".

The man stopped instantly whilst Frank whined "For god's sake listen to him, he's the original Dead Eye Dick with that gun. I've seen him in action".

"Now here's how it's going to go down" Mick had seen more than his fair share of gangster movies and had the patter down to a tee.

"I don't doubt that you've got a tribe of gung ho warriors surrounding the house" As he spoke he reached up and took an innocuous looking tin from a shelf at his left hand.

"This is a trigger for enough explosive to blow this house and a large chunk of the surrounding district to kingdom come. If anyone tries to come in here I will press the button and we'll all get blown sky high. I'm not messing about here, Frank knows how paranoid I am about unsuitable people getting hold of this technology. If he doesn't, he should, God knows I've told him often enough. I reckon my death and all of yours would be a small price to prevent that".

Frank turned deathly pale and stammered. "Mick, for pity's sake, there's about a hundred fully armed and dangerous men outside. You don't have a small dog's chance in hell of getting out of here. You have no reason to assume that we'd put your invention to any unethical use. We are only interested in the good of all humanity. Please accept reality and let's settle this amicably".

"By amicably I suppose you mean my handing the secret over to you and whatever brain dead twerps are going to be developing it. I assure you that I really mean it when I say that we'd all be better off dead than that. Ethical people don't break into other's houses and surround their property with stormtroopers. Now pay attention to me, and I'm addressing this to the leader of the troops outside. I've no doubt that he's listening in to our conversation.

Now I'm going to ask you nicely to kneel on the floor with your two hands through your legs whilst Wilson ties you up. We'll do this one at a time, your friend first Frank, and you and me can go over here to the other side of the room.

Frank's companion with a look which would have smouldered asbestos submitted to Wilson's ungentle ministrations and Mick took erstwhile friend aside.

"Mick, for the sake of our friendship, don't do this. You can't get away. We're just too strong for you and we desperately need this technology. Not everybody in the world is pleased and excited about our current prosperity and we badly need to defend ourselves against powerful aggressors"

"What friendship?" Mick snarled disgustedly "You're no friend of mine. You're a spineless little arselicker. If I never see you again it'll be too soon. If I meet you in the street in future I'll cross over to the other side rather than speak to you".

While they were talking Wilson finished trussing up the other man and Mick said "Take this lily livered turncoat and tie him up also. Make sure they're at either end of the room so they can't open each other's ropes".

Mick then said in a louder voice "I'm addressing the leader of the stormtroopers now. Wilson and I are leaving the room to have a private conflab. I don't doubt that you have two way contact with this pair of losers. By all means talk all you like to them and formulate whatever plans which occur to you, but mark my words, Do Not Attempt to Invade My House. I will not hesitate to blow it to smithereens and all of us, including you with it. I don't know Michael O'Reilly personally but I've made a study of dictators and I can assure you that if you survive my death and the loss of my technology, you will wish for an easy end to your miserable existence. If you're in any doubt as to whether I mean what I say, ask Frank, he knows me very, very well".

Going out Mick put his finger to his lips and gestured Wilson to follow him into the small bedroom which had been converted into an office. He quickly scribbled a note and at the same time said

"I really have no idea as to how we get out of this Wilson, do you". Pointing to the note.

Wilson picked it up and read.

"I reckon they've got parabolic mikes trained on every window in the house and they can hear every squeak we make. If you value your freedom, play up and keep talking. Don't pay any attention to what we say but follow my lead".

"Mick, I'm scared" Quavered Wilson "I don't think it's a good idea going up against these guys. They have the battalions after all and they will have been trained to take no prisoners".

Mick scribbled another note "Follow me, I have a plan" and he beckoned Wilson downstairs all the while continuing the conversation "I have a plan" he said loudly, "We'll hold these two losers to ransom and demand safe passage back to the hotel. Once there we can pick up the bike and we'll be free as the wind then. We might have to rough them up a bit just to convince the stormtroopers that we're serious but I believe we're safe for the moment from attack. They know that I'm determined not to give up my secrets, even if it means our deaths in the process". Here he tipped Wilson a heavy wink.

Chapter Twenty Two

Further Consequences

"But Mick" Wilson seemed to be in a total panic "I don't want to die. I've a whole bucket list of things to do before that happens. I really think you should reconsider your options and see if you can't strike some sort of a deal with Frank and his Glorious Leader".

During this conversation the lads had entered the garage and climbed into the Mustang, Mick having first fitted the flux capacitor. "Hold onto your hat Wilson" Mick whispered and turned the ignition key, at the same time raising the garage door with his door opener. He eased the car out into the driveway, relying on the element of surprise to confuse the captain of the stormtroopers momentarily.

As soon as the car cleared the garage Mick engaged the time drive and they found themselves back in their own timeline again, outside Micks house.

"Sorry if that last bit was a tad scary Wilson" He said "I couldn't engage the drive inside the garage or we would have materialised in the same space as the original Mustang. I'm not entirely sure what would have happened in that event but better safe than sorry".

They then ventured into the garage and found, not altogether to Mick's surprise, that the Mustang was not there. "Apparently no two versions of the same object can exist in the same timeline. That makes sense if you think of it. Think of the mess there would be if we were to meet ourselves in another timeline. I don't know about you but in my opinion two Wilsons at the same time would be a bit more than the world deserves".

"Mick, I've been thinking" Said Wilson.

"Oh dear, that can't be good" teased Mick.

"No but, I'm delighted we got away from Frank and the stormtroopers, but the motorbike, the Travellator and, not least the house, are still in their possession. All of them are time travel compliant so, aside from saving our bacon what have we accomplished. They still have the technology".

Mick gave a short bitter laugh.

"You and Frank always thought that I was too paranoid about the time travel gig and the necessity to keep it tight between ourselves. I would never in a million years have credited that Frank would betray me like that. Aside from any other consideration he was always on about ethics and the necessity to behave in a responsible fashion. This Michael O'Reilly guy must have cast a spell on him or something to make him abandon his principles like that.

"By the way, there's no need to worry about anyone getting their hands on a flux capacitor. All machines, including the house are routinely disabled when I leave them and I also take the capacitors out if I'm going to be away for a while. They're stored in a safe place and nobody but me knows where. So all Frank and his merry men have is one suburban house, one antique motorbike and one Winnebago, all in their original, unenhanced condition and good luck to anyone who can make anything out of that!"

"We do need to do something about Frank though. He knows altogether too much about time travel and he's actually travelled back in time with me. So he knows it exists and that it works. He doesn't have any idea about the mechanics of it, fortunately he's a mechanical moron. I can't be sure that if they put him under deep hypnosis he mightn't have seen or heard something useful to his glorious leader, so drastic action is called for".

Wilson shrugged philosophically.

"OK, so we track the little shite down in this timeline, tie a rock around his neck and drop him in the Liffey under cover of darkness. Then he won't ever meet with Michael O'Reilly and the job's a good one". He was getting into the Dublin argot thing.

"I've told you before, we don't kill people. That's not negotiable. We need a plan that's more subtle otherwise there's a risk of unintended thingummies. I've given some thought to why Frank would drop me in it like that and while the old power corrupts thing is undoubtedly a factor I'm also wondering if I did something to tick him off".

Wilson almost had an apoplectic fit "What the hell do you mean" He yelled "How could you have ticked him off? We just left him the other day in this timeline and you were the best of buddies then. The next time we see him it's 2025 and he's turned into a sycophantic lackey of a power crazy dictator who's bent on interstellar domination. How could you cause that?"

"As we stand at this moment my first thought

regarding Frank is that he's a traitorous rat. My inclination is either to do him harm or cut him out of my life completely. Suppose I do either or both of those things and we never see him again. At this point in time Frank hasn't done anything to me so he must be totally confused and upset. Suppose he tries to contact me and I cut him dead. Next time he comes across us it's 2025 and we call him, all hail fella well met. By this time he's a mover and shaker in the Government. In that scenario, what would you do if you were in his shoes?"

"Goddam it Mick, you have a rare talent for convoluted thinking. You're like the economist with three hands, on the one hand, and on the other hand, and on yet another hand. No wonder you always get up early. You need all the time you can get just to keep up with yourself. I still think the simple answer is to top the creep".

"There will be no topping of creeps. At this moment Frank is totally innocent of anything and is, in fact, my oldest friend. We can't go around topping people just because they have the potential to be troublesome for us in the future. If we started down that road we'd have to spend all our time running up and down the timelines shutting down bad guys before they got going. It's just not on, Wilson. Do you understand?"

Muttering darkly to himself Wilson said "I'm going to make a cuppa, do you want one?"

Mick replied, "No, I'm good thanks. I think I'll go for a walk and try to work something out about this Frank thing. Don't wait up for me, I might be late back".

Mick wandered aimlessly for an hour and then

found himself outside the Porterhouse pub in Phibsboro. Sitting drinking his solitary pint and contemplating Frank's treachery he became more and more convinced that his take on the situation was right. But how to resolve the matter caused him some deep consideration.

At some point he began to get an uncomfortable feeling that he was under observation. Casting surreptitious glances around he noticed a red haired woman who appeared to be looking in his direction. Mick was not accustomed to being an object of scrutiny by beautiful women and the hairs on the back of his neck immediately rose up.

When she saw that she had attracted his attention she rose to her feet and made her way to his table.

"Pardon me" the girl said "You're Mick Brennan, aren't you".

Mick looked over his shoulder to see if there was another Mick Brennan in the vicinity to whom she might be talking. Seeing that he was the only one of that description he replied.

"Yes, I'm Mick Brennan, who's asking?"

"You can call me Anita, it's as good a name as any I suppose. It's critical that we talk. I have a message for you and the fate of the entire universe depends on your response to it".

"Oh good" said Mick "No pressure then?"

"This is not a subject for levity" Even frowning in disapproval she was stunningly beautiful. "I've come back from the year 2025 to try to get you to do something about a chronological anomaly which has arisen. This trip has potentially cut me off from all my friends and relatives by my time travelling, so it's not for joking".

"You're a time traveler then?" Mick asked in surprise "I don't understand the cutting off all your connections thing. We've been up and down the timelines regularly in the recent past and we've always managed to get back to where we started. Why can't you?"

"We haven't got your version of the time drive, ours is one way only. Back into the past. That's what I mean when I say I've cut all my ties. Unless you agree to bring me back to my time, I'll be stuck here for the rest of my life"

"OK, I get that you need to go home but the fate of the universe bit is hard to swallow. I imagine there is more you need to tell me about this matter. I don't know why your time device is a one shot, one way only option. Mine works in both directions and back again. Tell you what, why don't we go back to my house and talk about this, the pub here is a bit public for confidential chat".

Chapter Twenty Three

Schemes and Stratagems

Back in the house Mick roused Wilson from a doze in front of the TV and introduced him to Anita. Wilson was suitably impressed and even more so when he discovered that she was a time traveler herself.

"Now" Mick said "You need to clear some things up. How did you get onto me, why can't you travel in time like we do, what's with the fate of the universe gig and last but not least how can I help the fate of etc.?"

"It's a rather long story but to shorten it as much as possible, here goes. There is, in America a very famous political family known worldwide. They have two presidents in their lineage and several senators, not to mention numerous congressmen. They are, of course phenomenally wealthy too. Before entering politics the younger members of the family are expected to serve some time in the family law firm before commencing a career in public service followed by inevitable election to office. We needn't mention the name as it's very obvious who we are talking about.

Apparently the antecedents of this family are shrouded in mystery and rumours of ill-gotten gains as a foundation of the family wealth abound. Furthermore there is no record of the family prior to the late 1880s. They seem to have sprung from nowhere, filthy rich, around about then. Early members of the family may have been associated with law enforcement, such as it was in those days.

In the recent past a black sheep younger son of the family has offered for publication, a book which he says is based on the real life adventures of his great, great Grandfather. The tale is, to the uninitiated, a tissue of half-truths and outright lies. To those of us in the know, however, it carries startling claims, mainly relating to successful back and forth time travel.

I am a member of a tightly knit team of people researching time travel and, as I indicated to you, we have successfully designed and commissioned a device which is partially fit for purpose. We have not, as yet, managed the holy grail of unhindered travel in both directions as and when required.

In this book you are prominently mentioned and, indeed, you are credited with the invention of the time machine mentioned. It was relatively easy to identify you and to track you down to the exact timeline from matters discussed in the book.

We wrote to the author requesting sight of the original documents on which the book was based. Sadly having agreed to share his sources with us and two days before an agreed meeting between us he was savagely beaten and murdered in his bed. Nothing was stolen from his apartment but his documents were in considerable disarray.

We have conducted a very confidential investigation into this death and we are totally satisfied that it was carried out by agents of the Irish Government at the personal behest of the Glorious Leader Michael O'Reilly who, apparently, has a deep interest in the intricacies of time travel, and the matter of interstellar flight.

At this moment Michael O'Reilly and his Minister for Information Frank McGuinness don't know about the existence of our little group, but as you know, these things have a nasty habit of leaking out.

These guys are seriously vicious folks and if they can find you, we figure you're chances of a future free of confinement is about a million to one against. It is well known that Mick O', as he's colloquially known is not satisfied with being dictator of a small country on the fringe of Europe but that he has designs on the entire world and, if he lives long enough, and he might, the galaxy and on to the complete universe. He must be stopped Mick. And you're the only man who can stop him".

When Anita paused to take a breath Wilson turned to Mick and blurted out.

"That unmitigated, brainless, good for nothing Freddie has landed us in it again. He's managed to reach out of the grave and put us in danger once more. I told you time and time again that we should have left him on a glacier in the last ice age. That's about the only we could keep him out of mischief. And as for that toad Frank, words fail me".

"I've already pointed out that Frank is, at this very moment entirely innocent of any wrongdoing and the same applies to Michael O'Reilly. I'm sure he's busily managing his transportation business, as we speak, with no idea that dictatorship lurks in his future. We all know the old adage about absolute power. Who of us can blame him if his success has gone to his head? He does have a lot to be proud of, after all. And bear in mind that he didn't ask for the job. It was forced on him, after all. So rather than casting aspersions on anybody, why don't we put our heads together and come up with a scheme to get us out of this pickle. Freddie can't be blamed either except to the extent that he's obviously passed on his tainted genes to this descendant pillock".

"I strongly suggest that we go back into the past and hire a bunch of ninja assassins to be set upon the whole boiling of them, Frank, Mick O', Freddie and the descendant pillock. That should nicely clear up our current dilemma". Wilson's feral instincts were fully aroused by this latest news.

Whilst Anita gazed at Wilson in open mouthed horror Mick said.

"Will you please knock of the assassin scheme? I've told you repeatedly that we're not going to do any killing, I'm totally opposed to killing myself and the law of unintended consequences looms over us at all times". Mick went on to say "We don't know for sure that Mick O' and Frank have sent a hit squad to kidnap me and we're fairly sure that at this moment they don't have the secret of time travel.

However we shouldn't rest on our laurels for long. They may find a way to screw the secret out of Anita's colleagues and it's just possible that they'll come knocking on the door at any moment. So the sooner we suss out a plot to thwart them the better for me. They will only be looking for me, of course, so I reckon that both you guys should get as much distance away from me as possible in case of collateral damage. After all they don't need you for the secret of the flux capacitor so they might just kill you to ensure your silence".

"Goddam it Mick" Burst out Wilson "You hardly expect that after all we've gone through I'm going to leave you in the lurch, do you? I'll leave that sort of carry-on to the twin toads Frank and Freddie".

Anita here put in her tuppence worth.

"You are my only hope of getting back to my own time and, not incidentally, foiling the ambitions of Wilson's twin toads, so you couldn't scrape me off with a stick. I'm in it for, literally, the long haul".

"Thanks gang" Mick was jubilant "With you guys in my mob I reckon we're like the Three Musketeers or something. Anyway we'll be unbeatable. So, let's settle down and figure out how to deal with our latest dilemma".

"Upon reflection we do have one thing going for us" Said Mick "We have Freddie's unbreakable covenant to his descendants which binds them to give us as much assistance as we need if we find ourselves up a greasy pole. The way I see it, this is the epitome of a greasy pole. The time has come to invoke the unbreakable covenant, what do you think guys?"

Wilson was not at all convinced, in fact under 'unconvinced' in the Oxford English Dictionary is a picture of Wilson's face as a perfect representation of unconvincedness.

"Mick, you know I'd follow you into hell and out again but anything to do with Freddie gives me the willies. In fact, not to put too fine a point on it, I'm unconvinced about using anything with a smell of that pathetic loser about it. Mind you, I don't have any better ideas either".

"OK here's what we'll do" Mick was at his most commanding "We'll go see these lawyers in Cleveland and try to suss out how much stuff Freddie left after himself which might point in our direction. If absolutely necessary I'll try to appeal to their better nature, though appealing to a lawyer's better nature seems like a peculiarly perverse course of action. Anyway I'll ask them to destroy the files or, as a last resort, sell them to me, If that works it should neatly stymie the descendant pillock and leave us free from Mick O's attention when he comes to write the book. If we can't convince the lawyer, either through principle or bribery, we'll just have to go to PlanB".

Suitably impressed by the facility with which Mick had come up with this brilliant scheme Anita still needed some reassurance.

"That sounds all well and good Mick but it means we'll need to convince a hard headed American lawyer who's never seen or heard of us before, first of all to give us an appointment and secondly to part with the family documents. And in the event that PlanA fails, what exactly is PlanB?"

Chapter Twenty Four

Babes in America

A few days later the Three Musketeers found themselves outside a towering skyscraper in Cleveland Ohio. Emblazoned in brushed stainless steel across the front of the building in letters three foot high was the legend:

Schuster, Levi and Mulligan. Attorneys at Law.

"Are you really sure about this Mick?" Queried a clearly worried Wilson. "I don't know how you managed to wangle an appointment with the senior partner of a prestigious firm like this and I might remind you that you never introduced us to PlanB".

Mick gave a carefree laugh and replied "If you have a bank account as healthy as mine, senior partners are more than anxious to talk to you and the letter from Freddie was also a great help. As for PlanB, I'm convinced we won't need it so don't get your knickers in a twist about it. Leave the talking to me and we'll be OK".

Rather like the Lion, Scarecrow, Tin Man and Dorothy in the Wizard of Oz, they linked arms and strode up the imposing steps to the grand entrance of the skyscraper. Mick was distracted by how good it felt to have his arm linked to Anita's and felt a warm glow of satisfaction as they entered the reception area.

Speaking to himself he said in a low voice "Focus Mick, Focus!"

Anita asked "Did you say something just now Mick?"

"It was nothing. Just a stray thought" Mick blushed mightily, secretly happy that the lighting was not overly bright.

Immediately on entering they were met by a tall blonde girl in a tightly fitting business suit.

"You must be the Mick Brennan party" She cried with a dazzling smile. "Mr Jedediah Bush is waiting impatiently to meet you, he's been looking forward to it ever since he got your letter a couple of days ago. Let me introduce myself, I'm Gloria, Mr Bush's private secretary".

"Of course you are" Leered Wilson sotto voce.

Mick kicked him savagely on the ankle and said in an undertone "Keep a lid on it or you'll be getting dropped in the ice age yourself".

Anita addressed herself to the statuesque Gloria "I thought we were going to meet the senior partner, what about Messer's Schuster, Levi and Mulligan. Is one of them not the senior?"

Gloria gave out a trill of laughter. "Oh no, all those gentlemen died at the close of the nineteenth century. The partnership is in the ownership of the Bush family ever since.

He was the Grandfather of the first President Bush, you know. The firm has been solely owned by family ever since".

Wilson nudged Mick and whispered "The Bush family! Is that the same Bush family I'm thinking of? Wasn't he the one who was famous for his gaffes?"

"I'm not going to justify that by a reply" Mick snarled "But if you won't keep your trap shut you can leave right now and we'll pick you up at the hotel later".

Wilson grimaced and subsided into subvocal muttering as they were ushered into

Jed's office. The first impression was of enormous space. The space was at least as big as the whole ground floor of Mick's house. It featured two suites of deeply cushioned settees, a fully stocked bar and a desk on which one could land a Harrier Jump Jet.

"Jesus save us" Burst out Wilson when he saw the man behind the desk who was just rising to greet them. "It's Freddie" He gasped pointing a shaking finger at the room's occupant. "But he must be well past his hundredth year, how has he managed to stay so young?"

Jed Bush laughed and said "I've been told that I bear a striking resemblance to my great Grandfather. You must have seen pictures of him at my age. I wonder where you got them, he was notoriously camera shy. Obviously we have some catching up to do. I'm looking forward to having a long session with you guys, in my position I have to listen to a lot of bullshit but something tells me that you have a tale worth hearing".

Mick had warned the others that all talk of time travel was most definitely off the agenda for this meeting. He had prepared a story which was true in its essentials, if somewhat heavily edited in fact.

"An ancestor of mine apparently met your Great Grandfather in Tucson Arizona back towards the end of the nineteenth century. At that time they were both peace officers in what was the American Frontier. Our family legend has it that your ancestor was central to the apprehension of a desperado with the unlikely name of Brazen Bill Brazelton. It seems that during the shootout involved with Bill's capture my ancestor, also named Mick, may have saved your Great Grandfather's life. The actual details are somewhat blurred but that's the story I was told in my younger days".

"But why does your large friend refer to my Great Grandfather as Freddie? His name was William George Bush. There's no record of a Freddie in our family".

"Well the details are a bit hazy, it's a long time since I heard the tale but if memory serves me it went something like this:

My ancestor had emigrated in the 1850s and somewhere along the way he met with yours. The two of them made a significant amount of money somewhere, it was never clear how. We always assumed it was a gold strike. The story goes that there may have been something murky in your Great Grandfather's history. In any event he decided to change his name at some point. Originally, it seems his name was Freddie Fortune, or Foreman, I'm not entirely sure which.

At any rate they both invested heavily in Standard Oil and made significant fortunes. By an amazing coincidence I recently received a letter from your ancestor which had gotten lost in the post for over a hundred years. It was a letter from Freddie, as my ancestor knew him, to

the original Mick. In this letter Freddie refers to an
unbreakable covenant placed in the care of this law firm.

I'm in the process of researching my family
history and I'd appreciate sight of this covenant and any
other documentation you might have on file concerning
the original Mick".

With a tight smile Jed replied.

"It may surprise you to know that I asked for those
documents to be brought to me when I received your
letter. They contain some amazing tales which, to tell the
truth, strain my credulity. I know that what you've told
me is true as far as it goes but there is much that you've
left unsaid. I suggest that you and your friends accept my
hospitality and stay at my house for a couple of days
while we trawl through the papers together. What do you
say?"

Mick decided to take the man at face value and
agreed to stay for a few days. He consulted with the others
as to whether they too would like to stay or if they wanted
to do the tourist thing in Cleveland. Both Anita and
Wilson agreed that their preferred option was to stick
close to Mick.

Later that evening found them assembled in the
library of a very large and very gracious house quite close
to the centre of the city but secluded from its clamour by
high walls and spacious gardens. They had dined very
well in the house which was occupied by Jed alone,
except for an aged manservant who looked after Jed's
modest needs. They were now convened with snifters of
very old brandy with the stated objective of investigating

Freddie's documents.

"In the interest of full disclosure I should tell you that I know that my Great Grandfather's name was Frederick Fortescue and that he had some connection with Her Majesty's armed forces".

Mick listened with sinking heart as Jed commenced proceedings with this statement. "That part of his story is quite clear from these documents. It gets a bit murkier the deeper you get into it. He insists that he was born in 1977, patently impossible since, to my certain knowledge these documents have been lying undisturbed under lock and key in my vaults since 1899. I am satisfied, beyond doubt that I am the first man since then to access that particular safety deposit box. In what appears to be deranged ramblings he describes arriving in America in a flying machine, and not just any flying machine but what is obviously a jet plane by his description.

Freddie goes on to describe driving to Tucson in a motor car, not a horseless carriage of which there were some in existence in those days but by motor car. He also describes his interaction with your assumed ancestor, the mysterious Mick Brennan.

Most of these writings could be taken as the ramblings of an unbalanced mind with an amazing ability to predict accurately trends in business and politics except he is credited within the family with never making an investment decision which was anything but a resounding success. Realistically this would seem to stretch the bounds of coincidence to their utter limits.

The latter part of his story is so far off the wall that I'm not even going to repeat it, at least at this point. However to add to all the list of coincidences you arrive bearing the name Mick Brennan and your companion gives every indication that he recognizes me. It's not possible that he should recognize me as to my certain knowledge we've never met. It is not beyond the bound of possibility that your friend has had sight of a photograph of Freddie/William but, again, to my certain knowledge no such photograph exists, as the old man steadfastly refused to have his picture taken.

The list of coincidences is growing ever longer and I believe it's now time for you to come out with the whole truth!" This speech had been delivered in a calm and deliberate manner but it was totally clear to all concerned that Jed was in deadly earnest.

"I am not prepared to comment on the documents until I see them" Mick declared "But I am prepared to admit that there is more to the Freddie story and I know at least some part of it. Why don't you get out the papers and we'll have a look at them and we'll talk about their veracity afterwards. How does that sound to you?"

"OK, I would have preferred a more outspoken reply to my request but we'll go with your proposal for now" Jed was plainly not best pleased but he accepted the situation for the present.

Some three hours later Wilson was the first to speak.

"Wow, this old guy sure had a wild imagination. Where did he get all this stuff about planes and cars away back in the old west? This stuff reads like a science fiction thriller and I didn't know science fiction existed back then".

"Well in point of fact H.G.Wells wrote 'The Time Machine' in 1895 so Freddie could have had access to some of the stuff in these memoirs. In that and other books Wells predicted many things including the invention of the Atom bomb. It's quite possible, indeed even likely that Freddie was trying to write a fictional account and that it has been preserved with his other less speculative works" Mick was well aware that he was reaching with this theory and, worse yet, that Jed was not buying it.

Jed said, with a tight smile which was becoming familiar to the three.

"Lissen guys, I'm an old hand when it comes to someone trying to pull the wool over my eyes and you people are just not in the premier league of liars. In fact you're not even in the top ten of the leagues. So why don't we cut the bullshit and you tell me what is going on here?"

"Look" Mick said, "I agree that we haven't been totally open and upfront with you, but there is good reason for our caution I assure you. Freddie left an unbreakable covenant with your firm way back when. Can we open that covenant and have a look at it before we go any further? I think it will help us to move on to a mutually agreed end point of our discussion".

Chapter Twenty Five

The Hiberno- American Alliance

Jed agreed and produced the document which read:

To Whom it may concern:

I assume that the reader is a descendant of mine either by blood or by business. I further assume that he, or she, is a person of some power and influence in the community and held in high regard in that community.

I have no doubt that you are fully aware of the huge debt owed to me by my successors due to the shrewd investment and sagacious decisions put in place by me at the founding of the firm.

The intent of this covenant is to place all of the influence and goodwill of the firm to be used to the fullest extent in order to further the aims and ambitions of one Michael Brennan of Dublin Ireland.

I place an onus on you to help Michael Brennan in any and all ways possible in any enterprise in which he might be engaged, however unlikely such a venture may appear.

I place the burden of this duty on you because Mick helped me, above and beyond the call of duty and indeed good sense at a time when I was at a low ebb. In a very real sense there would be no Schuster Levi and Mulligan Attorneys at Law, nor indeed any Bush family but for the decency and trust of the said Michael Brennan.

"Wow" Mick breathed "That is one helluva good reference and no doubt about it". Turning to Jed he asked "What's your response to this blast from the past? If we open up to you can we depend on your absolute and total discretion? I'd like you to think on your answer and reflect deeply about it. What we have to tell you is known only to we three and the knowledge may, of itself, be dangerous to know".

Jed said triumphantly "I knew there was something hinky about you guys, and indeed my revered ancestor. You really need to come clean with me now. I give you my word of honour, and I don't do that lightly, that I will abide by Freddie's covenant provided you don't ask me to do anything illegal".

"OK, but in fairness some of what I tell you will seem utterly impossible and also beyond the bounds of belief". And saying this Mick continued on to relate the full story of Freddie and their connection to him, including their travels in time.

As the story unfolded Jed's eyebrows rose progressively higher and higher until they almost met his hairline. When Mick finally paused for breath he released a pent up gasp of stunned disbelief.

"I don't know whether to call for the men in white coats or the bunko squad. This is, without exception, the wildest farrago of nonsense I've ever heard. Can you really be asking me to believe that you've invented a means of travelling through time and that you've been up and down the centuries creating mayhem everywhere you go and all devised and built in your own backyard, so to speak. Freddie did allude to this in his memoirs but I didn't believe it then and I find it hard to believe even now".

"The matter of your disbelief is easily dealt with, I can take you on a trip through time to any date you'd care to designate. All I need is a suitable vehicle to which I can affix a piece of equipment which we have whimsically given the name of Flux Capacitor, after a famous movie. We can use your own car if you like. The rest of the story gets a bit harder and our reason for being here takes a leap of faith on your part for us to persuade you that we're on the side of the angels here". Mick had decided that laying his cards on the table was the sensible course of action but he wasn't sure that Jed was prepared to take all this new information on board.

"Could you bring me back to meet Freddie?" Jed queried "He's been a hero of mine since boyhood and it would be a rare honour to actually meet him in the flesh, so to speak".

"Interacting with your ancestors can be a tricky proposition. I have a hang up about unintended consequences relating to this time travel gig. We have to be very careful that we don't materially change the past because it could have far reaching and possibly catastrophic effects on the present. It's not impossible that you could cause your Grandfather to meet a different woman and maybe to die childless. If that was the case, where would it leave you? You understand my reservations, don't you?

"Maybe I'm as mad as the rest of you. "Said Jed "But I'm prepared to let you demonstrate this thingumajig if you say you can. Let's leave the Freddie visit until a later date. We'll choose a different date for the demo. Tell you what, how about we go to Woodstock.

It was a rock festival in Bethel, New York, 1969. It's in Sullivan County, 43 miles from Woodstock, New York".

"You want to go to a rock festival?" Wilson queried "I wouldn't have pegged you as a rock music fan".

"Of course I'm a rock fan" Jed said indignantly "I'm fifty years old next year and I was six when Woodstock happened. I've grown up with the legends surrounding that event all my life and always bitterly resented missing it. If you guys can do what you claim then I'd be a mutt to pass up the opportunity. Woodstock wasn't just a rock festival, it was a music festival, based on the theme of 'An Aquarian Exposition'. I have a collector's copy of the program from the festival demonstrating this idea. This was the height of the Hippie movement, with peace and love and drugs and rock and roll everywhere. The theme song from the 1967 musical Hair encapsulated it all 'This is the dawning of the Age of Aquarius, when the Moon is in the seventh house and Jupiter aligns with Mars then peace will guide the planets and love will steer the stars'. There was a real feeling in those days that such high ideals were possible. Sadly we've become a much more cynical people since then"

He had the good grace to look a little embarrassed at his extreme enthusiasm.

"OK" Mick said "What sort of car do you drive? We don't want to seem too obvious when we get there so an ostentatious modern limo would be seriously out of place".

For the first time since meeting him, they saw genuine amusement on Jed's face. "Come with me. I think we can probably fix you up with something suitable".

Jed took them to a large barnlike building behind the house, he opened the door with a remote control device and as the large roller shutter rose the lights inside came up. The three gasped in appreciation at what was revealed inside. "There must be twenty five cars here" whispered Wilson in awe. "These are vintage and classic cars from every era of great American Automobiles. Look there's an original Oldsmobile from the year 1901, the first high volume petrol driven car manufacturer. God knows what this collection is worth".

Jed proudly led them down the line of cars and pointed out a 1965 Chevrolet Corvair.

"I think this would do us for your demonstration" He said to Mick "It's in perfect mechanical order and ready to drive. It'll carry all four of us in considerable comfort and if you can fit the flux thingy I reckon it's the car for us. OK?"

Very early the following morning Mick fitted the flux capacitor to the Chevy and they all climbed aboard.

Jed remarked "It seems that fitting that thingy is a very simple process, aren't you nervous that someone could swipe it and use it themselves? After all if it does what you claim it's worth all the money in the world in the wrong hands. I mean, one conk on your head and a swift rummage through your kit and the thief is off to the races, with all the winners sorted in advance, no?"

"It's not as simple as it looks" Laughed Mick "The thingy, as you call it, is biometrically connected to me in such a way that if anybody else tries to use it, or tamper with it in any way it will immediately shut down and fuse into a solid lump of metal. I got the technology to do this from far in the future and I've only used it for the flux capacitors. It is, I assure you utterly secure and cannot be hacked. Maybe at some point in the far future the technology to crack it will exist, but not now and not anytime soon".

"See now" Jed retorted "This story just gets more and more unbelievable. Technology like you've described would be of incalculable value. A man with that knowledge could have all the money in the world".

Mick laughed and said

"I have all the money in the world, or at least as much of it as I need, or want. If I didn't have a very healthy bank account I would never have gotten past your office reception, Freddie's letter or not. Am I right? That account is only one of hundreds I have established all over the world. Ask Wilson, my motto is not 'Am I Paranoid?' but 'Am I Paranoid enough?'".

At this point they were travelling north on I98 intending to take a leisurely drive to Woodstock. As they approached the town of Euclid Mick slowed the car and turning to Jed he enquired "Do you notice anything strange around here?

Jed looked around and replied "I'm not very familiar with this area so I'm not sure what I should see normally. What is it you are suggesting?"

Mick just nodded and pulled into an old fashioned looking gas station. "Why don't you go into the store and buy a paper" he suggested to Jed.

Jed did what he was asked and returned with a puzzled frown to the car. "What was all that about?" He demanded.

"Look at the date" Mick smiled.

Jed gazed open mouthed at the paper "Merciful God" He gasped "It says August 15th 1969. How can this be? You're pulling some form of scam on me. We just left Cleveland in 2012 and now you want me to believe we're back in 1969? No way. How could that happen?"

Mick called the petrol attendant over. "Hey buddy" He asked "What day is it today?

"It's Tuesday 15th August 1969 the attendant replied"

"I probably should have warned you" Said Mick "I engaged the time drive about five miles back when we were the only car on the road. It generates considerable interest if the car in front disappears as you're travelling along, so I like to transit time as quietly and unobtrusively as possible. You'll probably feel disoriented for a while. It's not the time travel which does it but the effect of finding yourself in a totally different timeline. Everything is strikingly similar and at the same time distinctly different. Don't worry, the effect wears off after a while".

As they continued on their journey to Woodstock Jed was more and more amazed the further they travelled.

"I'm finding this difficult", he said "I mean, I see the old road signs and the antique advertising hoardings, I hear the programs on the radio and I've spoken to people on the way, but it still takes a real leap of faith to believe that we've travelled back forty three years in time. It just defies belief. I still have a doubt in my mind that you guys have in some way drugged me or hypnotised me. That scenario would be easier to take".

Wilson grinned from the back seat and said "You ain't seen nothin' yet. Wait till we get to Woodstock. It'll be epic man".

Anita, always a practical person piped up

"We don't have any reservations for accommodation for this gig. Shouldn't we phone ahead or send an email or something. As far as I understand from you guys, we'll be there for a couple of days at least".

"Accommodation will be the last thing on our minds in Woodstock" Wilson crowed "There will be a half a million people in an open field in the middle of nowhere. White Lake is a sleepy one horse town in upstate New York and the town of Woodstock is about fifty miles away".

"That doesn't sound at all comfortable or, indeed hygienic". Was Anita's somewhat acerbic reply.

"You know" Jed mused "I've got an original David Byrd poster for Woodstock, it gave the venue as Walkhill in New York State, for some reason they shifted it to White Lake and redesigned the poster. I think my poster is better than the one they finally chose. It's more psychedelic, if you know what I mean".

"Is it possible that we're getting through to you Jed?" Wilson enquired "You seem to be getting into the swing of the Woodstock thing even though you doubt the whole time travel paradigm".

"If you guys are conning me I'll make your lives miserable. Woodstock has been an inspiration to me all my life. Messing with it would be like blasphemy. It marked the height of the hippie movement which promoted peace and love for all people. Sadly the movement collapsed and we fell back into our ancient, self-centred ways. It was a dream, but a beautiful one".

"You surprise me" Wilson had decided to be whimsical. Truth to tell, he was looking forward to the festival as much as Jed was, but he could not resist taking a rise out of the older man.

"I always understood that young children were kidnapped in infancy and taken to lawyer school. There they had their soul sucked out and replaced by statute books, points of law and precedents. And here we find that you are an old softy really, deep into philosophy, universal love and good will towards men. This image doesn't fit with your public one of a hardnosed man of the law".

"Mock if you like" Jed replied calmly "I guarantee you will all look on the world differently after living through this festival which was billed as: 'An Aquarian Exposition: Three Days of Peace & Music'. I am, as you say, settling into a state of suspended disbelief about this entire expedition. I hesitate to call it a trip because of the associations with mind altering substances connected to that word, but this feels like a road trip. One thing strikes me as we travel. Mick seems to be paying for everything on the way, why is that?"

Mick smilingly replied "I'll take that question. You are, no doubt, familiar with the term 'Your Money's no Good Here'. Well that's literally true here. Any money you have in your pocket is 'modern' in our terms and wouldn't be recognised as legal tender. Needless to say, credit cards are not in use yet. Over the past number of years I've built up a stock of currencies appropriate to the place and times we might visit so I'm the only one with 60s era cash. Therefore I pay. You can reimburse me later if you like, though it's not necessary. I literally have no need for money, I have absolutely as much as I need and more".

It would be superfluous to describe the events of the Woodstock Festival. That has been done by many others, including the movie which was shot during the proceedings, named not very originally 'Woodstock'. Suffice to say that all four enjoyed the experience enormously and whilst they did not over indulge in alcohol and they avoided even so-called soft drugs at Mick's absolute insistence, they nevertheless arrived back at Jed's vast house in 2012 in a state of near collapse, having not slept for almost seventy two hours.

Without any further discussion they staggered off to bed, resolving to discuss everything the following day.

Chapter Twenty Six

Convincing Jed.

Next day Mick rose late and finding nobody about he decided to take a walk around the estate.

Estate is probably not a grand enough term for Jed's house and grounds. The house itself dated from the late eighteenth century and included some fifteen bedrooms together with a ballroom, a fully equipped business centre, swimming pool, the barn containing Jed's collection of classic and vintage cars and a stables containing several thoroughbred horses.

As Mick approached the stables he noticed Anita leaning over the fence surrounding the paddock. His breath caught in his chest as he saw her stroking the forehead of a noble Arabian.

"What's going on here?" He asked himself "She's undoubtedly a beautiful girl. And she's interested in time travel and other stuff which I find interesting, but what is it about her that makes my pulse race when I catch a glimpse of her".

"Hi Mick" Anita called "Come and see this lovely mare and her colt. Aren't they the cutest thing?"

"They are definitely lovely, though not the loveliest thing to be seen around here this morning". Mick riposted gallantly.

Anita flushed a delicate pink and said "Do you think we convinced Jed about the time travel thing? I'm desperately worried about Mick O' and Frank. They are so deep into their own agenda that it will take something phenomenal to shift them off the path they've set themselves on". Whilst saying this she could not help noticing how alert and clear eyed Mick looked this morning.

Putting aside romantic notions to be entertained at a more appropriate moment Mick said

"Tell you what, why don't we go inside and wake the other two up. We'll get some breakfast, or lunch, or whatever and have a grand conference. Jed seems a reasonable kind of bloke and anyone who thinks Creedence Clearwater Revival are the greatest ever can't be all bad, even if he is a lawyer".

"So Jed" Mick opened the conference with a direct challenge "How do you feel about our story now? We've been to Woodstock. I'm quite sure that being, as you are a cautious man, you've had your bloods checked out for drugs to ensure we didn't put anything in your food or drink. We'd have to be hypnotists of extreme ability to construct such a scenario and to execute it seamlessly. All things considered I reckon you must be convinced, No?"

"I still retain some vestiges of disbelief" Jed replied "You must admit that this is a big bite to swallow in one lump. I am, however, more than half convinced and I'm also somewhat disturbed. The implications of this technology are mind bending, to say the least. You guys have, at your fingertips, the ability to fundamentally alter the very shape of civilisation. You could go back and strangle Hitler, Stalin or Genghis Khan in their cradles with far reaching and possibly catastrophic effect on the subsequent history of the world. You, Mick seem to have a firm grasp on the potential for havoc which you've created but if it fell into other hands I shudder to think what the outcome could be".

"Funnily enough that's why we've come to you". Mick assumed his most persuasive manner "It turns out that your revered ancestor has stirred up a hornets nest. He was undoubtedly a good person in his own way" Here Wilson snorted in disbelief "But he wasn't really the sharpest knife in the drawer when it came to interpersonal relationships. We got tangled up with him and Wilson here when the British Secret Services attempted to capture me and steal the secret of time travel. We foiled their plot but in the process we compromised Freddie's position in the Royal Marines. In order to solve this situation I gave Freddie the numbers for the upcoming Euro Lotto and he won a large fortune. We also expunged all trace of his involvement with us in the records of GCHQ.

Unfortunately, I've already mentioned his ineptitude with people, he became involved with a gold digging harpy and came to me to help out. As you know, I'm paranoid about messing with the timelines and I was forced to refuse him aid. He then made a clumsy attempt at blackmailing us, threatening to expose us to the Secret Services.

Needless to remark I couldn't allow that. Not to put too fine a point on it, I kidnapped him and brought him back to Tucson in 1878. Once there I helped him to capture a notorious outlaw and thereby started him on his career of law enforcement. He changed his name and the rest, as they say, is history".

"Dear God" Jed cried "You've upset everything I ever heard about Freddie, as you call him, I was always told that he was a fearless lawman in the old west and that he later joined the law firm of which I am now the senior partner. He was a pillar of society in the early part of the twentieth century and the foundation of our family's fortune and place in society. Now you tell me he was some sort of idiotic philanderer who got himself shanghaied and somehow landed on his feet, more by luck than by good judgement? That's not what a good Great, Great, Grandson wants to hear about his revered ancestor".

Mick had been thinking about this matter and replied

"What you've just said is undoubtedly true. From the time he got a second chance in Tucson he obviously made good, as the saying is, and laid down secure foundations for his descendants. You can't hold a man's past against him for his youthful indiscretions. The mark of a man is how he gets past such road bumps and gets on with his life.

Sadly not all his legacy will turn out for the good. You have, I believe, a nephew called GeorgeIII. I have been doing some checking and I find that he is not exactly an exemplary character. He has a reputation for being a ladies man and a spendthrift. He also has a name as a person who is, to say the least, averse to the work ethic".

"I can't imagine where you got that information from" Spluttered Jed "GeorgeIII has been led astray by some bad companions whom he picked up in college. I've taken him on board in the law firm and I have no doubt

I'll be able to turn him into a productive member of society. He's a good lad at heart. What has he got to do with anything, anyway"?

Mick said "I think I'll let Anita take up the tale from here, she knows more about the situation and it'll become clear as she explains".

"I know you've been bombarded by new information for the past week and it's understandably hard to take it all on board, but my story might strain the bounds of your credulity even more". Anita was conscious that her tale would be upsetting for Jed and she was proceeding cautiously.

"I was born in the millennium year 1987, I know I look far older than 12 years and I am. I'm actually thirty five years old. I've come back from the future on a one way trip to try to rectify a great wrong. I was, or am, employed in a think tank in the year 2025 whose main is to attempt to travel through time. We have been somewhat successful in this and are able to travel backwards through time. But we cannot return.

You must be familiar with the Irish entrepreneur Michael O'Reilly, well in 2025 Mick O' as we call him to distinguish between our Mick and the other, has established himself as effective Dictator of the Irish state, with total power over all aspects of society there. He started out as a decent, principled person but we all know about power and corruption. He now has an iron grip on Irish society and he is a despot comparable to Hitler at his worst. He has recently come across information which causes him to believe that our Mick has the secret of time travel completely sussed out.

This information comes from two sources, one is Mick's childhood friend, Frank McGuinness, now Michael O'Reilly's right hand man and the other is a book written by your nephew George Bush 3 containing verbatim the information hidden safely in your vaults. It seems your vaults are not as impenetrable as you'd like to think. Mick O's intention is to use time travel to help him establish himself as overlord of the world and, ultimately, the universe. He must be stopped.

Somehow this information must be suppressed. That's why we've come to you. We need to sanitise Freddie's papers before GeorgeIII can get his hands on them. Mick will deal with Frank".

"You're asking me to believe that you have information now, which implicates my nephew in at the very least a gross breach of confidentiality at some date long in the future. I accept that up until now he hasn't been an exemplary character, but this goes too far. He is, at bottom, a decent person. I have utmost confidence that you are totally on the wrong track as far as this scenario is concerned. On this matter my family honour is at stake and I cannot, nay, will not accept that GeorgeIII would do such a thing". Jed was obviously deeply hurt that this slur could be cast on his family's spotless escutcheon.

At this point Mick stepped in to bolster Anita's pitch "We don't want to antagonise you in any way Jed" He said "But you must, in conscience, admit that there is, at the very least, a remote possibility that what Anita has outlined might just possibly occur. We don't want you to do anything to GeorgeIII, nor do we want to come between you and him on family matters. In this case the solution is very simple and needn't ever come up between you and him in the future. We'd like you to put the documents which refer to me, time travel and Freddie Fortescue entirely beyond the reach of anyone who might, in any circumstances, misuse them.

I would be honoured if you would give those documents to me. I will give you my solemn word of honour that I will keep them safe. I will further undertake that if you ever want access to them at any point in the future you have only to contact me and I will personally deliver them into your keeping for as long as you want them".

Jed was not convinced "I'm a lawyer" He said "We like to go on evidence, you guys are all nice people and there's nobody I'd rather go to Woodstock with, but you need to see this from my perspective. Three total strangers land in my office with an outlandish tale and whilst the trip to Woodstock was convincing and also great fun, I still remain unconvinced about all the rest of the stuff you've told me. I'm also a reasonable man, so I have a bargain to offer. Why don't we all go forward to Anita's time and you can allow me to check out her story myself. Even doubting Thomas was convinced by the evidence of his own eyes. What do you say?"

Chapter Twenty Seven

Back To the Future

Anita was first to respond "I'd love to go back to my own time. When I travelled back to meet Mick (here she turned a dazzling smile on him, which immediately sent him into a dizzy spin) we had only solved one way travel, as far as I was concerned there was no way back. Now due to Mick's genius we can go either way and as far as we like. We need to be careful though, Ireland is a very dangerous place for independent minded people in that era. Mick O' and his people have a tight grip on the population and their spies are everywhere. I've read my history and I assure you that they are as bad, as or worse than, the Gestapo or the KGB. They also have agents all over the world, so even the USA is not safe from them".

"We don't have to go near Ireland" Said Jed "My law firm will have extensive contacts throughout the world and within a couple of hours in their library I'll be fully up to speed on the situation in Ireland and around the world".

"One little problem" Mick pointed out "Your law firm will not recognise you. You'll be thirteen years younger that they expect you to be and they won't let you anywhere near their library or inside the building. If you turn up there they'll probably send for the police, or the men in the white coats".

"If Freddie could do it, so can I. I'll just set up an irrevocable covenant of my own. I'll make it that anyone who resembles my photo can access the files, under strict terms of confidentiality. That should fix that issue".

"I would plead with you to put the documents in a safe place off the office site to ensure that they don't fall into the wrong hands in the meantime. I know this goes against the grain, but it cannot be stressed strongly enough how critical this is. In fact it's a deal breaker. No security for the documents, no more time travel". Mick was adamant on this point.

Jed reluctantly agreed "It sticks in my craw to accept that there is even the slightest possibility that any member of my family could act dishonourably, but I recognise the strength of your reservations also, so let's do it".

Mick chose a late model, electrically powered town car from Jed's stable of available vehicles as their transport and fitted the flux capacitor.

"I reckon that this car won't stand out too much in fifteen years' time" He said "And we might need to impress somebody with our elegance when we get there. We need an explanation for our need to access the documents and why we are all there so here's my idea. I'll be the driver of the car and Wilson the bodyguard, he's big enough, God knows, and if he assumes a menacing scowl most people won't want to mess with him. As far as it goes Anita, the least questionable role for you is as personal assistant to Jed. If they get the impression that there's something more to the relationship, so much the better. How does that sound? Jed had better be a previously unknown family member who's looking into something deeply confidential and must be given unfettered access to the documents and news feeds".

Three days and thirteen years later the impressive town car drew up outside the offices of Schuster, Levi and Mulligan. Attorneys at Law. The offices were in as good a condition as they had been back in the earlier days and just as grandiose. Mick jumped out, dressed in his chauffeur's uniform, and deferentially touching his cap he held the door open for the others. He then drove off to find parking for the car while the others entered the grand portals of the office block.

Once inside Anita approached the receptionist and explained their mission.

"Mr Bush is here to use the library and research services, this has been arranged with the librarian. Please expedite this matter as a matter of urgency as Mr Bush is a very busy man".

This demand was couched in such a commanding and imperious fashion that the unfortunate receptionist had no option but to call the librarian instantly, explaining the urgency of the matter. Anita overheard her telling the man on the other end of the phone

"She says he's Mr Bush and he looks very like Mr Bush but he also looks much younger than Mr Bush does. Perhaps he's another family member".

The librarian arrived in very short order. "Mr Bush?" He queried "I don't believe we've met but the family resemblance is remarkable".

Jed smiled, delighted at his subterfuge. He, of course, was very familiar with the librarian from his earlier time. He noticed that the man had not aged well and wondered if he was entirely well. Remembering

Mick's injunction that the less said on any subject the better, he decided not to pursue that line of enquiry.

"I understand that you are looking for access to the library and research facilities Sir. That's an unusual request, may I enquire what you are interested in particularly?" The librarian was suitably deferential but felt that access to these facilities should not be given to all and sundry on demand.

"Nothing confidential to the company" Said Jed "I'm interested in current conditions in Ireland at present. I'm considering investing there and I want to get a thorough grounding on the labour conditions there specifically".

"No problem" The librarian said enthusiastically "We have extensive contacts in Ireland and our database is bang up to date on the current situation there. I believe the labour conditions are exceptionally favourable for investors at the present time. I'll introduce you to Gloria, she's a research assistant and she can help you with anything you need while you're here".

"That won't be necessary" Jed declared "Anita here is fully competent to assist me. If you'll just show us to a terminal we'll get onto it immediately. I don't expect to need to spend any more than three or four hours here. That should be more than enough time to do what I need".

Several hours later a very relieved Mick saw his friends emerging from the office block with thoughtful looks on their faces. He immediately jumped out and held the door of the car for them and, as soon as they were aboard he drove off. Driving towards the freeway he called over his shoulder

"Well, how did it go, guys?"

Jed replied "in one sense it went very well, in another disastrously. If you can get us back to our own time I'll tell you exactly what my thoughts on the matter at hand are".

He fell into a moody silence as Mick expertly brought them onto the freeway and, as soon as it was practicable, back through time to their own timeline.

"So, what's the story" Mick demanded. He was not used to being on the outside and waiting for others to bring him up to speed and he disliked the feeling immensely.

"We've done an exhaustive trawl through both public and private sources to assess the current state of affairs in Ireland and Anita is quite correct. It is an effective dictatorship with your friends Mick O' and Frank McGuinness at the top of the pile. Freedom of the press and freedom of expression are totally squashed. Religion has been suppressed except for Scientology and any flickering signs of dissent are ruthlessly stamped out. These guys combine the worst excesses of the Nazis and the KGB together. As bad as this is for the Irish, the malign influence of the dictators is spreading throughout the European Union and signs are that within the next few years Mick O' will be crowned Emperor of a new European Empire. There is ample evidence that he will not stop there. He is well known to have world domination on his mind and he has been heard to boast that his ambition extends to the whole galaxy, in time.

This guy really needs to be stopped". A chastened Jed looked very unhappy when telling this story.

With an uncharacteristically sympathetic glance at Jed Wilson took up the tale "One of the newspapers had a story running about GeorgeIII having written a book which was touted to blow the roof off the family law firm. So Anita was right about that too. Apparently the law firm is seeking an injunction to prevent him publishing the book, but he claims he has powerful backers in Dublin who will do it for him. The Irish government, Mick O' and Frank by the looks of it, have unilaterally abandoned the international protocols about injunctions and claim that they don't apply in Ireland and that Europe will soon follow suit. I'm sorry about that Jed".

"No good comes of crying over spilt milk" Jed said "We need to work out a strategy for dealing with both situations and get cracking on it right away".

Chapter Twenty Eight

Blood is...

"OK, first off we need to either destroy these papers, put them in secure, offsite storage, or redact all mention of time travel and Freddie and you guys". Jed had evidently given this matter some serious thought. "All things considered I think that destruction is the best option, then nobody can get their hands on them and cause chaos further down the line".

Mick was greatly relieved "That seems like a very drastic option but realistically speaking it's definitely the most secure one. I'm sorry it's turned out like this, but obviously Freddie wasn't as discreet as I would have hoped he'd be and GeorgeIII seems to have inherited some of his less attractive characteristics. Let's do it! A bonfire would be nice".

In the grand gardens later that evening Jed lit the barbecue and consigned the papers to the flames. As the fire caught the papers burst into flame and flew up into the night sky, scattering around the barbecue pit. Everyone, except Wilson who had overindulged, rushed around picking up half burned pages and stuffing them back onto the fire.

Jed did a final cast about and said "That's the lot, we got them all. I'm saddened to have to destroy Freddie's papers. I told you guys that he was a childhood hero of mine, and I'll have to do something about GeorgeIII. He's obviously further off the rails than I had realised. Some form of intervention is in the cards for that young man, I can tell you".

Mick extended his hand to Jed and said

"I can't thank you enough for your hospitality and help here. We need to be getting back to Ireland, the matter of Mick O' and Frank still needs to be dealt with and Anita would, I'm sure like to go home to her own time"

Here he cast a longing look in her direction

"We'll keep in touch and let you know how things turn out. If you're ever over in Ireland look us up and we'll have a reunion".

Hardly had the taxi driven out of his drive than Jed reached for the phone

Gloria, get me GeorgeIII".

Two minutes later Jed was talking to George.

"You remember that project I gave you recently to research the old files in the office? Well something's come up. Get over here right away, time is most definitely not on our side in this matter".

Meanwhile, heading to the airport Mick noticed Wilson fingering a piece of charred paper with a puzzled look on his face.

"Hey Mick" he said "Do you notice anything strange about this paper?" He handed Mick the page.

"It looks like an ordinary page to me" Mick replied "What's so strange about it?"

"It's one I retrieved from the bonfire when they all flew up in the air" Wilson said hesitantly "But look at it.

It doesn't look like something from the early part of the twentieth century. In fact it looks like plain, ordinary computer paper, and" He added squinting at the page held sideways "This isn't done with a typewriter, it's printed off a bloody computer printer. It's a fraud. That bloody man has conned us. We should have left Freddie on an ice floe in the Arctic like I said. He was bad news back then and his bastard spawn is bad news now!"

"It certainly looks like he played me for a sucker" Mick admitted ruefully "Oh well, it looks like the only option is PlanB".

Wilson was not enthused about PlanB. In his admittedly short acquaintance with Mick his PlanBs tended to be a bit hairy.

"PlanB?" he queried "What's PlanB? I'm not too keen on your B plans, they often mean that we get into bothersome tangles".

"We don't really have any options. If Jed is turned against us, then extreme circumstances call for extreme measures. I had a PlanB on hold anyway before we met Jed. I wasn't altogether sure we'd be able to convince him of the necessity for killing the effect of Freddie's heritage" Mick didn't look too happy about the prospect of the PlanB option.

Wilson was almost apoplectic "Killing the effect? Killing the effect" He shouted

"You haven't forgotten that I wanted to kill that gobshite, Freddie. You're the one who's always going on about unintended consequences. See where your soft hearted, and soft headed, instincts have gotten us now.

You do realise that right now not only are we probably the target of a snatch squad for you and a death squad for Anita and me from the Irish goons, but Jed will most likely set his knuckle draggers on us too".

"Actually" Mick admitted "I believe you're right. Jed is hardly only interested in his family's unsullied reputation. A hard headed lawyer like him will have sussed out the advantage of time travel to him. God knows but Mick O' might get some competition in the dictator stakes if Jed could swan about up and down the timelines at will. We're in a deeper pickle than I first thought. This makes PlanB even more imperative".

Back in Cleveland GeorgeIII strolled into Jed's office with studied nonchalance.

"Hi Uncle Jed" He said "What's up. You sounded a bit upset on the phone. What have I done now?"

GeorgeIII was very accustomed to being in his uncle's bad books. He didn't seem to realise that in his own youth he had been known in Cleveland as something of a wild child himself. However Jed did have his hands on all the levers of family power and total control of George's trust fund. Antagonising the old man would not be a good idea.

"George" Jed glared icily at his nephew "There are times when I despair of you. You behave like a spoiled two year old most of the time and on the rare occasions when you put your brain in gear the result is almost always catastrophic. Is it possible that you thought I wouldn't find out that you had copied some of the documents I asked you to get from the vault? Do you think everyone is as stupid and careless as you? I know very well that you have a secret plan to write a book exposing all the Bush family secrets. If someone else doesn't wipe you from the face of the earth, I may be forced to pay an assassin to do it for me" His stony stare put the fear of God into his nephew.

"Now listen to me" Jed ordered "This time travel stuff is much too valuable to leave in the hands of a couple of Irish peasants. The Mick person has presented a conundrum in that he seems confident that he, and only he, has the key to the technology. I don't like the idea that the thing will melt into an inert lump if someone else attempts to access it. However there is more than one way to crack that particular nut. He seems smitten with the Anita person, not that I can blame him for that. She is a very pretty little thing".

"The other Mick, this O'Reilly person is another kettle of fish. He is very thoroughly in control in Ireland and has tentacles out all over the world. He is, however, just another bogtrotter from a backward country on the periphery of Europe. With our connections we should have no obstacles to disposing of him whenever we choose to do so. The only question is whether we should join forces with him in our quest to get hold of the time travel device or proceed with that project alone. We are in a fortunate position in that we have foreknowledge of events in the future and Mick O', as they call him, is blissfully ignorant of the future. That's a huge advantage".

GeorgeIII had been staring in open mouthed amazement at his uncle throughout this soliloquy. He had thought that his literary ambitions were a closely guarded secret. In fact, so far as he could remember, he had told no one else in the world about them, whilst in his sober senses at any rate. As to the rest of Jed's rant, he was totally at sea. He had no idea who the people under discussion were and even less about what Jed was talking about. Deciding that discretion was the better part of valour, he remained silent.

Jed meanwhile had been mulling over his options "OK. Here's what we'll do. We'll open a new project folder, confidential to you and me only. I want you to get the full lowdown on all the people involved in this matter. Mick, Anita, Wilson, Frank McGuinness and Michael O'Reilly. I want detailed dossiers on all those on my desk in two days. Money is no object, but do not screw this up or, nephew or not, you will suffer I promise you".

Chapter Twenty Nine

More Schemes and Stratagems

Mick and the others had reached the airport and paused in the coffee shop to consider their options. "Well it's pretty obvious that I seriously misjudged Jed. From this moment on we'd better be a lot sharper if we're to come out of this with whole skins".

"First off we'd better take the flight from Cleveland to Kennedy. I have no doubt that Jed has connections that will be able to pinpoint our movements with no problems. If we're seen to be heading for Ireland he'll be thrown off sufficiently for us to double back and put PlanB into operation".

"Wilson" Mick asked "With your undercover connections is there anyone in New York we can get to help out?"

"I do know some people, but just what do you want from them? They are not exactly the most welcoming of individuals at the best of times and just now with Homeland Security breathing down their necks I have no doubt they'll be even more prickly".

"We need to stay in the States but we also need Jed to think we've gone home. What I want is three people who would like a first class, all expenses paid, holiday in Ireland. They should look enough like us to pass a passport check, but God knows that shouldn't be a big deal. People leaving the States only get a cursory glance from the authorities in Kennedy and when they get to Ireland they just get waved through. Coming back they can use their own American passports".

"That shouldn't be a big deal" Wilson was confident that his contacts could pull this off "We'll need to get our passports back immediately so I'll make it a condition that they're posted back to us, as soon as they get to Dublin. Only then will I hand over the final payment. Speaking of payment, this'll cost a pretty packet".

"Don't worry about the payment" Mick smiled nastily "As part of PlanB I intend to fine Jed heavily for his breach of trust. He won't know what he did to deserve the fine, but he'll feel the effect right enough".

"OK. Wilson's got the decoys on the plane from Kennedy so we should be under the radar as far as Jed is concerned. Now for PlanB. We go back in time to when they were building Jed's company headquarters. I've looked up the historical records and find it was in 1972. We inveigle ourselves into the space of the vaults and time shift to a couple of years before all this GeorgeIII stuff came up. We steal the Freddie papers and burn them right there and then and shift back to 1972 and make our way home. That way we'll never come up on Jed's radar and we're in the clear". The gang were meeting in Mick's motel room outside Cleveland two weeks later".

"But how do we get into the vault, even in 1972 that won't be easy". Wilson was being awkward as usual.

"We get building inspector's passes and dress the part. This is all before the 9/11 outrage and America still reckons it's safe from anything the likes of which I'm proposing. If we act like we are entitled to be there nobody will give it any thought, trust me. I haven't let you down yet". Mick was not sympathetic to Wilson's fit of the collywobbles. "Besides as far as anybody in 1972 is concerned we'll only be in there for a quarter of an hour".

Two days and some forty years earlier on Whiskey Island in Cleveland's waterside a 1972 Oldsmobile popped into existence on the deserted road at four o'clock in the morning. Mick had reckoned that the traffic at that place and time was likely to be at a very low ebb and calculated that their chances of being seen transitioning into the timeline was as close to zero as he could make it. In the event, he was quite right and they neither met, nor saw any other traffic, vehicular or otherwise.

Mick heaved a great sigh of relief and said "OK, we're here and nobody's noticed. We'll get rooms in a motel and put the plan into operation tomorrow".

Next morning they drove up to the building site, dressed in suits and wearing hard hats and steel toe capped boots, and demanded to see the site manager. Brandishing the building inspectors passes which Wilson's contact in New York had assured him were 'more authentic than the real thing' Mick said in a supercilious voice:

"I'm the chief building inspector for the State of Ohio and we've been informed that things on this site are not as they should be. My associate Miss Gilligan here is going to inspect your paperwork whilst Mr Wilson and I conduct some sampling of various places on the site. Please ensure that we have free and clear access to all areas and we'll be out of your hair as soon as possible".

Anita went off with the site manager while Mick and Wilson headed towards the workplace. Mick had a large tool bag which contained a drill and several phials of serious looking chemicals. Tucked in at the bottom was a miniature version of the flux capacitor.

The manager had sent a man with them to check that they did not get into trouble on his watch. He looked on with great interest as Mick drilled some random hole in floors, buttresses and stairways. The resulting drill cores were placed in vials and mixed with a combination of chemicals.

"What's this for?" Enquired their guide.

"We need to check the precise composition and strength of the concrete mix at various places throughout the site" Mick explained. "The colour of the chemicals change with the different mixes. You can see that the stuff in the buttresses and that in the floors is different, whilst the stairs are different to both"

The guide looked a little worried but Mick hastened to reassure him "That's OK, the various parts are made to survive different stresses so their composition is meant to be different in each case. Concrete is not just concrete you know. So far everything checks out OK. What's on the lower basement level?"

"That's the vault" replied the guide "It's not finished, of course, we're waiting for the door to be installed and then the security guys can lock it up and we'll be done with it".

"I'll just take a sample of the floor then" Said Mick, "I'm sure it's top notch but I have to check".

Just prior to using his drill on the vault floor Mick tipped Wilson a surreptitious wink. "Where's the restroom?" Queried Wilson on cue "I shouldn't have had that curry last night". He looked a bit pale about the eyes as he said this.

The guide looked from Wilson to Mick and said "its two floors up and towards the back of the building" He said, pointing in the direction of the stairs.

"Do you think you could show me?" Wilson now looked to be in serious distress.

"I'm not supposed to leave anyone down here alone" The guide said, looking doubtfully at Mick.

"You needn't worry about me" Said Mick "I've one more hole to drill and then pack up. If you're going upstairs I'll be about two minutes behind you. The state Wilson is in, I'll probably catch you up before you get to the top step. You better go, I've seen him in this state before, and it can get pretty messy".

As the guide brought Wilson up the stairs he heard a soft popping sound from below. As he hesitated Wilson groaned loudly and looked even more upset. The guide rushed Wilson to the restroom and returned to the head of the stairs.

As soon as the other two had left him alone in the vault Mick stood on a little carpenter's stool which had been lying there and activated the flux capacitor.

He stumbled and fell off the stool and found himself in a very different vault. The floor was some twelve inches higher and covered in a metallic compound.

He blessed his foresight in standing on the stool as, otherwise he might have seriously injured his ankle by arriving on a floor which was higher than anticipated. The vault was lighted and contained a series of drawers which were large at the bottom and got progressively smaller as they neared the ceiling.

As he studied the drawers Mick heaved a sigh of relief. They were locked with standard locking systems. Apparently the vault was considered to be unassailable so drawers did not need high tech locking systems. Mick smiled triumphantly and drew from his tool bag a device he'd picked up in one of his future trips. Checking out the drawers he found one of the larger ones with Jed's name on it. Slipping the thin end of the device into the keyhole he wiggled it about for a couple of seconds. He felt an almost imperceptible click and the drawer fell open at his touch.

Inside the drawer was a veritable treasure trove of items.

Mick rapidly scanned the drawer's contents, a large stash of currencies from different countries, including Rubles, Swiss Francs, Euro and other notes of various denominations all told several hundred thousand dollars' worth. There was also an extensive collection of jeweler, the value of which Mick could not estimate. Down at the bottom mick recognised Freddie's handwriting on a thick bulky package 'Private and confidential, not to be opened until after the death of Mr George Bush the First'.

"That'll be it" Mick thought as he hurriedly opened it and scanned the contents. In his hand were copies of the documents which Jed had shown them before the barbecue, but on older paper and with much of it handwritten.

Also stashed in the drawer were numerous bearer bonds which on a quick scan Mick estimated to be worth many millions of dollars. He extracted three of these bonds and together with the Freddie documents stuffed them into the false bottom of his tool bag. He then quickly reset the time travel device and popped back to 1972.

Emerging an instant later than he had set out he set off up the stairs and met the guide as he started down.

"I was just coming down to see if everything was alright" the man said.

"No worries" Mick replied "All done, I'm happy to say that everything checks out and providing the paperwork checks out we can give you a clean bill of health for this construction".

As he came out of the building he found Wilson standing outside casually smoking a cigarette. "You look much better" He said.

"Yeah" Wilson replied "That food I ate last night certainly did not agree with me, but I'm feeling OK now".

Mick thanked the guide and shaking hands with him left and went to pick up Anita in the office. As he entered the room an older man in a business suit was coming out accompanied by a boy of about ten years of age. The man thrust out his hand and said "Hello, I'm Jed Bush, the senior partner in the law firm whose building this is. I've just been talking to your Miss Gilligan, charming girl, and she tells me that the paperwork checks out. I assume that everything is good on the site also?"

Mick smiled widely and said "I'm delighted to be able to give you a certificate of compliance for the work done here. I wish every site was as competently managed as this one. Who is this fine young man?"

"This is my son Jed Junior. I'm taking him around to see the site. Someday I hope he'll be senior partner here himself"

Chapter Thirty

Dealing with Mick O's Minions

Back in Dublin and quite satisfied that the Freddie thing was completely neutralised, they had minutely examined the documents which Mick had filched and were satisfied that they were the genuine article, the next item on the agenda was how best to deal with Mick O' and Frank and their minions.

"By the way" Anita asked "What's with the three million in bearer bonds you filched from Jed's safety deposit box? I thought you had all the money you needed, or wanted"

"That's my fine on Jed for screwing with us over GeorgeIII's book and the other stuff. He was more interested in the time travel lark than he let on. I guess if you spend all your life grafting on behalf of big business, you'll get sucked in finally yourself. I don't need the money and, in fact, I've already given it to charity to relieve famine in Africa. Jed probably doesn't even know it's gone and, with any luck, when he finds out he'll blame GeorgeIII. That should soften both their coughs". Mick smiled contentedly at the mind picture thus presented.

"Jeez" Anita said "Remind me not to get on your wrong side OK?"

Mick frowned distractedly "That was a relatively easy gig. Jed had no idea what he was dealing with. Mick O' and Frank are a very different kettle of fish. They have resources at their beck and call that Jed could only dream of. I'm very uncomfortable about that computer programme, Daneel. That thing could have immense power and if they really set it loose on the time travel idea there's no knowing what it might come up with".

Wilson, ever the pragmatist said "Why don't we whack the pair of them before they can get into a position of power. That will put a permanent kink in their hosepipe of life and remove them from the equation".

"I'm getting a little tired of the same old tune from you. We will not be killing anybody. In the first place it's wrong and in the second if it's not them running the show it might be worse. In this case the devil you know could very easily be better than the one you don't. We need a much more subtle approach to the situation".

"OK, we need to get to Michael O'Reilly before he becomes the dictator of Ireland" Mick had been thinking about this intensively. "He's into cheap flights, pedigree cattle, horse racing and rugby. Somewhere in there is a soft spot. We have to find it and exploit it. If we can come up with a total Wow factor it'll put him on a different track and when he's offered the dictator gig he'll blow it off. So what do you think guys?"

As Wilson and Anita were considering Mick's proposition there was a shattering crash from the back of the house, followed by the blaring of an alarm.

"There's someone trying to get in through the back windows. Well they're in for a little surprise". Mick said and turning he switched on the TV.

The set showed a split screen view of the front and

back of the house and Anita gasped in shock when she saw three men at the front and two at the back. The two at the back were behaving oddly, staggering around with their hands over their eyes and evidently in some serious distress. The three in front were obviously confused. One, who looked to be the leader was shouting into a handheld device which looked very like a mobile phone. Mick turned up the volume and they could hear the leader shouting "What's going on back there. Have you gained entry? Seamus, report in, what's happening?"

Meanwhile in the back garden the two men were still weaving and stumbling. Anita and Wilson listened as they whimpered

"My eyes, my eyes, I'm blind. I can't see a thing. Seamus, what's happening?" Seamus was fumbling with his mobile device but he couldn't see to press the correct button. He dropped the phone and swore as he frantically scrabbled around to find it.

Mick was laughing fit to burst. He wiped tears from his eyes as he explained to the others.

"When Anita told me that we might expect visitors from the future, I took some simple precautions. If someone attempts to force entry to the house by way of either the windows or doors a light bomb of two thousand watts goes off in their faces. It'll be a week before either of those bozos are any threat to anyone".

"Now look what the frontal assault looks like". Out front the leader turned to one of his remaining troops and said "Go around back and check see what those brainless morons are at".

Mick chuckled and mused "That could be mistake number two".

Tracking the intruder as he went towards the back of the house Mick waited until he was in line with the kitchen window. He then pressed a switch located on a remote control device which he had taken from a drawer in the TV console. A slim opening appeared in the frame of the window and when Mick was satisfied it lined up correctly he activated another button on the remote. A hidden Taser shot out and connected with the intruder. He experienced 6,800 kV for some five seconds, incapacitating him and dropping him to the ground immediately.

"Now I think we should deal with the front door pair" Said Mick.

"Let me do it" Pleaded Wilson. He had been raring to go ever since the first assault but stunned into quietness by Mick's preparedness.

The two out front had not waited for their cohort to return from the back of the house. Rushing forward, one of them produced a device like the one which Mick had used to pick the lock of Jed's safety deposit drawer and inserted it into the lock of the front door. Using a third button on his remote, Mick sent a high voltage, low current electrical discharge through the lock, sending the unfortunate would be intruder into convulsions and rigor. His comrade unwisely tried to pull him free only to find himself hopelessly trapped also.

Mick called out to Wilson

"Don't open the door for a couple of seconds.

Then we can collect up all these gallant heroes and ask a few questions".

Mick helped Wilson to drag the intruders into the house together with a couple of tool bags which they had dropped in their distress. Wilson examined the bags and grunted in satisfaction "These guys came prepared to kidnap us, right enough. There's cable ties and chloroform in here but no weapons. They must have been under instructions to bring us all back to their masters for questioning. That's reassuring, if it had been me I'd have wasted me and Anita and only tried for Mick. He's the brains of this outfit after all!"

Mick was busy tying up the villains with the cable ties as they slowly came back to consciousness.

"Not everyone is as bloodthirsty as you Wilson. If Frank was behind this I'm totally convinced he wouldn't want to hurt us. He just wants to screw the secret of time travel out of us. He is most likely a true believer of Mick O's. In fact they probably are both utterly convinced of the righteousness of their cause and look upon us as misguided fools".

"That's Mick's main fault" Said Wilson to Anita "He's determined to think the best of everybody, no matter how hard they try to convince him otherwise".

"You leave him alone" She riposted spiritedly "He's kept you out of trouble up until now!"

Wilson grinned knowingly and bent to help Mick with trussing up the villains.

By the time they were done with the tying up of

their prisoners those gentlemen were wide awake and taking notice. Mick and Wilson had decided that a good cop - bad cop setup would be best for questioning them.

"I'll be the good cop" Said Mick "You look a lot scarier than me so you can be my evil sidekick".

"So" Wilson growled kicking the soles of the lead intruders shoes "You're pretty incompetent burglars and breaking and entering was not your best subject in criminal school, was it?"

The villains had obviously been warned to keep quiet if captured and said nothing in reply to Wilson's goading.

Turning to Mick Wilson demanded "Give me the Colt and I'll make them talk"

With every sign of reluctance Mick handed over the Colt saying "You won't do anything rash, will you Wilson. Remember these guys probably have backup somewhere and if we ill treat them we might suffer for it later".

Wilson laughed fiendishly and replied "Dead men tell no tales. By the time I'm finished with this bunch of big girl's blouses there'll be no trace left of them for anyone to blame us for anything" and reaching down he grabbed the smallest by the scruff of his neck. He dragged the unfortunate terror stricken wretch out of the room and the others could hear him tramping down the cellar stairs accompanied by the thump, thump, of his victim's feet hitting each step of the descent.

Five minutes later, after some scuffling and

thumping noises followed by a gunshot, Wilson emerged back into the room looking somewhat dishevelled and with suspicious red stains on his shirt.

"He was a harder nut to crack than I expected. He didn't crack, unfortunately for him. Still we have four more, by the time I get to the end the last guy will be singing like a canary".

"For God's sake Wilson" Shouted Mick "I told you to go easy. I'm sure there's no need for bloodshed. Violence never solved anything" and turning to the intruders he appealed to them. "You guys need to tell us everything. When he gets into this frame of mind there's no stopping him. He has the only weapon in the house so he can do anything he likes. I really want you to tell us who sent you and what your orders were, otherwise I won't be responsible for what happens".

"OK, enough talk" Snarled Wilson grabbing the next in line and dragging him towards the cellar door. His victim was almost speechless with horror and cried out to his leader "Please Jimmy, tell him what he wants to know. Please mister" This to Wilson "I don't know anything. Jimmy got the gig and roped me in. I haven't met the guy who gave the orders. Jimmy is the one you want, tell him guys" He frantically appealed to the others. All except Jimmy nodded and agreed volubly.

"Well Jimmy" Wilson smiled "It looks like you're next. What limb do you think you need least? Leg or arm, right or left. Come along with me down to my little cellar where we can chat without interruption".

Jimmy, evidently deciding that good sense should

prevail said

"OK, you win. I'll tell you everything I know. Just please don't let him bring me down to the cellar" He pleadingly addressed Mick.

"There's not a lot to tell really" Jimmy was only too eager to assist with the enquiries by now "This guy approached me in a pub in North Strand and asked if I was up for a gig. He told me he wanted three people brought to him and promised a grand for me and another to be spread amongst the other guys, half up front and the rest on delivery. He was very insistent that nobody was to be hurt. He gave me the chloroform and told me to sort out the rest".

"And you just jumped in?" Wilson said, thrusting his face into Jimmy's with menace in mind.

"No, he told me you guys owed him money on a deal which had gone sour and all he wanted to do was collect. I'm not into rough stuff and I'm sorry I took the gig in the first place". Jimmy replied contritely.

"So where and when is the delivery planned to take place?" Mick asked.

"I'm to give him a call on his mobile to tell him we've got you sorted and arrange a meet. I don't know where or when because he didn't tell me".

"Well you'd best give him a shout then" said Wilson, looming large over the trussed and bound Jimmy.

"I don't think it'd be healthy for me to ring him and lie about things. To tell the truth, he kinda scared me. He had a sorta crazy look to him and unlike me I think violence would be no problem to him, so if you don't mind I think I'll give the ringing ting a miss".

Wilson checked the chambers on the Colt and said "Jimmy, I think you didn't get the message earlier. So I'll ask again, which limb do you think you need least? I don't want to have to ask that question again but if put to it I can ask as many times as needed. I figure four limbs, two shots apiece makes eight shots in total. By shot number three at the most I guess you'll be more than happy to help me out with the little phone call. C'mon up on your toes and we'll go downstairs and have a little chat".

"No, no, no" pleaded Jimmy "I'll do it. Please don't take me down the cellar. I'll do whatever you want. Just give me my phone, it's the green one on the countertop".

"No funny business now" Menaced Wilson "If you give me the least idea that you're trying something on it'll be the last joke you'll play in your life. Don't get the notion that I'm kidding. I don't kid".

"Hey man" Jimmy said into the phone "We've got the goods. Where would you like them delivered to? OK, and what time? Right, the back of the Magazine fort in the Phoenix Park at Two in the morning, got it. Bring the money Right?"

"That's it" He said "Now can we go? We'd like to be far away when his nibs' finds out we double crossed him".

"No you bloody well can't go" Roared Wilson "You have a starring role to play in our upcoming midnight revels in the Park. And besides, what about your poor unfortunate mate down below?"

"If you like, you can give him to us and we'll get rid of the body for you, we've done it a few times already. But we'd need to be going now, there's people waiting for us and if we don't turn up they'll be getting antsy".

"The only thing that'll be turning up is your toes if you continue to bullshit me" Wilson said in his most menacing tone.

"And what are you going on about getting rid of a body?" He turned and going to the cellar door he reached in and pulled the bound and gagged but otherwise unhurt intruder into sight.

"Oh dear God" Said Jimmy "There goes our only excuse for screwing up this gig. We're all dead".

Chapter Thirty One

Revels in the Park

The night had come on dark and dreary with a miserable drizzly rain which soaked anyone foolish enough to be out in it to the skin. Mick and his friends, together with the five, now thoroughly cowed intruders, had taken up positions near the meeting site much earlier.

"Do you think anyone will come?" Whispered Wilson "And if they do will we recognise them, will it be someone we know, like Frank or Mick O', do you think".

"I'm quite sure someone will come" Said Mick "But I very much doubt it'll be Mick O' or Frank. They will be much too busy plotting how to take over the world and other nefarious stuff. Besides neither of them will be willing to drop everything to take a one way trip back into the past.

"I assume" He continued to Anita who was huddling close to his side under the trees "That they must have found out about your group and either persuaded or forced them to send someone back after us".

"I very much fear so" She replied "I'm totally satisfied that they wouldn't agree to voluntarily assist the baddies but they are not the most discreet people in the world and one of them could have let the cat out of the bag. I hope none of them have been hurt by those guys".

"I reckon that the guy will be a heavy from Mick O's storm troopers. Dictators always have storm troopers at their beck and call. I'm prepared for a certain degree of resistance from him and as long as he's alone we should be more than a match for him. If he has backup along things could go a bit wobbly. I'd like you, Anita, to hang back under the trees when the meet takes place. We'll leave a shotgun with you and you'll be our PlanB, if necessary. Wilson, you take the driver's side and sneak up on him from that direction. I'll be out front, dressed as one of the others, with Jimmy and as soon as he stops, you stick the colt in his ear and subdue him. Is that OK?"

Soon after there was the sound of a heavy engine approaching and the lights of a large jeep came into view. Mick and Jimmy stood at the edge of the road with Jimmy's van parked behind them. Jimmy was most reluctant to be a part of the reception committee but Mick whispered that Wilson was behind them in the bushes, armed with the colt and Anita was hidden in the trees so he settled down albeit unwillingly.

The jeep drew to a halt beside Jimmy and the driver's door opened. As it did so, Wilson sidled up next to the vehicle and, exactly as planned, stuck the colt in the driver's ear. "Just keep completely still" He hissed "and everything will be totally peachy".

As Wilson was triumphantly preparing to frisk the driver for concealed weapons he felt a cold sensation on the back of his neck.

Unfortunately he had neglected to check the rear seat of the jeep, an understandable error as the rear windows were heavily tinted, a voice spoke in his ear "It would be very much in your interest to drop your weapon and release my buddy".

Wilson dropped the colt and turned and found, to his horror that he was confronted by a tall man brandishing a Mac 10 machine pistol with silencer attached, a weapon which has the dubious distinction of being the most widely used handgun in criminal circles in America, where it is known as a 'spray and pray' weapon, for obvious reasons.

"I guess you managed to outwit Jimmy" said the man "Well I shouldn't be too surprised. He's not exactly the sharpest knife in the cutlery drawer after all. I'll just have to choose more carefully in future. Now without any further messing about, where's Mick and what's her name, oh yes, Anita. We'll gather them up and go on about our business and leave Jimmy here to contemplate the price of failure".

Jimmy intervened at this point "What do you mean, price of failure, I've brought them to you just as you demanded. You owe us a couple of grand. Don't even think of doing us out of our dues. We're no pushovers I can tell you". He finally stopped yelling when Mick jabbed him in the back with a sharp stick which he had picked up and he finally realised that the big man had not recognised Mick.

"Go and put the van out of action" The big man called to the driver "I'll soon get this gink to tell me where the other two are hidden out".

He didn't have very long to wait until he heard Anita speak from behind him "One of the other pair is right here" She said "I wouldn't turn around if I was you. My finger might slip on the trigger of this shotgun and, as bad as I am with guns, I could hardly miss from two feet behind you. Now, turn the ugly gun around and hand it nicely to Wilson and we can proceed in a civilised fashion".

The big man swore in frustration and did as he was bid. Meantime the driver, who had gone to disable the van, returned calling out "Boss, Boss, there's something going on here. There's four dead bodies tied up and lying in the van. I think we've been double crossed by Jimmy and his gang".

"No shit" grunted the boss "Now he tells me".

As the driver rushed forward Mick stuck out his foot and tripped him. He then promptly sat on his head and speaking to Jimmy said

"How would you like to earn the other two grand and get a little payback on these guys into the bargain?"

"That sounds cool to me boss" Cried Jimmy "What do you need me to do. You want this pair of low lifes to be wasted, say the word and they're gone, like that!" And he snapped his fingers triumphantly.

"We're going to bring these Muppets back to my place and ask them a few polite questions. I'm not altogether certain that they don't have other guys knocking about for backup. I want to hire you guys to keep an eye out for any strange looking types in the neighbourhood and maybe help us out if it comes to rough stuff.

"Listen" Jimmy said "As far as these guys are concerned we'll happily do anything you like with them. I hate people who double cross ordinary decent criminals, and mostly I hate guys who try to outwit me. I'll even throw in the disposal of the bodies for free if you like".

"No, no, disposal of the bodies is not necessary" Mick replied "Just keep your eyes open and a little bodyguarding duty and I'll see you right".

"Can we stick around for the 'polite' questioning?" Asked Jimmy "I'd kinda like to see it working from the other side, having had it practised on me" He had an evil grin on his face as he ungently poked the boss man in the ribs with his sharp toed boot.

Once safely back in the house Mick commenced the 'gentle' interrogation of his prisoners.

"OK" He said to the boss man "I don't have to be a genius to figure out who sent you so all I need to know is how you received your instructions and how you got here. We can do this the easy way or the hard way, but make no mistake, we'll get the info out of you one way or another. It's plain to us that our lives or, at the very least, our liberty is at stake here and whilst Anita and me don't like violence, Wilson is a totally other story".

"Listen" the boss man replied "I've been thinking since you captured me and I believe I'm completely out of my comfort zone here. I was told that you had stolen some proprietary information and hidden it somewhere and my task was to retrieve that info. Listening to you guys talking it's clear that that story was bullshit. So here's the story, mind you, you might like to lose the outsider before hearing me out" And he nodded towards Jimmy.

Mick took the hint and bringing Jimmy outside he gave him a large wad of cash saying "Here's the money you were promised along with a nice bonus. We won't need you or your guys any more. Give me a phone number where I can contact you if I need you in future and I'll get in touch if necessary".

"Wow" Jimmy gasped "That's really cool, you're a real gentleman Mick. Don't hesitate to give me a shout if you're passing my way again" and gathering his cronies he drove the dilapidated van off into the rising dawn.

The boss man started by introducing himself "My name is John Maher and I'm an officer in the Irish National Guard, a military organisation formed by Michael O'Reilly and Frank McGuinness. Its charter is to protect and advance the aims and objects of the Irish State and People as represented by our Great Leader, Michael O'Reilly. The main reason for its existence is the great depression of the early years of the twenty first century. Michael O'Reilly has ordained that never again will Ireland and her citizens be held in thrall to international forces whose only interest is to preserve their own ascendency over other, smaller, nations".

"You do know" Said Mick "That what you've just announced is the manifesto of every dictator in history and that once you embrace that philosophy you are on a slippery slope which leads inevitably to repression and the crushing of civil liberties?"

"As it happens, since coming back to capture you I've been looking around and it's not like we were told it was in 2012. Sure, there's poverty and the politicians are pretty crappy but not a great deal different from our own lot in. Listening to you and the others talking I'm less inclined to believe that our future leadership is actually doing us any favours on the international stage. Before joining the National Guard I studied history and on reflection I'm coming around to the notion that we may be heading for a confrontation with the major powers. No matter what, I don't think we would survive a faceoff with the entire rest of the world".

"What was your mission" Asked Mick "You were on a one way trip, unless Anita is mistaken. How were you expected to report back?"

"First thing I did on arriving back here was to set up a safety deposit box and a method to make the key available to my future self. So I just drop my reports into the box and it acts as a time capsule. My job was to capture you and persuade you, by whatever means, to give up the secret of two way time travel. I would then drop it into the box and Hey Presto! It appears in the future. Make no mistake, Mick O' as you call him, is desperate to get this technology. He's totally convinced that it's the ultimate key to world domination".

Wilson, ever suspicious demanded "You're remarkably open about all this stuff. It looks like a suspiciously swift conversion. Why should we accept what you have to say? It may be a ruse to put us off balance and let you get the better of us in some way".

"I can see how that might appear to you" Replied John "I told you I was a student of history and I've been a member of a secret underground opposition group whose aim is to unseat Mick O' and replace him with a democratic, representative government. I'm a sleeper agent placed in the Guard in order to take any opportunity to advance this cause. I volunteered for this trip precisely in order to try to gain your support in our endeavours".

"That's all very well" Said the ever suspicious Wilson "But how do we corroborate it? We can hardly go forward and ask Mick O' or Frank to vouch for you. Either they'd say you were one of them or they'd terminate you with extreme prejudice, as the old fashioned term goes".

"Corroboration is quite simple. I'll give you access to two safety deposit boxes in separate banks. In one I've kept copies of my reports to be forwarded to Mick O' and in the other I've kept copies of those I've sent on to the underground. By revealing the underground contact to you I'm placing his safety and possibly his life in your hands. If that doesn't convince you I can't think of anything which will".

Mick and Co. withdrew to another room to discuss these revelations. Wilson, predictably was all for extreme measures

"Let me top this guy" He pleaded "He knows far more than is good for either him or us. It's just too dangerous to leave him wandering around loose. God knows what damage he could cause".

"Oh give it a rest" Mick pleaded "Anita, what do you think? You've got a different perspective than we do, coming from that timeline as you do".

"There were persistent rumours about an underground movement in my time. We never got in touch with them because we weren't sure that the devil you don't know wasn't worse than the one you do. I am very worried that he managed to come back to this timeline because it means the Mick O' and Frank have somehow gotten their hands on our version of time travel. This doesn't augur well for my colleagues who developed that technology. They were as determined to keep it out of unsuitable hands as you are Mick. Things do not look good for them I'm afraid". Anita looked distressed and tearful.

"We don't need to worry too much about that" Mick said in his most comforting way "If we can solve this 'Master of the Universe' scenario with sense and discretion, then everything else will automatically sort itself out accordingly. The issue as I see it right now is whether we can trust John, next door".

"Goddam it" Wilson cried "We've left him unsupervised in there for the last twenty minutes. He could be gone with one of the flux capacitors by now!"

"You persist in underestimating my paranoia" Said Mick heading into the other room "I make very sure that they are kept under lock and key in a very safe place and, even if someone could get his hands on one and mess with it, it would immediately melt into a homogenous lump of an unknown compound, leaving no possible clues as to what it did or how it functioned".

In the other room John was quietly watching a current affairs programme on TV. Turning as Mick entered he said:

"This is exactly what I mean about our timeline as against this. We could no more imagine a TV programme which criticised Mick O's policies than we could think of eating ice cream on the face of the sun. It just couldn't happen. Admittedly your politicians don't seem to be any better than ours, but at least they are answerable to some extent to the public. Ours just do as they like without let or hindrance".

Chapter Thirty Two

Yet More Schemes and Stratagems

Mick was determined that now that Jed was out of the equation the next issue of Mick O' and Frank be dealt with as soon as possible.

"OK guys" He said, John was now included in his band of adventurers, despite Wilson's evident discomfiture "We need to deal with this problem and, the sooner we start, the better. Have you got any ideas as to how we should proceed?"

Wilson was, needless to state, in favour of direct, and terminal, action and to his great surprise, and gratification he was fully supported in this strategy by John.

Mick cast his eyes up to heaven and said to Anita "Bloody soldiers! They have only one solution to any problem and that issues from the mouth of a gun, the bigger the gun, the sooner the problem is resolved for them".

"We're not going to kill anybody. It's not just that killing is ethically wrong, though that's a good enough reason. It simply doesn't work. If the assassination plots against Hitler had succeeded do you think that some of his underlings, possibly even worse than him, wouldn't have taken over? Goebbels or Goring would possibly have been nastier dictators and, what would be catastrophic altogether, maybe more competent at the business of maintaining the Nazi state. We need to deal with the root of the problem, not the symptoms".

"When dealing with time anomalies, we need to treat time like a raging river. If we blow up the watercourse the river will just rage onwards and continue unheeding on a new course. We need to find one small current in the time flow and tweak it such that we obtain our desired outcome with least consequences, except the intended ones".

"We know that Mick O's interests are his transportation business, horse racing and rugby. Frank is also an avid rugby fan. I wouldn't be a bit surprised if their shared interest in rugby is what brought them together in the first place. I reckon we could leverage that shared interest into something which we can exploit to our advantage".

Anita had been paying close attention to Mick's mini lecture and said "It strikes me that Mick O might be interested in a solution to the fuel question for his transportation fleet. I notice that fuel in this timeline is almost exclusively carbon based and very expensive. It's also getting scarcer and harder to find, besides being hell on the environment. If we could offer him access to safe and cheap hydrogen production or even cold fusion technology that might divert his attention into something more useful and less megalomaniacal than his 'Ruler of the World' gig, as you call it".

"My God Anita" Mick cried, grabbing her and giving her a big hug "I believe that's the way to go". Suddenly realising that Anita was still closely held in his arms he blushed furiously and stumbled back in utter confusion.

In a rare display of tact Wilson intervened in an attempt to spare Mick any further embarrassment

"Hasn't cold fusion been totally debunked? I read an article recently where some gink had invented it and was displaying it to the scientific world but it was proved to be a fraud". He knew as much about cold fusion as the cat knows about stellar physics but he felt that he was obliged to help Mick out of this impasse.

Recovering her composure Anita replied

"It's back on the respectable agenda in 2025. Still theoretical of course but there are a number of knowledgeable physicists who are making encouraging noises about it. Cheap hydrogen is not yet fully developed either but in both cases the wrinkles should be ironed out by 2050, according to research papers I've read".

Mick was still in a state of confusion and embarrassment but he manfully struggled back into the conversation.

"Here's what I propose" He said, avoiding eye contact with Anita "We'll hop forward to 2050 and check out these options. If at all possible we'll get complete schematics of them and come back to the current timeline. We'll call 2012 base timeline because that's when I first made the original flux capacitor. Once back here we'll contact Frank and using his rugby connections we'll arrange a meet with Mick O' and offer him the technology. If we're convincing enough he'll go for it, hook, line and sinker".

"We need to remember" Anita interjected "By 2050 Mick O' will have a stranglehold on the economy of a significant portion of the world. Or he'll be deposed and someone else will be in his place if Mick's scenario come about. What I'm trying to say, is that we need to be extremely careful about how we go about this. Remember Daneel, or the latest iteration of that insidious technology will probably be even more pervasive in that timeline. These things tend to develop over time you know".

"I hadn't thought of that" Said Mick "Thank you Anita. This might be where Wilson and John's military expertise comes in useful. We can send them out to scout the lay of the land whilst you and I hang back in a support position".

Mick suggested that all and sundry take the evening to consider the proposed agenda, sleep on it and return in the morning to round out any items which might require tweaking before putting together a concrete plan of action.

As they were leaving the room Wilson tapped Mick on the shoulder and said "A word in your ear, please Mick".

"There's no use going on at me about topping people" Mick said "I'm totally against it and I won't even consider it unless one of us is in imminent danger of death".

"That's not what I wanted to say" Wilson interjected "Though I have to repeat, I think you're not thinking the thing through with that attitude. No, what I wanted to say was that it's about time you did something about you and Anita".

"What are you talking about?" demanded Mick

"what about Anita and me? There's nothing going on between me and Anita. Don't apply your own low standards to me and even more important don't sully a great friendship with your smutty thoughts"

"Ah c'mon Mick. You know as well as I do that you have the hots for her and nobody could blame you for it, she is, after all, a very beautiful girl. By the same token I've seen her looking at you when your attention is elsewhere and I can tell you, and I have a lot of experience in these things, that she fancies you too.

"Look" Mick said "I admit I like and admire Anita and maybe more than like and admire her, but it's just ridiculous to suggest that she fancies me. I don't have anything to offer a gorgeous girl like Anita".

"Nothing to offer! That's total bullshit and you know it. You are the smartest person I know, you've access to more money than God and you have mastered the secret of time travel. And added to all that you're young and not bad looking. What more could any young girl want?"

"But she's never shown any indication that she fancies me". Whined Mick.

"A girl's got her pride after all Mick. It's your place to make a move. I'm telling you she is waiting for you to go first, but she won't be around forever".

Mick decided that faint heart never having won fair lady that he would invite Anita out for a date.

Never one to allow his ideas to cool off by overthinking them He went to Anita's room and tapped on the door.

"Come in" Said Anita.

"Is it possible" thought Mick "that a short phrase like 'Come in' could sound so sweet in anyone's mouth other than Anita's?. This girl has totally enthralled me since I met her, I've never felt like this before in my whole life".

He entered the room, which in her short stay she had made her own and stamped her personality on and said

"Anita, I'd very much like to take you out to dinner. We've been so busy thrashing around, up and down the timelines that we haven't had time for a normal conversation. I'd love to get to know you better, what do you say?"

"I'd like that very much" She replied, with a look which melted his already half melted heart "When had you in mind?"

"No time like the present" replied Mick "How about tonight. The head chef in Chapter One is a personal friend of mine and he'll find us a table, I'm sure".

"You'll need to give me an hour to get ready" Anita told him smiling enchantingly "But Chapter One sounds very nice. Mind you McDonalds would be a treat for me. It doesn't exist in my time, apparently they offended Mick O' at some point and he had them all closed down".

Mick floated downstairs and rang Ross Lewis in his restaurant "Ross" He pleaded "You've just got to find me a table for two for tonight. I know its short notice but I've met this girl and the only restaurant I could dream of bringing her to is your place".

"My God Mick" Ross replied "Is it possible that my favourite Irish bachelor is smitten? The place it booked to capacity but the chef's table in the kitchen is free. Would that suit the case?"

"Absolutely ideal" Said Mick "But you need to promise to keep your distance. I know what you're like with the ladies and I don't need the competition tonight. This is important to me".

The splendid meal which they enjoyed that evening was utterly lost on both diners, so wrapped up were they in each other. If Mick had asked Mick in later times what he had eaten he could not have reliably answered. He could, however describe in minutest detail how Anita looked and sounded throughout the evening.

After dinner having floated up the steps, on a cloud of delight, from the basement restaurant in the fine Georgian house in Parnell Square, Mick suggested a stroll around his beloved Dublin City. Anita readily agree and the pair set out on a Dublin Saunter.

The remainder of that evening is in no way germane to the progress of this story and so a decent veil will be drawn over it. Suffice to say that a bond was formed that night which endured throughout two long and eventful lives.

Next day it was business as usual with the exception of Wilson's heavy handed comments on the star struck nature of the lovers.

"Enough of this guff" said Mick "We have serious business to do. Has anybody anything to add to the agenda we discussed yesterday? No? OK, we'll go on that so. I think it would be too dangerous for us to pop up in Ireland in 2050. That's Mick O's heartland and presumably his stronghold. I think France would be a better bet. The French are the most chauvinistic people on earth and will resist Mick O's influence more than most. Britain will go where the money is and you can bet that Mick O' has a firm grip on that commodity. Germany has a long history of love affairs with strong leaders and Mick O' certainly fits that bill, so, is it France?"

The others having agreed with Mick's assessment and proposal they set about arranging their adventure.

Chapter Thirty Three

Back to the Future - Again!

At four o'clock on a stormy November morning in the year 2050, with the familiar soft thunderclap the Travellator emerged on the Avenue Foch, in the neighbourhood of the Arc De Triomphe. A small group of revelers who had dined and drunk well, if not wisely were startled when it appeared as if from nowhere.

"D'où cela vient-il? (Where did that come from?) Said one member of the group, less inebriated than his companions.

"Je n'ai pas vu quoi que Ce soit" (I didn't see anything)" Said his less sober companion and shrugging in inimitable Gallic fashion they proceeded on their way.

"Hey Mick" Wilson teased

"You're getting to be the right risk taker, aren't you? Not so long ago you would have gone a thousand miles out of your way to avoid notice like that and tonight you land smack in the middle of a major city".

"I figured that anyone about on a night like this would not be in a position to comment on our sudden arrival, even if they had seen us. It was a calculated risk and it seems to have paid off". Mick had found a new urgency in his quest to deflect Mick O' from world domination since the development of his relationship with Anita.

"We can't use computers to suss out information

in this timeline. There's no way to be sure that Daneel hasn't got his tentacles into the French public library system. So if Wilson and John will go to the National Gendarmerie barracks on the rue St Didier in the XVI° district and find a local bar, with a bit of circumspection they should be able to pick up some military gossip. That's where the Special Forces guys hang out. Bring two of the translator phones with you, but for God's sake, be careful. You don't want to get banged up in a French prison, it's not good for your health".

"Anita and I will go to the BIBLIOTHEQUE PUBLIQUE D'INFORMATION and look up their newspaper archive. Between the lot of us we should get a handle on the stuff we need. You guys see if there's any talk about Mick O' and we'll look for stuff on energy sources. We'll meet at the camp ground this evening for dinner".

Wilson and John found themselves in a dingy cafe bar in the rue St Didier having a Parisian soldier's breakfast of petit pain and absinthe. They fell into conversation with a grizzled old ex-serviceman named Jacques who sat down, uninvited, at their table.

"You guys are not from around here" He said in somewhat garbled but recognisable English. "I'd say that you're from Ireland if I had to make a guess. Am I correct?"

"What's it to you?" Demanded Wilson, always a bit cranky in the early morning, especially when sleep deprived.

John hastened to pour oil on waters which could

easily become troubled. "Hey Wilson, there's no need to be rude, the man's only making conversation". And turning to Jacques he said, in rapid French "You've a good ear for an accent friend. You have the sounds of the Languedoc about you, yourself, though I'd imagine it's a long time since you've been back there".

The old soldier laughed and complimented John on his excellent colloquial French. "You talk French like a Parisian born" He said. "Yes, I've been all round the world in the French Foreign Legion. I've served in Embassies and hovels in all the continents and seen my share of action too. The Languedoc is quite beautiful but a little too genteel for an old squaddie like me".

"How are things in Dublin" He queried "I was on duty there in 2035 for two years and it was a wild place then".

"We wouldn't know" Said John "We've been doing a bit of travelling ourselves this past few years and I wouldn't be surprised if you know more about the current state of affairs back home than we do".

"I'd guess that there's reasons why you haven't been home for a while" Jacques twitted John

"The place might be a little bit too hot for you, hey? It's a very different place from what it used to be since they closed the borders in 2046. They've become very parochial and insular with all their great wealth. They're also afraid of their neighbours and they might have reason for their paranoia. There's many a regime in Europe that looks with envious eyes at the Great Irish Resurgence, as it's called in the newspapers. That man

Michael O'Reilly seems to be an economic marvel. Unfortunately we also hear disturbing rumours of repression of dissent, worthy of Josef Stalin at his worst and that the state has become entirely totalitarian. The story also goes that they have an international network of spies and informers in every major city and state.

There's even talk that the Irish are considering territorial expansion. That wouldn't be popular with their older, more established neighbours. I think a lot of it is bullshit, myself. But you never know, do you?"

"Listen" Wilson said "We'd like to invite you to lunch, we're very interested in what you've told us so far and we'd like to hear more. You choose the restaurant and we'll pay".

Jacques gladly accepted and the remainder of the day was spent in a grand round of bar hopping through the many soldiers dives of Paris.

Mick meanwhile was finding it difficult to keep his focus on the task at hand. Here he was, in Paris, the romance capital of the world with the most beautiful girl in the world. More remarkably she seemed to be as fascinated with him as he was with her. Consequently a great deal of time was lost as they explored Paris and each other's likes, dislikes and past histories.

Finally they found themselves standing outside the BIBLIOTHEQUE PUBLIQUE D'INFORMATION and Anita said "We'd best get on with our quest, hadn't we?"

Mick reluctantly agreed and with typical single mindedness immediately set about researching energy sources, using only hard copy sources as to use computers might bring them to the notice of Daneel or his successor digital entities.

After several hours of research they had come to the conclusion that the introduction of cold fusion was as far from a viable solution as it had been back in the twentieth century. It remained the holy grail of energy sources and as mythical as that iconic vessel was.

Cheap hydrogen production was a very viable option and required only abundant energy and water for its successful production. The trick, of course was to use hydrogen, once produced, to continue to produce more of itself by cracking it from water. The initial investment in hydrogen production was of such an order that no private enterprise could amass the seed capital required and so it fell to national governments to prime the pump, so to say. There were only two sources for this energy, electrical and solar. Nuclear energy by 2050 was so denigrated that it was, except in rare cases, totally decommissioned, having been demonstrated to be utterly cost inefficient, especially when waste management costs were factored in.

As their research progressed it emerged that the world leader in hydrogen production was located in the Somali desert on the coast of the Indian Ocean. Here a visionary scientist named Wolfgang Schroder has built a massive solar furnace capable of generating temperatures in excess of 1000^0 Celsius. Using this massive energy capacity, the production of plentiful hydrogen proved to be relatively simple, safe, environmentally neutral and, most importantly, extremely cheap. Further research revealed, not too surprisingly, that much of the initial capital for this project had been provided by an Irish millionaire in the early twentieth century, one Michael O'Reilly by name.

Mick was greatly excited by this information but Anita was significantly cooler about it. "I don't see how it advances our cause Mick" She said "In fact it looks like Mick O' happened on this discovery before we came on the scene and had a grip on it well in advance of his elevation to High King of Ireland".

"I don't think so" Mick replied "In fact I think we are probably the spark that started this project in the first place. Don't you see, if we can get Professor Wolfgang and Mick O' together in base timeline and if we can provide a large donation to the Prof, he could produce a working model of his solar furnace? With such a model he could, and probably did, convince Mick O' to back his full scale production facility. With a bit of luck and careful planning we should be able to steer Mick O' away from his grandiose plans for world domination and at the same time raise the gross national product of both Somalia and Ireland".

"It's like I say, we only need to untangle one thread and the effects are multiplied out of all proportion".

Later that evening at a campsite on the Bois de Boulogne, near Paris both parties sat down to compare notes.

"It's bloody cold in here" Said Wilson "We've been traipsing around all day in the fog and rain and I, for one, would appreciate a bit of heat".

"No problem" Said Mick "I'll need to start the engine, but as its hydrogen driven it's neither noisy nor an environmental pollutant, so it won't offend our neighbours"

"So, how did you guys get on? I notice you didn't stint yourselves on the Vin Ordinaire at any rate".

"We didn't drink so much" Said John "But we had to stay in character so a couple of glasses were essential. You seem to be dead on the button regarding things in Dublin. Mick O' has the country in a grip of iron and rumour has it that he has even larger ambitions. The 'Great' powers are not too pleased about this but, apparently, there's not a lot they can do about it. Frank seems to be a regular Machiavelli in international affairs, he's managed to pit them all against one another so each one is terrified that the other will gain an advantage. The end result is that they are tripping over themselves trying to stay in Ireland's good books".

"Meanwhile, we'd be well advised to keep our guard up whilst in this timeline. Apparently they have spies and informers everywhere. We shouldn't get too cosy or feel too secure, even here".

"Well" Mick said "Anita and me have sussed out a potential approach to the question of how to tilt Mick O' off his 'Ruler of the Universe' kick. It seems that hydrogen fuel is widely available in this timeline and that Mick, himself, is behind the largest producer. If we can persuade him to get into that before he's promoted to King of the World status he may be persuaded to devote his energies to good ends rather than evil ones. Furthermore if hydrogen energy is produced by an Irish entity that in itself might drag us out of the depression we find ourselves in without the necessity for his intervention in the governance of Ireland".

Just then the Travellator was lit up from outside by a glaring light, front and back. An amplified voice blared out:

"You in the Winnebago. Come out with your hands raised. We have you surrounded. Resistance is futile".

John twitched the curtain aside and peered out. "It looks like the Gendarmerie have arrived" He said "There seems to be hundreds of them out there, all armed and looking pretty fierce in their riot gear".

"I'm not totally surprised" Mick seemed to be very calm, considering this new development. "I guess Frank has pull with officialdom in France and somehow we've given ourselves away. I wouldn't be surprised if someone picked up on you guys in the rue St Didier. It probably wasn't wise of me to send you there".

Chapter Thirty Four

The Art of Successful Negotiation

Mick switched on the external speakers which he had built into the Travellator and speaking through his Android translator phone he said:

"I would like to speak to the commanding officer please". At the same time gesturing to the others to leave the talking to him.

"My name is Commandant Mathurin Cordier" Boomed a voice over the loudspeaker "Surrender and come out with your hands on your heads".

"Good evening Commandant" Said Mick in his most civil tones "Why don't you come, alone and unarmed, in here and we'll discuss this over a glass of good wine, like civilised people? If you like we'll send some wine out to your troops whilst we talk. I'm sure they'd like that. It's very cold and windy out there".

Cordier turned to his second in command "What the bloody hell is going on here. We were told that these are dangerous terrorists. I've never heard of terrorists inviting the military for a drink during a siege situation, have you?"

His subordinate shrugged in typical Gallic fashion and replied "Non mon Commandant. It's not your typical desperado behaviour. Do you want me to put a couple of rounds through the door, just to get their attention, you know?"

Returning to his loudspeaker Cordier broadcast "You must know that such a proposal is impossible. We are the Gendarmerie. We do not sit down with suspected terrorists, drink wine and discuss things. That's not how this goes. You need to come out here, with your hands on your heads and surrender to the lawful authority".

"Listen" Mick answered "I can understand that you might be reluctant to come into an unfamiliar place, alone and unarmed, but we don't have enough space in here to entertain all the guys you've brought here tonight.

Tell you what. Why don't you bring your second in command with you and if you'll keep your pistols holstered we'll overlook the unarmed bit. To sweeten the pot I'll deposit one million Euros in gold outside the door as an earnest of our good faith. Feel free to examine it before you come in, if you like, but you have to promise to give it back if you leave. Is it a deal?"

"This is, without doubt, the most bizarre thing I've ever been involved in" Cordier said to his subordinate. I'm going to accept their invitation. You stay here and if I don't come out in fifteen minutes you can storm the truck. If I haven't convinced them to surrender in that time I'll create a diversion to allow you a window of opportunity".

The second in command was horrified. "But sir, you can't just hand yourself over to these people. They're terrorists. We have it on the highest authority from Dublin that they've been involved in all sorts of villainy in Ireland and elsewhere. What will I tell the General if this goes badly wrong?"

"I'm doing this on my own responsibility" Said

Cordier "Whatever else they are, these are not common terrorists. There's something else going on here that isn't obvious to us. Furthermore news out of Ireland is very suspect these days. I'm more inclined to think that the Irish government are the most likely terrorists around. Remember - fifteen minutes and then do the business like we've been training to".

A moment later Cordier entered the Travellator and confronted the alleged terrorists.

"I see you've come unarmed" said Mick, gesturing to Wilson to open a bottle of Vin de Pays d'Oc from the Languedoc region which he had laid on for the occasion "And you didn't ask for the gold, that's very civil. Can I ask you why you've come after us, mob handed, like this? As far as I know we've done nothing to deserve such treatment. We're peaceful tourists just here on a visit to the City of Light. Why all the guns and lights?"

"We've received some disturbing reports from external sources" Said Cordier "And upon investigation we cannot find any record of your arrival in France. That's not a big deal normally, given our open borders, but together with other information given to us we chose the path of valour over discretion".

"This wine is excellent" He continued "But time is short. You have exactly twelve minutes to tell me what's going on here before my men storm the truck. If that happens it won't be good for you".

Mick took it upon himself to explain their presence in Paris.

"I've no doubt that your information comes from

official sources in Dublin" He said "I've even less doubt that you are well aware that the Irish government is on a par with the Nazi regime in the middle of the last century. The French, more than most people, should know that such people are not to be trusted. I give you my word of honour that we are dedicated to solely peaceful initiatives in our quest to overturn the totalitarian cohort who currently reign in Ireland".

"Now I'll tell you what I'd like you to do for me" He continued "We'd like to leave this place and depart from France, quietly and without fuss. I am obliged to inform you that your men will not succeed in storming this vehicle. It is clad in armour which is impervious to anything short of your most powerful explosives, which I am sure you do not have ready access to and it is capable of quite extraordinary speed. Furthermore it drives on hydrogen, a highly explosive gas itself, if by some unlikely circumstance you did pierce the skin of the truck, the resultant explosion would probably take out a half city block along with most of your troops".

"I propose that you withdraw your troops to a distance of about three hundred metres and allow us to go, peacefully, on our way". Mick finished with a straight face.

The Commandant had listened to this farrago of nonsense with increasing incredulity. "What you ask is utterly impossible" He bellowed "Surrender immediately and things will go easy for you, any further resistance is futile. Now, I must return to my men, your time is up. I am reluctant to harm you, you seem to be good folks but whatever happens next is on your own heads".

Cordier pulled open the door and strode towards his command post, as he walked he heard a soft sound like a muted clap of thunder from behind him, and felt a breeze ruffle the back of his neck.

Turning around he was astonished to see that the Travellator was gone.

"What happened" He demanded "Where's the truck gone?"

His second in command was equally astonished "I don't know. One second it was there and the next it was gone. It just disappeared, I wouldn't believe it except I saw it with my own eyes".

"How in the name of all that's holy will I explain this to the General" Pleaded the unfortunate Commandant.

Meanwhile, back in 2012 on the Bois De Boulogne Mick and the others were convulsed with laughter.

"I'd dearly love to see his face" Wilson crowed, wiping tears of laughter from his eyes "He seemed like a nice enough guy but he was a pompous ass, wasn't he".

Mick quickly put an end to the merriment.

"We need to get to this Professor Wolfgang Schroder as soon as possible". He was looking pensive

"It's not outside the bounds of possibility that Mick O' could send someone else back in time to waylay us and an obvious place to find us would be in the vicinity of the said Wolfgang. He won't have overlooked the possibility that we will be following leads to future technologies and he might easily have targeted the hydrogen project as a likely mark".

A quick search through the University records found eleven postgraduate students in various colleges throughout Europe. Further sifting left only three working in the field of theoretical physics with a particular interest in alternative energies. This left Mick with the task of identifying the specific individual concerned by means of a test of their abilities.

Shortly afterwards an advertisement appeared in several Physics journals as follows:

Bursary

Postgraduate Studies in Physics

With particular concentration on

Alternative Energy Sources

Contact Dean Of Studies

For Further Information.

"That should draw them out" Said Mick, and indeed it did.

All three of those identified on the short list of possibilities appeared in the group seeking the bursary and after interviewing all three Mick and Anita decided on their candidate, a gangly young man from Westphalia in Germany.

They took the young man to dinner and quizzed him on his interest and ambitions. As expected he professed a desire to advance the use of hydrogen as a safe, economical and widespread fuel to replace fossil fuels.

"OK" Mick said "We have a particular interest in the production of hydrogen fuels. What we'd like you to do is to design and construct a small scale model of an efficient and economical method doing this. We have an individual who would be very interested in this technology and if we can convince him of its viability we can persuade him to fund full scale manufacture. We are satisfied that you can accomplish this and we are prepared to pay for the small scale modelling phase. I have an engineering background and I'm also prepared to provide technical assistance if needed".

Needless to say, Wolfgang was more than delighted to accept this generous offer and the bursary in the Physics Department of the University of Heidelberg, where he spent the following two years perfecting the theory and design of his small scale prototype Solar Furnace, maintaining close contact with Mick throughout.

Chapter Thirty Five

Within the Hiatus

Leaving Wolfgang to his labours and with no immediate necessity for any further action Mick asked Anita to marry him. "Oh Mick" She cried, throwing her arms around his neck "I'd love to marry you, but with all this Mick O' stuff going on is this the right time?"

"No better time than now" Replied Mick "Wolfgang is busy with the solar furnace project, that'll take a couple of years, and we've neutralised Mick O's troops for the present moment. Things will get hotter later on, but we have a bit of a hiatus at present. So what do you think?"

"Mick, you impetuous fool, let's do it"

Wilson and John were delighted at the news and some three months later the happy couple married in St Francis Xavier Church in Gardiner Street. At Anita's request Mick had taken the Travellator forward to her own timeline and collected her collaborators on the time travel project which had brought herself and Mick together and they celebrated her glorious day as one big happy family.

The honeymoon was spent in the Travellator, time jumping from one momentous occasion in history to another and to all the romantic scenes which are to be found in literature, both old and new.

When after some time, they returned to the Drumcondra house they found that Wilson and John had moved out and bought a house of their own in Portmarnock. It emerged in conversation that John was an enthusiastic surfer and Portmarnock suited him perfectly. Wilson spent most of his time ogling the long legged, bikini clad lovelies playing volleyball on the long strip of golden sand under his bedroom window.

Mick called a meeting of the group and said

"If we're going to split up we need a means of sending a signal if any of Mick O's goons show up. It needs to be quick and simple. The best thing would be to have a one word signal permanently programmed into our mobile phones so that at the first sign of trouble we could send off a text". The word chosen was 'Trouble'. Mick commented that he would sleep sounder after initiating this SOS system.

One morning at breakfast Mick opened his mail and found one from his sister. "That's odd" He said "We don't get along very well and it's unlike her to get in touch with me. Let's see" Opening and scanning the letter he snorted in exasperation.

"What's up Mick/" Queried Anita.

"The blasted cheek of this witch" Snarled Mick "It seems her gormless dope of a husband has injured himself rock climbing in the Himalayas and she has to go and ferry his fool arse home. That's not the worst bit. She wants me to look after her Daughter Gráinne and a couple of friends for a week until she gets back. I don't hear from her from one end of the year to the other and now she wants to dump a gang of ankle biters on me without warning!"

"Take it easy, it's not that big of a deal. How old are these ankle biters anyway" Anita had never seen Mick so thrown off balance before.

"I'm nearly sure I sent Gráinne a birthday present earlier in the year, about fourteen or fifteen maybe? I'm not sure. What do I know about teenage girls? There must be someone else she can dump them on".

"Oh don't be such a grumpy old curmudgeon, fourteen or fifteen is hardly ankle biter age" Said Anita "It'll be fun. We can bring them to the Zoo and I'm sure they will be interested in the new movie that I see advertised 'Madagascar 3'. It's only for a week, after all".

Just then the infamous doorbell sounded its raucous call "Godammit" said Mick "I meant to get that bloody thing fixed" and he headed out to open the front door.

"Oh Mick, you don't know what this means to me. I've been at my wits end trying to figure out what to do. You're my last hope" His sister Penny stood on the doorstep with three teenage girls behind her.

"Penny" Gasped Mick "I didn't expect you so soon".

Anita came forward and brushing Mick aside she graciously drew Penny and the three girls inside. "Hi, I'm Anita, Mick's wife. You'll be Penny and who are these young ladies?"

"Yes, I'm Penny" She replied, giving Anita a perfunctory hug. "This is my daughter Gráinne and her friends Tanya and Clara. You don't know how grateful I am for you keeping them for a few days. I've been out of my mind trying to sort them out. I must be in London tonight to catch the weekly flight to Nepal. I'll kill that muppet husband of mine when I get there. I told him repeatedly that a man of his age and state of health shouldn't engage in dangerous sports. Oh well, I'll be off. Have you got your bags, girls? That's OK then, see you next week. Thanks again". And with that she was gone.

"That was a bit strange" Anita whispered to Mick as the girls were getting settled in. "Is she always like that?"

"Yeah, she's a big business woman with interests in several high powered companies and she is in a constant state of rush. I'm not surprised that her husband is off in some God forsaken part of the world. If I was married to her, I'd be somewhere far away from her too. Mind you, when you get her on a good day, she's the nicest person on Earth".

Sometime later in the day Anita asked the girls what they'd like to do during their week. Gráinne, well used to being dumped on various relatives and friends, had a full programme of events planned out.

Mick was somewhat dubious about some of the items on the list. He was pretty sure that Copper Faced Jacks was an unsuitable venue for sixteen year old girls, so he vetoed that. The movie 'Fun Size' seemed to be an eminently suitable entertainment. What harm can a Halloween movie do after all?

Later in the week Mick treated them all to a dinner in, of all places, Chapter one. Mick had pressured his buddy Ross, the head chef, to reserve the Chef's Table for them. This table is located in the kitchen itself and the whole process of cooking and serving gourmet food is displayed in front of the diner's eyes. The restaurant is located in the Basement of the Writer's Museum in Parnell Square and as the girls were all into creative writing, in fact Clara is a school librarian, the evening promised to be interesting.

On the way home in the Mustang Gráinne said "That was pretty cool. Ross is a real nice man and those other chefs! Wow. The pace of that kitchen was really something. They must be wrecked after serving all those people".

"I wouldn't like to be stuck with the washing up" Said Tanya "Did you ever see so many dishes in your life?"

As they turned into the drive of Mick's house they felt a rending crash and the car was thrust sideways against the gatepost.

As they struggled out of the car, Mick sent the 'Trouble' text and was delighted to hear Anita's phone ring her message tone.

Anita emerged from the car, ignoring her phone, and checked to see that the girls were OK. Turning around she was startled to see three men clad in dark clothing and wearing black knitted hats jumping out of the car which had rammed them and rushing towards them.

"Just take it easy lady" Said the lead man "If you do what I say, nobody gets hurt. Any resistance will bring on a world of hurt".

"Oh, God" Anita gasped "Its Mick O's goons" And she grabbed her phone to send the signal, not realising that Mick had already done so.

"I'll take that" Said one of the goons and snatched the phone out of her hand "We wouldn't want you to be calling anybody, now, would we?"

Chapter Thirty Six

Pesky Ankle Biters

Tanya meanwhile was whispering to the other girls "OK, this is what the kick boxing classes were all about. Are you guys up for it?"

Grainne and Clara nodded enthusiastically and without further delay they attacked the goons whilst screaming like demented banshees. The astounded goons turned to face this totally unexpected assault and were met by a barrage of punches and kicks. The lead goon fell to the ground with a fractured ankle whilst the other two turned and fled with massive bruising to their arms and torsos.

Mick had taken advantage of the diversion to retrieve his Colt 45 from behind the front seat of the car and persuaded the groaning lead goon to crawl into the house.

Turning to the barely dishevelled girls he said

"My God girls, that was awesome. Where did you learn stuff like that?"

"We're enrolled in a dojo in Killester" Said Gráinne with a totally innocent smirk "We do Taekwondo, Ju Jitsu, and other martial arts but mostly kick boxing. A girl's got to be able to look after herself in the big bad world hasn't she?"

"It was incredibly brave of you" Said Anita "But what if they'd been armed? You might have been hurt, or even worse".

"No fear of that" Clara replied "We're trained in all the techniques for disarming attackers and disabling them whilst waiting for assistance. We were in no danger. In fact it's been a great opportunity to put our training to the test".

"Well you certainly passed that test with flying colours" Anita observed.

At that moment another car barrelled up the road and screeched to a halt outside the house. Wilson and John scrambled out and amidst a welter of questions and explanations they all entered the house and found Mick questioning the head goon.

"Hello Pete" John said to the goon "You've been sent back to snatch Mick too? It won't work. Our Mick is a wily character and it's difficult to catch him napping".

"It wasn't Mick" Said Pete, his professional pride piqued "We weren't told that he'd have three ninja banshee bodyguards protecting him. Please don't let them near me".

"We thought you must be dead when you didn't report back" Pete said to John with deep reproach

"I never thought you'd betray your country and our Leader. How could you?"

"It's a long story that started before I ever met you. I've been convinced for many years that Mick O' is well out of line and needs to be sorted out. Mick here has a plan which we hope will address the issue without bloodshed".

Sometime later, having bound up Pete's ankle and ascertained that the other two goons were hired muscle who would not pose any problems. Wilson and John placed him in the panic room for safe keeping whilst they figured out a method for dealing with him and the girls finally got talking to Mick and Anita about their experiences.

"What's all this stuff about time travel, Uncle Mick?" Queried Gráinne.

"Time travel" Blustered Mick "You must have misheard. Nobody was talking about time travel". He was a very unconvincing liar when confronted directly.

"Ah, Mr Brennan" Pleaded Tanya "Don't treat us like babies. I think we've demonstrated conclusively that we're well informed and clued up people. We certainly heard what we heard and it included references to time travel. So stop waffling and give with the goods".

"Call me Mick, please" Mick said distractedly. "You girls have stumbled on something very secret and very, very dangerous. I have developed a safe and reliable method of time travel. Now you might think that that's a good thing, and in some ways it is. On the other hand time travel in the wrong hands could be catastrophic. I really need a total commitment from you guys that never, under any circumstances, will you tell anybody about this. Can I rely on you for this?"

"You mean nobody?" Queried Clara "Does that include our parents?"

"Them and everybody else" Said Mick sternly.

"OK, but there's a quid pro quo" Gráinne was grinning all over her face as she spoke.

"What do you mean, quid pro quo?" Demanded Mick "This isn't a game, you know. It's deadly serious".

"Ah, Uncle Mick, will you lighten up. We'd just love to head off on a time travel adventure to see the past. We'll keep quiet about the time travel anyway because if we talked about it everybody would think we're nuts. They'd probably put us into a home for the bewildered or something".

Mick looked to Anita for support but found to his astonishment that she supported the girls.

"Why not Mick, it can hardly make things any worse. They already know about the thing anyway and they certainly deserve a treat after saving our butts last night".

"Oh my God" Moaned Mick "I'm in the clutches of the monstrous regiment of women. OK, but you need to do exactly what I tell you and its only one trip. Also I can't stress enough the absolute need for you to keep your mouths shut about this. If you study physics and are good at it, I'll let you join me when you finish college, but until then remember - A shut Mouth Gathers No Flies!"

The girls agreed and having expressed an interest in seeing Elvis Presley live Mick promised an experience not to be missed.

"First off we need to get rid of Pete" Mick declared

"He's not really a bad guy" Said John "He's been

blinded by Mick O' and Frank. They've been preaching their own brand of rubbish since he was a kid and he doesn't know any better. We should cut him some slack if we can".

"OK, what we'll do is bring him back to somewhere safe and isolated in 2050 and go from there back to see Elvis. That way we can kill two birds with one stone"

Wilson cast his eyes up to heaven in despair at Mick's magnanimity.

Having deposited Pete on the plinth of the Phoenix Monument in the park at an early hour of the morning Mick and Anita with the three girls travelled back to the end of July 1954. Mick had slipped back earlier and procured tickets for a Slim Whitman concert at the Overton Shell in Memphis at which Elvis and two buddies were making their first concert performance in support of Slim. Elvis was, at that time, completely unknown and was so nervous and caught up in the rhythm of the music that his legs started shaking, his wide cut pants emphasising his movements. The young girls in the audience, including Gráinne, Tanya and Clara, went wild screaming and stamping their feet.

When, at last the concert ended Mick brought the girls back stage where they met the pop icon as a young performer just on the cusp of his meteoric career.

Afterwards on the way home Clara piped up from the back seat

"Mick, did you mean it when you said we could work with you after college?"

"Of course he did" Anita retorted, "Mick never jokes about his work. He's the most single minded person in the world and nothing would prompt him to treat his work lightly".

"OK then. I'll take him up on that offer. I've never had as much fun as we've had in this past week and I can't wait to come back again".

Gráinne and Tanya enthusiastically agreed and also promised to come back again.

At the end of the week a large black limousine drew up outside the house and Penny jumped out. As she entered the house with a distracted nod at Anita, who had opened the door she called out "Gráinne, your father is waiting in the car outside, he can't walk very well so will you and the other girls please get your gear together and come down immediately".

Giving Mick a cursory hug, she turned to Anita she said

"Thanks for the help, I really was at my wit's end. Congratulations on your wedding, by the way, sorry I missed it. Busy with work, you understand I'm sure".

Gathering up the girls she hustled them, waving frantically, into the limo and sped off.

"Dear God but that woman is a dragon" Mick sighed theatrically mopping his brow. "I guess she means well but she's hard on the nerves. The girls were good fun to have around though. We'll ask them back again won't we?"

Going back inside the house Anita said "Well now

that that's all over I think we need to focus on doing something about Mick O'. This business of a bunch of heavies turning up on an irregular basis trying to kidnap us is getting old and tired. We need to speed up the agenda"

Chapter Thirty Seven

Dealing with Adversity

Mick called his group together for a conference.

"We need to deal decisively with this Mick O'
thing" He said. "I reckon Wolfgang has another year to go
before he's ready to demonstrate his hydrogen harvesting
technique. Given the tendency for Mick O's troops to turn
up at odd times, out of the blue, I don't think we can risk
waiting for as long as that. I propose that we jump
forward thirteen months and check in on Wolfie. If he's
ready then we'll set up a meet with the glorious leader and
pitch the alternative energy plan to him. If we can hook
him on that, it may divert him from being drawn into the
domination of the world gig. How does that strike you
guys?"

"That sounds good" Wilson interjected "But how
do we get to Mick O'? He must be plagued with people
banging on his door trying to interest him in any number
of cockamamie schemes. He'll have us unceremoniously
kicked down the stairs if we just turn up offering him vast
wealth and global influence. I know that that's a gift horse
I'd be giving an intensive dental examination to, myself,
in his place".

"You're not going to like this bit" Mick said.
"We'll bring Frank into the loop. He's an avid rugby fan
and if he doesn't already know Mick O', getting
acquainted with him, shouldn't present any
insurmountable obstacles. There'll be plenty of
opportunities at the after match knees ups and other social

occasions. Once he's gotten himself into the glorious etc's circle of friends he can broach the project and get us an appointment to demonstrate the HHT (Hydrogen Harvesting Technique)".

"You know as well as I do that if Frank is involved I think we will finish up on the sticky end of the greasy pole" Wilson waxed vehement "But I can't think of any better suggestion so let's get on with it".

Further up the timeline Mick met an excited Wolfgang.

"Mick, I'm glad to see you. I've got two wonderful pieces of news for you".

Oh dear" Mick thought. In his experience unexpected good news tended to be a mixed blessing at best.

"OK first tell me, is the demo ready?"

"Yes it is and it works perfectly and I've also been talking to a potential backer for the full scale production facility. He's very anxious to meet you to discuss terms so that he can start immediately".

"Wolfgang, are you out of your mind? You swore a confidentiality oath as part of your sponsorship deal with me. You know, or you should know that I hold all commercial rights on your work. Are you seriously telling me that you've be in touch with other interested parties without telling me? That is a breach of our agreement and a serious lapse in security on your part".

Wolfgang was utterly dismayed.

"I'm very sorry Mick, I thought I was doing a good thing. This guy seemed to be all right and as he claimed he knew you I assumed you had put him onto me. I'll cut off all contact with him and have nothing to do with him in future. I hope this won't interfere with our working relationship".

"It's not your fault" Mick was thinking rapidly "What's this person's name and how does he claim he knows me?"

"Hang on" Wolfgang was very eager to please. "I've got his business card here and his contact details". And after rummaging in the drawer of his desk he eventually produced a crumpled piece of pasteboard.

Straightening the card Mick was astonished and disturbed to see the name emblazoned on it Mr Frank McGuinness, Energy Consultant.

"Describe this man to me" He demanded of Wolfgang.

"He's about my age, very dark, curly hair. He looks to be fit and I also got the impression that he might have been armed. There was a suspicious bulge under his left armpit. Despite that he was very soft spoken and polite. He asked me to give his regards to you if you turned up and to let him know whenever you're in town".

"Goddam it" Mick snarled and turning to Anita and Wilson who had come with him he said "This is a set up. Frank must have sent another of his goons back to try and trap me. That description doesn't fit Frank himself. Maybe he's trying to send me a message. God knows how he cottoned onto Wolfgang, though I suppose an enquiry to the University authorities would give them sufficient pointers to enable them to suss it out. Thank God I didn't give Wolfgang advance notice of our visit today or we'd have been met with a welcoming committee".

"Wolfgang, we need to leave immediately. I'll be in touch with you in the next few days. In the meantime if Frank gets in touch don't tell him I've been here and keep him at arm's length about his proposed investment. Don't refuse to talk to him, just play it cool and whatever else you do, do not commit to anything. Get it?"

Once outside Mick said "We need to get away from here right now. This guy probably has Wolfgang under surveillance and he could arrive, mob handed, at any moment".

Without further discussion they hurried to the Mustang which was parked nearby. As Mick drove down towards the Motorway Wilson piped up from the backseat.

"I don't wish to worry anyone but I think that we're being followed by a black BMW with several passengers aboard. If you could manage to ditch them I think it might be a good idea".

"Right" said Mick, "It's time to get a bit proactive where these guys are concerned. I'm getting more than a little pissed off with all this harassment".

Wilson fervently agreed "Good on you Mick. I knew if they pushed you far enough you'd kick over the traces. Go get 'em tiger".

Diverting from his original destination Mick

turned off and drove to the car park at the foot of the cable car leading to the King's Chair, a forested high point very close to the old town in Heidelberg. The car park was almost deserted as it was the end of November and not many tourists wanted to brave the freezing conditions on the top of the hill. Happily they were just in time to catch a train, which was empty except for themselves, as it was about to leave the station. As the train set off to climb the hill the black BMW pulled in and Wilson derived immense satisfaction to see the occupants jump out waving their hands at the train driver, who either did not see them or chose to ignore them.

Mick meanwhile was on his mobile phone to John. "John they've turned up again as we thought they might. We need you at the top of the King's Chair as quickly as you can manage. Yes, if necessary use the helicopter. I know you don't have permission to land up there but do it and disable the bird and claim force majeure. Bring some troops with you and be prepared for some rough stuff. Whatever else you do, don't injure the leader, a guy called Frank McGuinness. He's an imposter but I suspect he may be high in Mick O's organisation. I particularly want a little conversation with this person".

"OK, we have the initiative here" Said Mick "Let's make good use of it. I'll wait at the upper station and you guys go hide in the trees. When John arrives with reinforcements, I want you to hold back till I see how this Frank fella plans to handle things. I'll give you and John time to quietly surround them and when I throw my mobile phone on the ground you guys move in and make certain sure that none of them escapes".

The train started downwards just as John's

helicopter fluttered down to a landing a little further up the hill.

Mick and Anita embraced and she whispered

"Be careful Mick, now I've found you I don't know how I'd cope if anything happened to you".

"No worries" Mick replied "In this case I'm sure we've got all the bases covered. John has a group of ex Special Forces men surrounding us and you'll be over there in the trees with Wilson. I'll be here at the station, apparently exposed. But we both know that the last thing they want is to harm me. They not only need to capture me, but they need me in an agreeable frame of mind. Otherwise they'll get no good out of me and if nobody else knows that Frank certainly does".

The motor on the cable car started and Mick said "OK doll, we're ready. You go with Wilson and we'll see about doing something decisive about these thugs".

As the car slowly ascended its tracks and prepared to enter the station Mick was surprised to see that it contained only one man. He emerged from the station with his hands held in the air and called out;

"Hello, you'll be Mick Brennan I'm sure. I'd like to talk to you about a very serious matter. I absolutely assure you that I'm unarmed and that I have no inimical intentions towards you".

"Stay where you are and talk then" There was something familiar about the young man but Mick was sure that they had never met.

"My name is Frank McGuinness". The young man

said "I realise that I'm not the Frank McGuinness you know but I'm Frank McGuinness just the same".

Chapter Thirty Eight

Strange Bedfellows

It dawned on Mick then "You're his son. I thought there was something familiar about you".

"Listen" Said Frank Jr. "This isn't the ideal place to have a discussion. Can I propose that we travel down and pick up your car and go someplace where we can talk in comfort? You needn't worry about the people I had in my car. I've sent them back to Frankfurt where I picked them up. I know from my father that you are a very careful man and I've no doubt you've taken security precautions. I suggest you bring some of your people down with us to ensure that the bottom station and car park is sterile. How does that sound?"

"Tell you what" Replied Mick "I'll go one better. I'll send my boys down in the helicopter and wait here for their all clear. Then we'll travel down in the car with some of my people".

Frank laughed and said "He said you were paranoid, but not how paranoid. Still it pays to be careful. I think that's a great idea. I've a flask of hot coffee in the station, why don't we have a sip while we're waiting?"

Mick, Anita, John and a couple of his Special Forces people climbed aboard the train with Frank in tow and started down. Mick was greatly relieved on reaching the car park to see that it was deserted and that the black BMW had gone. John dismissed the bodyguards and collecting Wilson they jumped into the Mustang with

Frank Jr. sandwiched between Wilson, who had hitched a lift in the helicopter, and Frank in the back seat.

Emerging onto the sparsely occupied ring road Mick took the first opportunity to shift timelines back to the year 2000. He had not been too picky as to the season chosen and they found themselves not in freezing conditions, but in blazing sunshine and 25 degree temperatures. The large container truck immediately behind them blasted his air horn in strident protest at their sudden appearance and, shaking his fist, overtook them gesturing wildly.

Frank Junior in the back seat was gazing around in open mouthed amazement.

"Did we just time shift" He asked

"Sure we did" Replied Wilson "You didn't think we'd stick around in a timeline where you knew when we were? We're not that thick".

"Look, I acknowledge that you've reason to be suspicious of me. My father has handled this business between us badly, sending guys back to snatch you. He realises that now. That's why I'm here. I guess that his man beside me is John Maher, formerly of the Irish National Guard. When he didn't report back we thought he was dead, either through some accidental happening or by extreme action on your part. When you delivered Jimmy back to his own timeline and we'd thoroughly debriefed him we realised that we'd gotten hold of the wrong end of the stick".

"We decided that we'd send someone back and attempt to negotiate with you in a civilised fashion. My dad volunteered for the job but, given your recent experience with him it was decided that he might not be the best emissary. I put my name forward and was accepted".

Frank Jr. continued as they drove to the ferry port and a voyage home to Ireland

"In my timeline there is growing unease about the style of government in Ireland and effectively throughout Europe. Mick O' and my father have been so unimaginably successful at everything they've set their hands to that they are, to all intents and purposes, rulers of the European Union, which they rejoined on very favourable terms in 2030, after impassioned pleas from the Germans and French after they had managed to make a total hames of the economy of the union.

"Not everybody is pleased about this state of affairs and the old adage about absolute power is raising its ugly head. My dad and Mick O' are really good guys but there are others in positions of power and influence who are quite prepared to subvert the good already achieved to their own ends. An enormous bureaucracy has grown up around them and they are buried beneath a massive mountain of responsibility, and demands on their time leave them no resources to deal with the imperfections of the system".

"At the same time, overseas, the Americans and the Russians, not to mention the Chinese are casting covetous eyes at the success of what has become known as 'The Irish Model'".

"As we speak there is evidence that a coup is

being plotted by members of Mick O's cabinet, supported by the CIA, the Russian secret service and, believe it or not, dissident Irish Republicans. The aim of this plot is to destabilise Mick O's government and take over the Irish state. This would be a disaster of unimaginable proportions. The Civil War in the 1920s would be a picnic by comparison and it's not impossible, given the delicate state of international politics that it could escalate into a full World War".

"We need desperately you to do something Mick". Frank Jr. said pleadingly.

With a jerk Mick pulled the car over to the roadside and stopped He turned to Frank Jr. and yelled

"Are you out of your freaking mind? Between the lot of you you've managed to drag the good name of Ireland into the mud, threaten the economic stability of Europe and bring the world to the brink of a war which might easily mean the extinction of the entire human species and you want me to 'DO SOMETHING'. What had you in mind? Even Superman would struggle with a conundrum like this and I assure you that I'm no Superman".

"I always said that Frank was an arrogant prick" Said Wilson "But this exceeds in scale even my low expectations of his character".

With a rare display of temper Anita interjected

"If you can't offer something constructive Wilson, you should keep your mouth shut. That sort of comment is of absolutely no help whatever in the present circumstances. Of course you can deal with this mess

Mick. In fact you're probably the only person on the planet who can. You have access to the entire spectrum of time from the Big Bang until the end of the Universe literally at your fingertips. All you need to do is construct a strategy and implement it. We've all seen you do this before, admittedly not on a comparable scale but I have faith in you".

"Bravo Anita" Cried John "With a woman like that behind you Mick, you can't fail. I'm with you".

"I'm sorry" Said Wilson "It's just that Frank senior seems to have gotten up my nose from day one. Of course I have total faith in you Mick. You've brought us through many scrapes and we've won out in the end. So, when do we start?"

"It's easy for you guys to talk. I've got to worry about the wellbeing of all the world, now and into the future. All things considered I think we should go ahead with my original idea. I'm sorry if this seems a bit off Frank, but given your antecedents we'll have to leave you out of the loop on this. It's just too sensitive to allow even the slightest element of risk.

I'll leave it up to you, do you want to go back to 2050 or would you like to sit out our response to the issue in relative comfort in the here and now?" Mick said apologetically.

"I can't go back to the future" Said Frank. I've been warned that my name is on a high level hit list compiled by the aforementioned spook services. I'm a marked man back there. I don't want to sit around on my butt in this timeline either. I'm convinced that I have a lot to offer you, if you can bring yourself to trust me. I get it that with my family connections I might be considered unreliable, all I can say is that our interests coincide here. You should remember the old adage 'My enemy's enemy is my friend'".

Chapter Thirty Nine

Meanwhile in 2050

"What is it now Frank?" Mick O' was sitting at his desk in his vast and impressive office atop the Presidential tower with its magnificent views of the Dublin mountains to one side and the broad vista of Dublin Bay, spread out in glorious sunshine to the other.

The tower was the hub of Mick O's burgeoning empire, now spread as far as the borders of Russia and reaching its tentacles into the African continent with strong footholds in Morocco, Tunisia and Libya.

Despite the passage of years, both men presented the appearance of strong healthy people in their mid-thirties, due to the use of nanotechnology which had been developed some twenty five years earlier.

Frank was, as usual, somewhat harried and upset.

"I haven't heard a peep from Frank Jr". He said "He was supposed to check in on a regular basis to update me on the progress of his trip back to try and contact Mick Brennan, but there has been no word since he first confirmed his safe arrival. I'm worried".

"Remind me again about the complicated system you set up for communications between you" Mick O' didn't really look as if he was deeply concerned. He had, after all, a fairly large slice of the planet to worry about and that was occupying a lot of his attention right then.

"He bought a computer first thing when he arrived

back in 2012 and found a secure, long term storage for it. It's still there all these years later. I check it out once a day, at the very least and he only left the one message on it for me to pick up on his first day back then. The system self-evidently works, but no messages since". Frank had explained all this to Mick O' when he'd sent Frank Jr. back, but Mick O' obviously hadn't been paying attention. In point of fact, Mick O's failure of attention was a source of concern to Frank. He felt that his commitment to important issues was flagging lately.

"I'm quite sure he's all right" Said Mick O' "You know Frank, I've been wondering lately if all this huffing and puffing is worth the effort. Don't you ever get the urge to just kick back and grab some rays on a deserted beach somewhere and let some other poor fool do all the worrying. I don't remember the last time I had a decent break, the Irish rugby team is a bunch of plonkers and couldn't kick their way out of a paper bag, ever since I quit the horse breeding thing I've lost interest in going to the races and my son Michael is doing a better job of managing the farm than I ever did. I really need a break".

Frank gazed at him in open mouthed horror

"Dear God Mick" He almost wept "don't even joke about such a thing. We have a serious situation here at home with a domestic underground movement, a possible coalition of foreign secret services coming at us from overseas and an upcoming fuel crisis following the destruction of the hydrogen production plant in the Horn of Africa. The last thing we need is for you to start navel gazing at this time".

"Navel gazing? What the hell do you mean, navel

gazing. I merely asked if you sometimes got tired of the constant demands for someone or something's immediate attention. Never mind, get on with your report. What's going on in the big bad world which requires my intense and focused concentration today?"

We've sussed out another underground cell of the insurgents, but on a worrisome note, they're armed with the most up to date weapons which must have been supplied by one of the governments or other. I suspect the Americans myself, but we'll probably never know. Our own gallant Presidential Guard went on a drink fuelled rampage in downtown Amsterdam last night and caused considerable damage to property and to the public also. The rank and file have been sentenced to fifteen years in the stockade but the officer in charge is your Cousin Joe's eldest son and Joe has put in a plea for clemency. This is a public relations mess. And it feeds right into the resistance agenda. How do you want to play it?"

"Joe can go and get stuffed. That son of his was trouble from the day he was born. I didn't want to sponsor him for the Guard but my aunt Winnie pleaded with me to give him a chance. Well she's gone to a better place now so the pressure is off. Send word to the Guard that he is to be treated exactly as any other soldier convicted of gross misconduct".

"I assume you ferreted out these insurgents by sending someone back in time to infiltrate them before they got too big for their boots?"

Mick O' was not normally deeply interested in the ins and outs of Frank's operations but today he was in a strange introspective mood.

"Yeah" Frank replied "But I'm getting a little uneasy about shooting people back into the past every time we hit a snag in our planning. Mick was always very adamant that if you weren't very careful that the law of unintended consequences would catch you by the hasp of the arse. We are all familiar with the concept of the 'butterfly flapping its wings in Brazil and causing a tornado in Texas'. I'm getting very dubious about the number of unpredictable, small, effects which our actions are causing which may ultimately have catastrophic consequences. I'll be much happier when we have cracked the two way time travel thing so that we can go forward and check out the results of our actions, so that we can modify them as necessary".

"My old mother used to say 'Piss in one hand and wish in the other and see which gets filled first" Mick O' suddenly snapped out of his unaccustomed mood and assumed his normal thrusting leadership mode.

"In other words wishing gets you nowhere. You need to get yourself focused, Mick Brennan can't be the only man in history to crack the secret of time travel. You're too set on getting him on board. The guys you have studying the problem are off the path. They're trying to find a result from our one way system and that's obviously a dead end. Mick Brennan was an uneducated tinkerer when he found his time travel device. It's as plain as the nose on your face that his route to the answer was an empirical one. He didn't know enough to be stuck in a cul de sac. He just kept trying different things until he lit on the right combination. That's the method you need to adopt and get rid of those eggheads with their inflated opinions and rigid notions".

"As far as the unintended blah de blah is concerned, we have an amazing tool at our hands to enable us to achieve our goals. My take on this is that we would be seriously negligent in our duties to our citizens if we failed to use all and every means at our disposal to make their lives better, safer and richer. I don't see that the consequences of our actions are bad, except for crusty republican groups, unwashed Russian ideologues, and smart arsed CIA types from across the water. The only drawback to us using time travel is that, for us, it's one way. Your focus should be concentrated exclusively on resolving that issue. I'll deal with the other matters".

As they were speaking the door was thrust open and five men, dressed in the uniform of the Presidential Guard, strode into the room.

"What is the meaning of this? Demanded Mick O' "Colonel Friedrich, don't you know I'm never to be interrupted by anybody when I'm in conference with Mr McGuinness. I hope you've got a good reason for this otherwise a very negative report will go to your superiors"

As he spoke Frank sidled behind the desk and towards the back wall of the office, putting as large amount of space between himself and Mick O' as possible.

Colonel Friedrich addressed Mick O' "Mr Michael O'Reilly I have been directed by the provisional council for the liberation of our oppressed peoples to place you and all your associates under arrest with immediate effect".

So saying he reached forward, grasped Mick O' by

the arm and deftly snapped a pair of handcuffs on his wrists.

Meanwhile Frank had managed to back up to the wall and reaching down he tripped a switch which instantly cast the room into darkness and caused a concealed door to swing open beside him. Taking advantage of the confusion caused by the sudden loss of light, he slipped quietly through the door and closed it gently behind him.

As he raced down the hidden staircase his mind raced. This was obviously the work of the coalition of disaffected nationalists, secret services and other interested parties. He was not sure if they knew about the time travel issue. This was a matter which had been kept extremely tightly under wraps with an inner circle of about ten people in total. If any of those had defected to the opposition things were dark, indeed.

Frank was nothing if not a planner. If he could get to the time machine before the rebels he could perhaps salvage the situation before it spiralled out of control.

Chapter Forty

Back and Forth

"Where did he go" Roared an infuriated Colonel
Friedrich "Lock down the building immediately, search
floor by floor, I want him back alive. This is a bloodless
coup so far, let's keep it that way".

Mick O' laughed sardonically

"You have no idea" He said "Frank and I designed
this building. There are more back doors throughout it
than there are members of your pathetic organisation.
Frank is a remarkably competent individual and before the
day is out you will have a counter revolutionary force
banging on the doors. I would strongly advise you to
release me and hand over your weapons before this gets
messy. At this point I can afford to be magnanimous but if
it escalates I won't be able to control it and the
consequences will fall on your head".

Frank, meanwhile, had reached the ground floor
where the time machine was located. Peering out of the
door of a supply cupboard where the hidden stairs had
terminated him carefully studied the corridor outside. At
the far end stood two Presidential Guards in full
ceremonial uniforms. Frank had no way of knowing if
they were loyal to Mick O' or not. Looking around his
cramped hiding place he found a cleaners overalls and a
trolley laden with cleaning supplies.

He quickly donned the overalls and finding a cap
in the pocket he stuck it on his head. Whistling cheerfully

he thrust open the cupboard door and headed for the door of the time lab.

As he keyed in his code to the locking mechanism a voice spoke from behind him.

"Have you seen the deputy President in this area?"

Turning around, Frank was hugely relieved to see that the question was addressed to the pair of soldiers guarding the other end of the corridor. He was less enthusiastic to note that the questioner was one of the Guards who had barged into Mick O's office earlier.

"I'm very sorry sir" replied one of the Guards "We were only seconded to this posting this morning. We wouldn't recognise the deputy President by sight, but there's been nobody in this corridor since we arrived an hour ago". Evidently the presence of a cleaner did not count as a person in their minds.

Not so the officer. Turning to Frank he demanded "You there, has there been any unusual activity on this floor this morning? We're looking for the deputy President. Have you seen him about anywhere?"

"No sir" Said Frank thanking his lucky stars that the cap he was wearing was a little oversized and covered his forehead, shading his eyes. "He doesn't usually come down here. It's mostly offices and things down here. He's mostly on the top floor with all the other big wigs".

"What's in here?" Demanded the officer as he pushed open the door which Frank had unlocked a moment before.

"It's a machine room" Replied Frank "I think it's a

new thing for air purification or something. I don't understand this stuff, I just keep the place clean".

The room contained very little except for a glass fronted cabinet and some computer controls. There was no place for a person to hide and after poking around the officer said

"If you see the deputy President, tell one of the Guards outside, they'll be in this corridor all day. Now go on about your business" And he stamped out the door, slamming it behind him as he went.

Frank heaved an enormous sigh of relief and went to the computer controls. Despite the many times he had been here when people were being transported into the past, he had never actually initiated the sequence himself. On close inspection he concluded that it was reasonably simple. He fired up the computer and it demanded a security protocol. Fortunately for Frank he had learned something from Mick Brennan about paranoia and had insisted that his security pass was good for everything in the building. He quickly allowed the obligatory retinal and fingerprint scans and the system booted up. In feverish haste he inputted the timeline he wanted to go to and set the initiation sequence for ten minutes. He then turned to another, smaller device located below the computer station and entered a completely different sequence of commands.

As he stood up a thunderous knocking sounded from the door and a voice shouted

"Open in the name of the Provisional Council for the Liberation of our Oppressed Peoples".

Frank stepped smartly into the glass fronted cabinet as the knocking was replaced with the sound of something smashing against the door. Fortunately for Frank his timing sequence counted down and he disappeared with the customary soft clap of thunder. As the door crashed open an ear shattering explosion occurred which completely demolished the room and all evidence of the existence of the time machine.

On the top floor Mick O' heard the explosion and smiling triumphantly he thought "Good for you Frank that should throw them off the time travel tack. I hope you managed to get clear yourself".

Frank staggered and almost fell down. This was his first experience of time travel, other than Mick Brennan's version and on close examination he was not enamoured of it. Looking around he found himself in the middle of a small park beside a muddy stream. Over to his right stood a statue of the Blessed Virgin, hands spread to encompass the whole world. He immediately breathed easier. He was in the little triangle of park at the corner of Drumcondra Road and Botanic Avenue, exactly where he need to be.

"So far, so good" He thought "Now to check exactly when I've got myself to"

He crossed the road and examined the newspapers racked outside the door. The date was November 4th 2014.

Having no currency which was current in this timeline Frank headed for Micks house, which was quite close by, happily for Frank who had lost the habit of walking in his recent career as deputy President.

He smiled wanly as the doorbell pealed its strident cacophony into the still night air.

"Well" He thought "Some Things never change".

Mick and his companions, including Wolfgang and Frank Jr. had only two days before returned from Heidelberg and on hearing the doorbell Mick peered at the CCTV screen beside the door.

"Dear God" He breathed "It's Frank himself. What brings him here?"

"Don't open the door" Wilson shouted "He's probably got a troop of goons hidden outside waiting to jump us as soon as they get the chance".

"Don't be ridiculous Wilson, I've checked the CCTV cameras and he's all alone. The road outside is also clear and there can't be anybody hiding in the garden because there's pressure sensitive pads dotted all over it. He's on his own, though what he expects from us after all that stuff with thugs and guns etc. is hard to figure". Mick shrugged philosophically and opened the door. "Come on in and take the weight off your feet".

Frank advanced tentatively into the hall.

"I hardly expected that you'd let me within an ass's bawl of you, given the treatment you've been getting from me in recent times" He said, somewhat shamefacedly.

"You definitely have a few things to answer for, but we go back a long way and I'm a forgiving type of guy, as you well know. Come on inside, there's someone here you'll probably appreciate meeting".

Chapter Forty One

The Effects of Unintended Consequences

After Frank had met and embraced Frank Jr. Mick called all the interested parties together to establish the current state of affairs and the preferred route to resolving the various issues.

"Frank, I think you owe us an explanation for your behaviour towards us, and particularly me. We've been friends since kindergarten and, to put it straight to you, your treatment of us has been appalling. Before we get to that I suspect that your presence here and now doesn't bode well for the future state of the world. So, first off, bring us up to speed on what's happening in your timeline".

Frank rapidly explained the recent developments in 2050 and his presence in the current timeline.

"I recognise Anita from our earlier dealings with the other time travelling group who have not been successful in cracking the back and forth issue. We were very concerned when she disappeared but it's quite clear what happened now. Despite what she and others may have told you our object in all of this was not self-aggrandisement. Admittedly being second in command to the effective ruler of half the world is an exhilarating experience, but we were, and are, primarily focused on making the world a better place for humanity. I understand that this may be hard to take from one such as me, but nevertheless it's true".

"Admittedly we made mistakes and some bad decisions were made, both by ourselves and on our behalf by overzealous subordinates, but our intentions were always for the best. Unfortunately we didn't take enough heed of Mick's constant admonition about unintended consequences and, in spite of our diligent efforts, word of our meddling with time travel has gotten to the ears of forces unsympathetic to our cause. The current situation in 2050 is that a cabal of disparate interests have attempted a coup. I can't be sure how successful they'll be but a high priority for the 'intelligence' elements of this uprising will certainly be the secret of time travel. We can be certain that if they get their hands on that information they will, most definitely, not use it for the greater good of the peoples of the world".

"The reason I'm here tonight is twofold" Frank looked haggard and drawn as he spoke "First, on my way out of the timeline I destroyed our time machine and all the records relating to it. Without those records it will be difficult, but not impossible, to achieve the desired goal. However it is, pretty much the case that once Pandora's Box is opened it can't be closed again, so there's no certainty that, with a determined effort, they won't find a way to recreate the technology. Even worse they might even stumble on a system like Mick's one. With two way time travel these people would with, absolute inevitability, destroy the world.

This brings me to the second reason for my presence. I want to appeal directly to you, Mick, as the only person on Earth who can effectively prevent what will inevitably result in catastrophe for us and all future inhabitants of the world. I'm acutely aware that I sound well over the top here, but I can only reiterate that these guys are not safe hands in which to have a secret as powerful as this".

Wilson intervened at this point "So, to sum up. You guys have totally screwed up and let the time travel cat out of the bag. Then you have the unmitigated brass neck to come crawling back here to ask Mick to wave a magic wand and resolve your cock up, and, presumably, restore your empire in the process. You really take the biscuit, don't you?"

Anita turned to Mick and said "You're very quiet, Mick. What's on your mind? You can surely intervene to resolve this issue. We've all seen the product of your paranoid intellect, it shouldn't be beyond your abilities to think up a satisfactory scheme for this gig".

She experienced a sinking sensation in the pit of her stomach as she looked deep in his eyes.

"Mick" She cried "What's wrong? You look completely beaten down. I've never seen you like this, it's the responsibility isn't it. You always get stuck with all the decisions, it's not fair".

Turning on the others in the room she stormed

"Why don't you guys come up with something instead of sitting there like sheep, waiting for Mick to clean up all the cosmic shit created by others like you?"

"It's OK, darling" Mick intervened as he gazed longingly at her. "This whole situation and all its entanglements is down to me. Without my invention of the time machine I wouldn't have met Wilson and

Freddie, he wouldn't have fathered a political dynasty which is most likely what's driving the 'intelligence' contingent of Frank's cabal. Mick O' and Frank wouldn't have been messing around in the timelines and, last but not least, we wouldn't have met".

"I've been trying to avoid this conclusion for weeks now. But the only option open to us, as I see it, is for me to go back and erase all my work on time travel from day one. Realistically speaking, I've been fooling myself from the start. My theory about unintended consequences is deeply flawed. It's not that we need to worry about the unintended matters, but that despite the best intentions, unintended consequences arise. They appear to be totally unavoidable and, indeed, inevitable. There is only one course of action which eliminates the possibility of bad results and that is to utterly avoid the whole concept of time travel completely".

With tears streaming down her face Anita pleaded "Please Mick, there must be some other solution. We've had such a short time together and if you do this, we won't even have our memories left to us. We'll revert to our original 2012 selves and we hadn't even heard of each other then. Time travel can't be entirely down to you. Others will stumble on the secret and the world will be back to square one, without any gains made".

During this conversation the two Franks had been engaged in an intense, low voiced discussion. Frank senior spoke up.

"That suggestion is not a runner Mick. Once the genie is out of the bottle you can't just stuff him back in and carry on as if nothing had happened. You talk of consequences, intended and otherwise, who is to say what the end result of your proposal might be? Before you started this train of events the world was embroiled in the worst recession in history, there were a series of nasty little wars in progress in various regions and at least two nuclear powers were squaring up for a fight which might easily cause to destruction of the planet.

As things stand with all the interventions, yours and ours we've had nearly forty years of global peace and prosperity. It may be a dictatorship and, admittedly, some injustices were done in the name of the regime, but as we speak there is no threat of global war in 2050. By reverting to the previous status quo you might be condemning us all to extinction".

Wilson felt obliged to stick in his tuppence worth

"Dear God, Mick, please don't tell me I have to go back to that hellhole in Cheltenham. If I have to spend time listening to the crap that Major Freddie hands out, I won't be responsible for my actions".

"I've already said that I have given this matter serious thought". Mick held Anita in a close embrace "It is the only way to resolve the issue. My only consolation is exactly what Anita points out. We won't remember any of this. We'll just pick up where we left off prior to my building the first time machine. I'm aware that someone else could invent something comparable but as things stand at the moment there is concrete proof that the concept works. If I go back and 'uninvent' it there will be no precedent for others to follow. I just hope that if it is reinvented in future that those who build it will be better at managing it than I was".

Chapter Forty Two

Two Franks

As Mick turned to leave the room and head for his workshop Frank Jr. stepped forward "Just a moment Mick" He said "I can't let you do this" And he produced Mick's Colt 45 from the back of his waistband where he had concealed it earlier.

"What do you think you're doing?" Gasped Frank senior. "Put that bloody cannon away, if Mick Brennan can't be convinced by rational argument, he sure as hell won't be cowed by force of arms".

"Dad, it's time for extreme measures. Mick can't just unilaterally decide to junk fifty years of progress on foot of a couple of reverses. You and Mick O' have worked for decades to bring peace and stability to the world. If in order to maintain that, we need to tinker with the timelines a little then I think it's a small price to pay for the enormous gains. Now stand aside and the rest of you move over to the corner where I can keep an eye on you".

Mick shook his head in exasperation "You guys just don't seem to get it". He said. "It's not acceptable for me, you or Mick O' to mess about in the timelines. It creates uncontrollable effects down the ages. Worse than uncontrollable, they are utterly unpredictable. One thing I have observed though, is that when people with power get their hands on the technology, they invariably use it to retain and strengthen their grasp on that power. The end result of this is a cascading sequence of disasters ultimately leading to an Armageddon scenario".

"By the way" Mick continued "Have you noticed that the gun has no bullets in it?"

Frank Jr glanced down at the colt and Mick taking advantage of his momentary lapse of concentration grasped Anita's hand, swept his hand over the light switch and slipped out the door, locking it after him.

Racing upstairs he said to Anita "We don't have much time. That door is quite sturdy but he'll blast the lock out with the gun and then he'll be on our heels directly".

As they ran up the stairs they head the ear shattering blast of the colt behind them. With their slender head start they managed to make it into the laboratory and slam the door.

"This should hold him off for a while" Mick smiled "This door is made of laminated steel and the lock is keyed to my retinal scan only. It'll take him a while to break it down. We haven't improved our situation all that much however. I can't get at the Mustang or the Travellator and activating the house time machine doesn't help greatly. We'd still be in here and Frank Jr would still be outside the door so I'm stuck for an answer".

"But Mick, haven't you still got the mini flux capacitor that you made for the raid on Jed's office in America?" Anita asked

"You are a genius" Mick said, giving her a quick kiss "That'll do perfectly for what we need".

"Mick" She said "Is there no way we can stay

together. My heart is breaking thinking of how little time we've had together".

"I'm desperately sorry" He replied, taking her in his arms "I've been thinking all this over for some time now and I just can't see any other solution. The only bright side to it is that we won't have any memory of each other when we push the reset button".

"That's no consolation" Anita sniffled "If one of us died at least we'd have our shared memories to console us but with your idea we won't even have that. I can't bear to even think about it".

"But you do understand the need to do this?" Queried Mick.

"Oh, Mick" She sighed "This is the hardest thing I've ever had to do, but you're right. You have always had a thing about the consequences of our actions and with time travel, the consequences are just too complex and unpredictable. Do it".

Outside the lab door Frank Jr, who had arranged for a squad of Mick O's crack troopers to be standing by, and had ushered them into the house as soon as he had broken out of the downstairs room shouted at the leader of the squad!

"We can't afford any delay. Blow the lock out of the door but remember, don't injure the people inside".

Wilson was handcuffed and restrained downstairs and in a state of incandescent rage. Lunging forward he head butted the trooper who had been left to guard him and knocked him down. As he stumbled awkwardly towards the stairs he was struck on the head and knocked unconscious by another trooper who had been stationed outside the door.

Meanwhile the shaped charge which the squad leader had fitted to the lock went off with a surprisingly muted thud.

"Do you want to use stun grenades Sir?" He asked Frank Jr.

"No need, they're unarmed and anyway Mick is a convinced pacifist. He won't be putting up any resistance".

So saying Frank Jr. pushed open the door and strode into the lab.

"Damn and Blast" He swore, "They've gone. We're screwed, there's no way of tracking them to wherever they're gone and Mick will have put his Armageddon plan into action before we know it".

Frank senior entered the room and hearing his son's negative comments sharply said

"Get a hold of yourself. He's gone without his various transportations. They will have the flux capacitors still attached and we'll find all his research and records here in this lab. If we act quickly we should be able to jump back through time ourselves and stymie any plan he might have to change things. Put the Mustang and Travellator under immediate tight guard and start a search for any and all documents right now"

As they frantically searched it became obvious that there was no documentary evidence that Mick had ever been interested in time travel.

"Blast Mick's paranoia. He's obviously kept his notes and everything else off site" Frank senior said. "We're wasting precious time here. Let's go and see if we can find what he called his flux capacitors in the vehicles. Maybe our technicians can reverse engineer them and give us the answer we need".

Here they were destined for disappointment. There was no sign in either vehicle that a flux capacitor had been fitted, nor if one had been fitted, where it might have been located.

Frank Jr. turned to his father and said

"Did you ever see one of these things? It might help if we had some idea of what size or shape of a thing we're looking for"

Frank stood back and thought deeply. He had known Mick since kindergarten school and was more in tune with his mind than anyone on earth.

"He's hidden them somewhere in this house" He said "There is no way that he would have trusted them far from his reach. There's a secret compartment somewhere in the house. We just need to find it".

They spent the next several hours probing and tapping all the walls, ceiling and floors of the house to no avail.

They questioned a now revived Wilson but finally gave up.

"That man would rather die than reveal Mick's

secret to us" Said Frank senior "More to the point I don't believe that Mick would have revealed the location of his stash even to one so close to him as Wilson, especially given how hard he finds it to keep his mouth shut on sensitive matters".

Just as they were on the point of abandoning their quest one of the troopers knocked on the door.

"Sir, the squad leader would like to see you in the lab, he thinks he may have found something" He said.

The two Franks raced up the stairs and burst into the lab.

"What's going on" Demanded Frank Jr.

"We noticed a strange, metallic, smell in here a few minutes ago and we think we've traced it to the back wall just about here" The squad leader pointed to a corner of the room.

Just then they saw a wisp of smoke rising from the corner which had been indicated.

"For God's sake" Cried Frank senior "There's something hidden in that wall, break it down quickly".

The troopers had come prepared for any eventuality and quickly produced tools to break down the wall. This proved to be unnecessary however as Frank Jr, investigating the smoke, discovered a trip switch which allowed a section of the wall to fall open, revealing a state of the art safe from which the smoke was seeping around the seals.

One of the troopers had been selected for his safe

breaking skills and he quickly set about decoding the password required to open the safe. His efforts proving fruitless, Frank Jr directed the demolitions expert to blow the door off the safe and stood back as he carried out the order.

As soon as the smoke cleared the two Franks rushed to the safe and gazed in disappointment at its contents.

The safe contained the ashes of some indistinguishable documents which, under the influence of the charge used to open it had spread them liberally throughout its interior. Nestled within the incinerated remains were three lumps of indistinguishable metal, obviously burnt beyond recognition and usefulness.

"Bring them with us" Said Frank senior "We might find someone in this timeline who could resurrect something from them, but I'm afraid Mick's paranoia wins out once again".

Chapter Forty Three

The End of Days

Anita awoke in the beach hut on the tropical island of Bali where she and Mick had spent ten days soaking up the sunshine and enjoying each other. By common consent they had not discussed the inevitable end of this blissful interlude.

She studied Mick's face as he slept. The sun had failed to give him a tan but it had brought out his freckles and reddened the tip of his nose. He had never looked more vulnerable and precious to her. She sighed deeply saddened by the prospect before them.

Mick's eyes slowly opened and a beatific smile lit up his face as he saw Anita looking at him.

"Good morning darling" He said, then his face darkened as he realised the reason for her downcast looks.

"Well" Anita sighed "This is the day, isn't it?"

"I'm deeply sorry my love" Mick held her hands "We are agreed that this is the only way to put the genie back into the bottle aren't we?"

Anita nodded.

"Anyway we have the trip home to Dublin to go before we need to put the plan into action. That'll take a couple of days, so this is not the final day really".

"OK" Anita replied "Let's get packed and off to the airport. It would be a terrible thing if we missed the plane, wouldn't it. Oh that's right, we still have the flux capacitor, we could just reset the time and we'd never need to be late for anything ever again. Remind me once more why we can't just put the thing into a continuous loop and stay here, in paradise, forever".

"I'm not sure of the actual physics involved but my theory is that if we make a change in the timelines, however tiny, it's like a pebble thrown into a still pond. The ripples spread until they run out of momentum. Think of throwing pebble after pebble into the pond. Very soon the ripples intersect with one another and soon the whole pond is a mass of conflicting wavelets. Now think about the effect of a large rock thrown into the mix, and finally consider the consequences of a meteor strike on the placid surface of the pond. Most of my interventions have been of the tiny pebble variety, but you must admit that some have been in the order of large rocks, if not small meteors. The end result is that the whole thing has reached such a pitch of unpredictability that the only sensible course is to reset the clock to where it was before I started messing around".

Back in Dublin once more a couple of days later Mick and Anita entered the house in Drumcondra, several months before Mick started on the time travel gig. Mick went to his desk in the laboratory and began riffling through the papers. Finally satisfied he removed some and replaced others in the ordered chaos on the desktop.

Within a nanosecond a ripple effect went through the time-space continuum. Mick and Anita disappeared, Wilson found himself at his desk in GCHQ, listening to Freddie's hectoring voice demanding coffee, and Frank was on yet another trip to Kazakhstan on a mission for the

Department of Education. Michael O'Reilly was back in charge of his transportation empire, other less critical characters had resumed their ordinary humdrum existences and the extended Bush family continued with grooming the next generation for high office.

Chapter Forty Four

Alternative

"What are you doing" Frank asked

"I'm designing a Solar Furnace" Mick answered as if that was the most reasonable thing in the world to be doing.

"What in God's name are you going to do with a Solar Furnace?"

"The one thing the world needs is a safe, cheap, reliable fuel source" Said Mick "Well it's all around us. The word is four fifths water and water is roughly two thirds hydrogen. Getting the hydrogen out of water is reasonably complex and requires large amounts of energy, hence the Solar furnace. There's a guy called Wolfgang Schroder who has written some very interesting papers on getting hydrogen from seawater using solar power. I figure if I contact him and we design and build a small scale demonstration of this technology, we can get someone with money to back us to build a facility in some part of the world where there's abundant sunshine, East Africa would be an obvious choice. The problem would be to get someone with loot to help us".

Frank looked pensive "I could maybe help with that. I am friendly with Michael O'Reilly, the transportation guy, he's always looking for cheaper fuel. If you get the demo model going I'll arrange a meet for you".

"That would be excellent" Said Mick "It's odd you

know, but I was clearing up my desk when I came across some notes I'd made on this subject and it got me thinking about the possibilities in it. I had forgotten all about it till then".

"Why don't we go up to the Porterhouse and get a pint" Said Mick "My head is wrecked with all this designing lark".

"You're getting very fond of the Porterhouse lately" Said Frank, putting on his coat.

"Well to tell the truth, there's this girl with the most gorgeous red hair who drinks there. I was thinking of asking her if I could buy her a drink or something

(Photograph © Volker Gebhart)

Hi. My name is Harry Browne and I've been writing for a couple of years.

Mostly I've done short stories, some of which can be found on my blog hbrowne4.wordpress.com.

If you would like to contact me try Twitter

https://twitter.com/hbrowne4 or hbrowne4@hotmail.com

I promise I'll answer all communications.

Made in the USA
Charleston, SC
25 April 2013